Stories from the Pentamerone

Giambattista Basile

Copyright © 2017 Okitoks Press

All rights reserved.

ISBN: 1973936771

ISBN-13: 978-1973936770

Table of Contents

I	4
HOW THE TALES CAME TO BE TOLD	4
II	7
THE MYRTLE	7
III	11
PERUONTO	11
IV	14
VARDIELLO	14
V	17
THE FLEA	17
VI	20
CENERENTOLA	20
VII	23
THE MERCHANT	23
VIII	26
GOAT-FACE	26
IX	29
THE ENCHANTED DOE	29
X	32
PARSLEY	32
XI	34
THE THREE SISTERS	34
XII	37
VIOLET	37
XIII	39
PIPPO	39
XIV	41
THE SERPENT	41
XV	45
THE SHE-BEAR	46
XVI	49
THE DOVE	49
XVII	53
CANNETELLA	53
XVIII	56
CORVETTO	57
XIX	59
THE BOOBY	59
XX	62
THE STONE IN THE COCK'S HEAD	62

XXI	65
THE THREE ENCHANTED PRINCES	65
XXII	68
THE DRAGON	68
XXIII	73
THE TWO CAKES	73
XXIV	77
THE SEVEN DOVES	77
XXV	83
THE RAVEN	83
XXVI	88
THE MONTHS	88
XXVII	91
PINTOSMALTO	91
XXVIII	94
THE GOLDEN ROOT	94
XXIX	98
SUN, MOON, AND TALIA	98
XXX	101
NENNILLO AND NENNELLA	101
XXXI	103
THE THREE CITRONS	104
XXXII	108
CONCLUSION	108

I

HOW THE TALES CAME TO BE TOLD

It is an old saying, that he who seeks what he should not, finds what he would not. Every one has heard of the ape who, in trying to pull on his boots, was caught by the foot. And it happened in like manner to a wretched slave, who, although she never had shoes to her feet, wanted to wear a crown on her head. But the straight road is the best; and, sooner or later, a day comes which settles all accounts. At last, having by evil means usurped what belonged to another, she fell to the ground; and the higher she had mounted, the greater was her fall—as you shall see.

Once upon a time the King of Woody Valley had a daughter named Zoza, who was never seen to laugh. The unhappy father, who had no other comfort in life but this only daughter, left nothing untried to drive away her melancholy. So he sent for folks who walk on stilts, fellows who jump through hoops, for boxers, for conjurers, for jugglers who perform sleight-of-hand tricks, for strong men, for dancing dogs, for leaping clowns, for the donkey that drinks out of a tumbler—in short, he tried first one thing and then another to make her laugh. But all was time lost, for nothing could bring a smile to her lips.

So at length the poor father, at wit's end, and to make a last trial, ordered a large fountain of oil to be set in front of the palace gates, thinking to himself that when the oil ran down the street, along which the people passed like a troop of ants, they would be obliged, in order not to soil their clothes, to skip like grasshoppers, leap like goats, and run like hares; while one would go picking and choosing his way, and another go creeping along the wall. In short, he hoped that something might come to pass to make his daughter laugh.

So the fountain was made; and as Zoza was one day standing at the window, grave and demure, and looking as sour as vinegar, there came by chance an old woman, who, soaking up the oil with a sponge, began to fill a little pitcher which she had brought with her. And as she was labouring hard at this ingenious device, a young page of the court passing by threw a stone so exactly to a hair that he hit the pitcher and broke it to pieces. Whereupon the old woman, who had no hair on her tongue, turned to the page, full of wrath, and exclaimed, "Ah, you impertinent young dog, you mule, you gallows-rope, you spindle-legs! Ill luck to you! May you be pierced by a Catalan lance! May a thousand ills befall you and something more to boot, you thief, you knave!"

The lad, who had little beard and less discretion, hearing this string of abuse, repaid the old woman in her own coin, saying, "Have you done, you grandmother of witches, you old hag, you child-strangler!"

When the old woman heard these compliments she flew into such a rage that, losing hold of the bridle and escaping from the stable of patience, she acted as if she were mad, cutting capers in the air and grinning like an ape. At this strange spectacle Zoza burst into such a fit of laughter that she well-nigh fainted away. But when the old woman saw herself played this trick, she flew into a passion, and turning a fierce look on Zoza she exclaimed: "May you never have the least little bit of a husband, unless you take the Prince of Round-Field."

Upon hearing this, Zoza ordered the old woman to be called; and desired to know whether, in her words, she had laid on her a curse, or had only meant to insult her. And the old woman answered, "Know then, that the Prince of whom I spoke is a most handsome creature, and is named Taddeo, who, by the wicked spell of a fairy, having given the last touch to the picture of life, has been placed in a tomb outside the walls of the city; and there is an inscription upon a stone, saying that whatever woman shall in three days fill with tears a pitcher that hangs there upon a hook will bring the Prince to life and shall take him for a husband. But as it is impossible for two human eyes to weep so much as to fill a pitcher that would hold half a barrel, I have wished you this wish in return for your scoffing and jeering at me. And I pray that it may come to pass, to avenge the wrong you have done me." So saying, she scuttled down the stairs, for fear of a beating.

Zoza pondered over the words of the old woman, and after turning over a hundred thoughts in her mind, until her head was like a mill full of doubts, she was at last struck by a dart of the passion that blinds the judgment and puts a spell on the reasoning of man. She took a handful of dollars from her father's coffers and left the palace, walking on and on, until she arrived at the castle of a fairy, to whom she unburdened her heart. The fairy, out of pity for such a fair young girl, who had two spurs to make her fall—little help and much love for an unknown object—gave her a letter of recommendation to a sister of hers, who was also a fairy. And this second fairy received her likewise with great kindness; and on the following morning, when Night commands the birds to proclaim that whoever has seen a flock of black shadows gone astray shall be well rewarded, she gave her a beautiful walnut, saying, "Take this, my dear daughter, and keep it carefully; but never open it, but in time of the greatest need." And then she gave her also a letter, commending her to another sister.

After journeying a long way, Zoza arrived at this fairy's castle, and was received with the same affection. And the next morning this fairy likewise gave her a letter to another sister, together with a chestnut, cautioning her in the same manner. Then Zoza travelled on to the next castle, where she was received with a thousand caresses and given a filbert, which she was never to open, unless the greatest necessity obliged her. So she set out upon her journey, and passed so many forests and rivers, that at the end of seven years, just at the time of day when the Sun, awakened by the coming of the cocks, has saddled his steed to run his accustomed stages, she arrived almost lame at Round-Field.

There, at the entrance to the city, she saw a marble tomb, at the foot of a fountain, which was weeping tears of crystal at seeing itself shut up in a porphyry prison. And, lifting up the pitcher, she placed it in her lap and began to weep into it, imitating the fountain to make two little fountains of her eyes. And thus she continued without ever raising her head from the mouth of the pitcher—until, at the end of two days, it was full within two inches of the top. But, being wearied with so much weeping, she was unawares overtaken by sleep, and was obliged to rest for an hour or so under the canopy of her eyes.

Meanwhile a certain Slave, with the legs of a grasshopper, came, as she was wont, to the fountain, to fill her water-cask. Now she knew the meaning of the fountain which was talked of everywhere; and when she saw Zoza weeping so incessantly, and making two little streams from her eyes, she was always watching and spying until the pitcher should be full enough for her to add the last drops to it; and thus to leave Zoza cheated of her hopes. Now, therefore, seeing Zoza asleep, she seized her opportunity; and dexterously removing the pitcher from under Zoza, and placing her own eyes over it, she filled it in four seconds. But hardly was it full, when the Prince arose from the white marble shrine, as if awakened from a deep sleep, and embraced that mass of dark flesh, and carried her straightways to his palace; feasts and marvellous illuminations were made, and he took her for his wife.

When Zoza awoke and saw the pitcher gone, and her hopes with it, and the shrine open, her heart grew so heavy that she was on the point of unpacking the bales of her soul at the custom-house of Death. But, at last, seeing that there was no help for her misfortune, and that she could only blame her own eyes, which had served her so ill, she went her way, step by step, into the city. And when she heard of the feasts which the Prince had made, and the dainty creature he had married, she instantly knew how all this mischief had come to pass; and said to herself, sighing, "Alas, two dark things have brought me to the ground,—sleep and a black slave!" Then she took a fine house facing the palace of the Prince; from whence, though she could not see the idol of her heart, she could at least look upon the walls wherein what she sighed for was enclosed.

But Taddeo, who was constantly flying like a bat round that black night of a Slave, chanced to perceive Zoza and was entranced with her beauty. When the Slave saw this she was beside herself with rage, and vowed that if Taddeo did not leave the window, she would kill her baby when it was born.

Taddeo, who was anxiously desiring an heir, was afraid to offend his wife and tore himself away from the sight of Zoza; who seeing this little balm for the sickness of her hopes taken away from her, knew not, at first, what to do. But, recollecting the fairies' gifts, she opened the walnut, and out of it hopped a little dwarf like a doll, the most graceful toy that was ever seen in the world. Then, seating himself upon the window, the dwarf began to sing with such a trill and gurgling, that he seemed a veritable king of the birds.

The Slave, when she saw and heard this, was so enraptured that, calling Taddeo, she said, "Bring me the little fellow who is singing yonder, or I will kill the child when it is born." So the Prince, who allowed this ugly woman to put the saddle on his back, sent instantly to Zoza, to ask if she would not sell the dwarf. Zoza answered she was not a merchant, but that he was welcome to it as a gift. So Taddeo accepted the offer, for he was anxious to keep his wife in good humour.

Four days after this, Zoza opened the chestnut, when out came a hen with twelve little chickens, all of pure gold, and, being placed on the window, the Slave saw them and took a vast fancy to them; and calling Taddeo, she showed him the beautiful sight, and again ordered him to procure the hen and chickens for her. So Taddeo, who let himself be caught in the web, and become the sport of the ugly creature, sent again to Zoza, offering her any price she might ask for the beautiful hen. But Zoza gave the same answer as before, that he might have it as a gift. Taddeo, therefore, who could not do otherwise, made necessity kick at discretion, and accepted the beautiful present.

But after four days more, Zoza opened the hazel-nut, and forth came a doll which spun gold—an amazing sight. As soon as it was placed at the same window, the Slave saw it and, calling to Taddeo, said, "I must have that doll, or I will kill the child." Taddeo, who let his proud wife toss him about like a shuttle, had nevertheless not the heart to send to Zoza for the doll, but resolved to go himself, recollecting the sayings: "No messenger is better than yourself," and "Let him who would eat a fish take it by the tail." So he went and besought Zoza to pardon his impertinence, on account of the caprices of his wife; and Zoza, who was in ecstasies at beholding the cause of her sorrow, put a constraint on herself; and so let him entreat her the longer to keep in sight the object of her love, who was stolen from her by an ugly slave. At length she gave him the doll, as she had done the other things, but before placing it in his hands, she prayed the little doll to put a desire into the heart of the Slave to hear stories told by her. And when Taddeo saw the doll in his hand, without his paying a single coin, he was so filled with amazement at such courtesy that he offered his kingdom and his life in exchange for the gift. Then, returning to his palace, he placed it in his wife's hands; and instantly such a longing seized her to hear stories told, that she called her husband and said, "Bid some story-tellers come and tell me stories, or I promise you, I will kill the child."

Taddeo, to get rid of this madness, ordered a proclamation instantly to be made, that all the women of the land should come on the appointed day. And on that day, at the hour when the star of Venus appears, who awakes the Dawn, to strew the road along which the Sun has to pass, the ladies were all assembled at the palace. But Taddeo, not wishing to detain such a rabble for the mere amusement of his wife, chose ten only of the best of the city who appeared to him most capable and eloquent. These were Bushy-haired Zeza, Bandy-legged Cecca, Wen-necked Meneca, Long-nosed Tolla, Humph-backed Popa, Bearded Antonella, Dumpy Ciulla, Blear-eyed Paola, Bald-headed Civonmetella, and Square-shouldered Jacova. Their names he wrote down on a sheet of paper; and then, dismissing the others, he arose with the Slave from under the canopy, and they went gently to the garden of the palace, where the leafy branches were so closely interlaced, that the Sun could not separate them with all the industry of his rays. And seating themselves under a pavilion, formed by a trellis of vines, in the middle of which ran a great fountain—the schoolmaster of the courtiers, whom he taught everyday to murmur—Taddeo thus began:

"There is nothing in the world more glorious, my gentle dames, than to listen to the deeds of others; nor was it without reason that the great philosopher placed the highest happiness of man in listening to pretty stories. In hearing pleasing things told, griefs vanish, troublesome thoughts are put to flight and life is lengthened. And, for this reason, you see the artisans leave their workshops, the merchants their country-houses, the lawyers their cases, the shopkeepers their business, and all repair with open mouths to the barbers' shops and to the groups of chatterers, to listen to stories, fictions, and news in the open air. I cannot, therefore, but pardon my wife, who has taken this strange fancy into her head of hearing the telling of tales. So, if you will be pleased to satisfy the whim of the Princess and comply with my wishes, you will, during the next four or five days, each of you relate daily one of those tales which old women are wont to tell for the amusement of the little ones. And you will come regularly to this spot; where, after a good repast, you shall begin to tell stories, so as to pass life pleasantly—and sorrow to him that dies!"

At these words, all bowed assent to the commands of Taddeo; and the tables being meanwhile set out and feast spread, they sat down to eat. And when they had done eating, the Prince took the paper and calling on each in turn, by name, the stories that follow were told, in due order.

II

THE MYRTLE

There lived in the village of Miano a man and his wife, who had no children whatever, and they longed with the greatest eagerness to have an heir. The woman, above all, was for ever saying, "O heavens! if I might but have a little baby—I should not care, were it even a sprig of a myrtle." And she repeated this song so often, and so wearied Heaven with these words, that at last her wish was granted; and at the end of nine months, instead of a little boy or girl, she placed in the hands of the nurse a fine sprig of myrtle. This she planted with great delight in a pot, ornamented with ever so many beautiful figures, and set it in the window, tending it morning and evening with more diligence than the gardener does a bed of cabbages from which he reckons to pay the rent of his garden.

Now the King's son happening to pass by, as he was going to hunt, took a prodigious fancy to this beautiful plant, and sent to ask the mistress of the house if she would sell it, for he would give even one of his eyes for it. The woman at last, after a thousand difficulties and refusals, allured by his offers, dazzled by his promises, frightened by his threats, overcome by his prayers, gave him the pot, beseeching him to hold it dear, for she loved it more than a daughter, and valued it as much as if it were her own offspring. Then the Prince had the flower-pot carried with the greatest care in the world into his own chamber, and placed it in a balcony, and tended and watered it with his own hand.

It happened one evening, when the Prince had gone to bed, and put out the candles, and all were at rest and in their first sleep, that he heard the sound of some one stealing through the house, and coming cautiously towards his bed; whereat he thought it must be some chamber-boy coming to lighten his purse for him, or some mischievous imp to pull the bed-clothes off him. But as he was a bold fellow, whom none could frighten, he acted the dead cat, waiting to see the upshot of the affair. When he perceived the object approach nearer, and stretching out his hand felt something smooth, and instead of laying hold, as he expected, on the prickles of a hedgehog, he touched a little creature more soft and fine than Barbary wool, more pliant and tender than a marten's tail, more delicate than thistle-down, he flew from one thought to another, and taking her to be a fairy (as indeed she was), he conceived at once a great affection for her. The next morning, before the Sun, like a chief physician, went out to visit the flowers that are sick and languid, the unknown fair one rose and disappeared, leaving the Prince filled with curiosity and wonder.

But when this had gone on for seven days, he was burning and melting with desire to know what good fortune this was that the stars had showered down on him, and what ship freighted with the graces of Love it was that had come to its moorings in his chamber. So one night, when the fair maiden was fast asleep, he tied one of her tresses to his arm, that she might not escape; then he called a chamberlain, and bidding him light the candles, he saw the flower of beauty, the miracle of women, the looking-glass and painted egg of Venus, the fair bait of Love—he saw a little doll, a beautiful dove, a Fata Morgana, a banner—he saw a golden trinket, a hunter, a falcon's eye, a moon in her fifteenth day, a pigeon's bill, a morsel for a king, a jewel—he saw, in short, a sight to amaze one.

In astonishment he cried, "O sleep, sweet sleep! heap poppies on the eyes of this lovely jewel; interrupt not my delight in viewing as long as I desire this triumph of beauty. O lovely tress that binds me! O lovely eyes that inflame me! O lovely lips that refresh me! O lovely bosom that consoles me! Oh where, at what shop of the wonders of Nature, was this living statue made? What India gave the gold for these hairs? What Ethiopia the ivory to form these brows? What seashore the carbuncles that compose these eyes? What Tyre the purple to dye this face? What East the pearls to string these teeth? And from what mountains was the snow taken to sprinkle over this bosom—snow contrary to nature, that nurtures the flowers and burns hearts?"

So saying he made a vine of his arms, and clasping her neck, she awoke from her sleep and replied, with a gentle smile, to the sigh of the enamoured Prince; who, seeing her open her eyes, said, "O my treasure, if viewing without candles this temple of love I was in transports, what will become of my life now that you have lighted two lamps? O beauteous eyes, that with a trump-card of light make the stars bankrupt, you alone have pierced this heart, you alone can make a poultice for it like fresh eggs! O my lovely physician, take pity, take pity on one who is sick of love; who, having changed the air from the darkness of night to the light of this beauty, is seized by a fever; lay your hand on this heart, feel my pulse, give me a prescription. But, my soul, why do I ask for a prescription? I desire no other comfort than a touch of that little hand; for I am certain that with the cordial of that fair grace, and with the healing root of that tongue of thine, I shall be sound and well again."

At these words the lovely fairy grew as red as fire, and replied, "Not so much praise, my lord Prince! I am your servant, and would do anything in the world to serve that kingly face; and I esteem it great good fortune that from a bunch of myrtle, set in a pot of earth, I have become a branch of laurel hung over the inn-door of a heart in which there is so much greatness and virtue."

The Prince, melting at these words like a tallow-candle, began again to embrace her; and sealing the latter with a kiss, he gave her his hand, saying, "Take my faith, you shall be my wife, you shall be mistress of my sceptre, you shall have the key of this heart, as you hold the helm of this life." After these and a hundred other ceremonies and discourses they arose. And so it went on for several days.

But as spoil-sport, marriage-parting Fate is always a hindrance to the steps of Love, it fell out that the Prince was summoned to hunt a great wild boar which was ravaging the country. So he was forced to leave his wife. But as he loved her more than his life, and saw that she was beautiful beyond all beautiful things, from this love and beauty there sprang up the feeling of jealousy, which is a tempest in the sea of love, a piece of soot that falls into the pottage of the bliss of lovers—which is a serpent that bites, a worm that gnaws, a gall that poisons, a frost that kills, making life always restless, the mind unstable, the heart ever suspicious. So, calling the fairy, he said to her, "I am obliged, my heart, to be away from home for two or three days; Heaven knows with how much grief I tear myself from you, who are my soul; and Heaven knows too whether, ere I set out, my life may not end; but as I cannot help going, to please my father, I must leave you. I, therefore, pray you, by all the love you bear me, to go back into the flower-pot, and not to come out of it till I return, which will be as soon as possible."

"I will do so," said the fairy, "for I cannot and will not refuse what pleases you. Go, therefore, and may the mother of good luck go with you, for I will serve you to the best of my power. But do me one favour; leave a thread of silk with a bell tied to the top of the myrtle, and when you come back pull the thread and ring, and immediately I will come out and say, Here I am.'"

The Prince did so, and then calling a chamberlain, said to him, "Come hither, come hither, you! Open your ears and mind what I say. Make this bed every evening, as if I were myself to sleep in it. Water this flower-pot regularly, and mind, I have counted the leaves, and if I find one missing I will take from you the means of earning your bread." So saying he mounted his horse, and went, like a sheep that is led to the slaughter, to follow a boar. In the meanwhile seven wicked women, with whom the Prince had been acquainted, began to grow jealous; and being curious to pry into the secret, they sent for a mason, and for a good sum of money got him to make an underground passage from their house into the Prince's chamber. Then these cunning jades went through the passage in order to explore. But finding nothing, they opened the window; and when they saw the beautiful myrtle standing there, each of them plucked a leaf from it; but the youngest took off the entire top, to which the little bell was hung; and the moment it was touched the bell tinkled and the fairy, thinking it was the Prince, immediately came out.

As soon as the wicked women saw this lovely creature they fastened their talons on her, crying, "You are she who turns to your own mill the stream of our hopes! You it is who have stolen the favour of the Prince! But you are come to an end of your tricks, my fine lady! You are nimble enough in running off, but you are caught in your tricks this time, and if you escape, you were never born."

So saying, they flew upon her, and instantly tore her in pieces, and each of them took her part. But the youngest would not join in this cruel act; and when she was invited by her sisters to do as they did, she would take nothing but a lock of those golden hairs. So when they had done they went quickly away by the passage through which they had come.

Meanwhile the chamberlain came to make the bed and water the flower-pot, according to his master's orders, and seeing this pretty piece of work, he had like to have died of terror. Then, biting his nails with vexation, he set to work, gathered up the remains of the flesh and bones that were left, and scraping the blood from the floor, he piled them all up in a heap in the pot; and having watered it, he made the bed, locked the door, put the key under the door, and taking to his heels ran away out of the town.

When the Prince came back from the chase, he pulled the silken string and rung the little bell; but ring as he would it was all lost time; he might sound the tocsin, and ring till he was tired, for the fairy gave no heed. So he went straight to the chamber, and not having patience to call the chamberlain and ask for the key, he gave the lock a kick, burst open the door, went in, opened the window, and seeing the myrtle stript of its leaves, he fell to making a most doleful lamentation, crying, shouting, and bawling, "O wretched me! unhappy me! O miserable me! Who has played me this trick? and who has thus trumped my card? O ruined, banished, and undone prince! O my leafless myrtle! my lost fairy! O my wretched life! my joys vanished into smoke! my pleasures turned to vinegar! What will you do, unhappy man! Leap quickly over this ditch! You have fallen from all happiness, and will you not cut your throat? You are robbed of every treasure! You are expelled from life, and do you not go mad? Where are you? where are you, my myrtle? And what soul more hard than marble has destroyed this beautiful flower-pot? O cursed chase, that has chased me from all happiness! Alas! I am done for, I am overthrown, I am ruined, I have ended my days; it is not possible for me to get through life without my life; I must stretch my legs, since without my love sleep will be lamentation, food, poison, pleasure insipid, and life sour."

These and many other exclamations that would move the very stones in the streets, were uttered by the Prince; and after repeating them again and again, and wailing bitterly, full of sorrow and woe, never shutting an eye to sleep, nor opening his mouth to eat, he gave such way to grief, that his face, which was before of oriental vermilion, became of gold paint, and the ham of his lips became rusty bacon.

The fairy, who had sprouted up again from the remains that were put in the pot, seeing the misery and tribulation of her poor lover, and how he was turned in a second to the colour of a sick Spaniard, of a venomous lizard, of the sap of a leaf, of a jaundiced person, of a dried pear, was moved with compassion; and springing out of the pot, like the light of a candle shooting out of a dark lantern, she stood before Cola Marchione, and embracing him in her arms she said, "Take heart, take heart, my Prince! have done now with this lamenting, wipe your eyes, quiet your anger, smooth your face. Behold me alive and handsome, in spite of those wicked women, who split my head and so ill-treated me."

The Prince, seeing this when he least expected it, arose again from death to life, and the colour returned to his cheeks, warmth to his blood, breath to his breast. After giving her a thousand caresses and embraces, he desired to know the whole affair from head to foot; and when he found that the chamberlain was not to blame, he ordered him to be called, and giving a great banquet, he, with the full consent of his father, married the fairy. And he invited all the great people of the kingdom, but, above all others, he would have present those seven serpents who had committed the slaughter of that sweet suckling-calf.

And as soon as they had done eating, the Prince asked all the guests, one after another, what he deserved who had injured that beautiful maiden—pointing to the fairy, who looked so lovely that she shot hearts like a sprite and drew souls like a windlass.

Then all who sat at table, beginning with the King, said, one that he deserved the gallows, another that he merited the wheel, a third the pincers, a fourth to be thrown from a precipice; in short one proposed this punishment and another that. At last it came to the turn of the seven wicked women to speak, who, although they did not much relish this conversation, yet, as the truth comes out when the wine goes about, answered, that whoever had the heart basely to touch only this quintessence of the charms of love deserved to be buried alive in a dungeon.

"As you have pronounced this sentence with your own lips," said the Prince, "you have yourselves judged the cause, you have yourselves signed the decree. It remains for me to cause your order to be executed, since it is you who with the heart of a negro, with the cruelty of Medea, made a fritter of this beautiful head, and chopped up these lovely limbs like sausage-meat. So quick, make haste, lose not a moment! throw them this very instant into a large dungeon, where they shall end their days miserably."

So this order was instantly carried into execution. The Prince married the youngest sister of these wicked creatures to the chamberlain, and gave her a good portion. And giving also to the father and mother of the myrtle wherewithal to live comfortably, he himself spent his days happily with the fairy; while the wicked women ended their lives in bitter anguish, and thus verified the proverb of the wise men of old—

"The lame goat will hop
If he meets with no stop."

III

PERUONTO

A good deed is never lost. He who sows courtesy reaps benefit; and he who gathers kindness gathers love. Pleasure bestowed on a grateful mind was never barren, but always brings a good recompense; and that is the moral of the story I am going to tell you.

Once upon a time a woman who lived in a village, and was called Ceccarella, had a son named Peruonto, who was one of the most stupid lads that ever was born. This made his mother very unhappy, and all day long she would grieve because of this great misfortune. For whether she asked him kindly, or stormed at him till her throat was dry, the foolish fellow would not stir to do the slightest hand's turn for her. At last, after a thousand dinnings at his brain, and a thousand splittings of his head, and saying "I tell you" and "I told you" day after day, she got him to go to the wood for a faggot, saying, "Come now, it is time for us to get a morsel to eat, so run off for some sticks, and don't forget yourself on the way, but come back as quick as you can, and we will boil ourselves some cabbage, to keep the life in us."

Away went the stupid Peruonto, hanging down his head as if he was going to gaol. Away he went, walking as if he were a jackdaw, or treading on eggs, counting his steps, at the pace of a snail's gallop, and making all sorts of zigzags and excursions on his way to the wood, to come there after the fashion of a raven. And when he reached the middle of a plain, through which ran a river growling and murmuring at the bad manners of the stones that were stopping its way, he saw three youths who had made themselves a bed of grass and a pillow of a great flint stone, and were lying sound asleep under the blaze of the Sun, who was shooting his rays down on them point blank. When Peruonto saw these poor creatures, looking as if they were in the midst of a fountain of fire, he felt pity for them, and cutting some branches of oak, he made a handsome arbour over them. Meanwhile, the youths, who were the sons of a fairy, awoke, and, seeing the kindness and courtesy of Peruonto, they gave him a charm, that every thing he asked for should be done.

Peruonto, having performed this good action, went his ways towards the wood, where he made up such an enormous faggot that it would have needed an engine to draw it; and, seeing that he could not in any way get in on his back, he set himself astride of it and cried, "Oh, what a lucky fellow I should be if this faggot would carry me riding a-horseback!" And the word was hardly out of his mouth when the faggot began to trot and gallop like a great horse, and when it came in front of the King's palace it pranced and capered and curvetted in a way that would amaze you. The ladies who were standing at one of the windows, on seeing such a wonderful sight, ran to call Vastolla, the daughter of the King, who, going to the window and observing the caracoles of a faggot and the bounds of a bundle of wood, burst out a-laughing—a thing which, owing to a natural melancholy, she never remembered to have done before. Peruonto raised his head, and, seeing that it was at him that they were laughing, exclaimed, "Oh, Vastolla, I wish that I could be your husband and I would soon cure you of laughing at me!" And so saying, he struck his heels into the faggot, and in a dashing gallop he was quickly at home, with such a train of little boys at his heels that if his mother had not been quick to shut the door they would soon have killed him with the stones and sticks with which they pelted him.

Now came the question of marrying Vastolla to some great prince, and her father invited all he knew to come and visit him and pay their respects to the Princess. But she refused to have anything to say to either of them, and only answered, "I will marry none but the young man who rode on the faggot." So that the King got more and more angry with every refusal, and at last he was quite unable to contain himself any longer, and called his Council together and said, "You know by this time how my honour has been shamed, and that my daughter has acted in such a manner that all the chronicles will tell the story against me, so now speak and advise me. I say that she is unworthy to live, seeing that she has brought me into such discredit, and I wish to put her altogether out of the world before she does more mischief." The Councillors, who had in their time learned much wisdom, said, "Of a truth she deserves to be severely punished. But, after all, it is this audacious scoundrel who has give you the annoyance, and it is not right that he should escape through the meshes of the net. Let us wait, then, till he comes to light, and we discover the root of this disgrace, and then we will think it over and resolve what were best to be done." This counsel pleased the King, for he saw that they spoke like sensible, prudent men, so he held his hand and said, "Let us wait and see the end of this business."

So then the King made a great banquet, and invited every one of his nobles and all the gentlemen in his kingdom to come to it, and set Vastolla at the high table at the top of the hall, for, he said, "No common man can have done this, and when she recognises the fellow we shall see her eyes turn to him, and we will instantly lay hold on him and put him out of the way." But when the feasting was done, and all the guests passed out in a line, Vastolla took no more notice of them than Alexander's bull-dog did of the rabbits; and the King grew more angry than ever, and vowed that he would kill her without more delay. Again, however, the Councillors pacified him and said, "Softly, softly, your Majesty! quiet your wrath. Let us make another banquet to-morrow, not for people of condition but for the lower sort. Some women always attach themselves to the worst, and we shall find among the cutlers, and bead-makers, and comb-sellers, the root of your anger, which we have not discovered among the cavaliers."

This reasoning took the fancy of the King, and he ordered a second banquet to be prepared, to which, on proclamation being made, came all the riff-raff and rag-tag and bob-tail of the city, such as rogues, scavengers, tinkers, pedlars, sweeps, beggars, and such like rabble, who were all in high glee; and, taking their seats like noblemen at a great long table, they began to feast and gobble away.

Now, when Ceccarella heard this proclamation, she began to urge Peruonto to go there too, until at last she got him to set out for the feast. And scarcely had he arrived there when Vastolla cried out without thinking, "That is my Knight of the Faggot." When the

King heard this he tore his beard, seeing that the bean of the cake, the prize in the lottery, had fallen to an ugly lout, the very sight of whom he could not endure, with a shaggy head, owl's eyes, a parrot's nose, a deer's mouth, and legs bare and bandy. Then, heaving a deep sigh, he said, "What can that jade of a daughter of mine have seen to make her take a fancy to this ogre, or strike up a dance with this hairy-foot? Ah, vile, false creature, who has cast so base a spell on her? But why do we wait? Let her suffer the punishment she deserves; let her undergo the penalty that shall be decreed by you, and take her from my presence, for I cannot bear to look longer upon her."

Then the Councillors consulted together and they resolved that she, as well as the evil-doer, should be shut up in a cask and thrown into the sea; so that without staining the King's hands with the blood of one of his family, they should carry out the sentence. No sooner was the judgment pronounced, than the cask was brought and both were put into it; but before they coopered it up, some of Vastolla's ladies, crying and sobbing as if their hearts would break, put into it a basket of raisins and dried figs that she might have wherewithal to live on for a little while. And when the cask was closed up, it was flung into the sea, on which it went floating as the wind drove it.

Meanwhile Vastolla, weeping till her eyes ran like two rivers, said to Peruonto, "What a sad misfortune is this of ours! Oh, if I but knew who has played me this trick, to have me caged in this dungeon! Alas, alas, to find myself in this plight without knowing how. Tell me, tell me, O cruel man, what incantation was it you made, and what spell did you employ, to bring me within the circle of this cask?" Peruonto, who had been for some time paying little attention to her, at last said, "If you want me to tell you, you must give me some figs and raisins." So Vastolla, to draw the secret out of him, gave him a handful of both; and as soon as he had eaten them he told her truly all that had befallen him, with the three youths, and with the faggot, and with herself at the window: which, when the poor lady heard, she took heart and said to Peruonto, "My friend, shall we then let our lives run out in a cask? Why don't you cause this tub to be changed into a fine ship and run into some good harbour to escape this danger?" And Peruonto replied—

"If you would have me say the spell,
With figs and raisins feed me well!"

So Vastolla, to make him open his mouth, filled it with fruit; and so she fished the words out of him. And lo! as soon as Peruonto had said what she desired, the cask was turned into a beautiful ship; with sails and sailors and everything that could be wished for; and guns and trumpets and a splendid cabin in which Vastolla sat filled with delight.

It being now the hour when the Moon begins to play at see-saw with the Sun, Vastolla said to Peruonto, "My fine lad, now make this ship to be changed into a palace, for then we shall be more secure; you know the saying, "Praise the Sea, but keep to the Land." And Peruonto replied—

"If you would have me say the spell,
With figs and raisins feed me well!"

So Vastolla, at once, fed him again, and Peruonto, swallowing down the raisins and figs, did her pleasure; and immediately the ship came to land and was changed into a beautiful palace, fitted up in a most sumptuous manner, and so full of furniture and curtains and hangings that there was nothing more to ask for. So that Vastolla, who a little before would not have set the price of a farthing on her life, did not now wish to change places with the greatest lady in the world, seeing herself served and treated like a queen. Then to put the seal on all her good fortune, she besought Peruonto to obtain grace to become handsome and polished in his manner, that they might live happy together; for though the proverb says, "Better to have a pig for a husband, than a smile from an emperor," still, if his appearance were changed, she should think herself the happiest woman in the universe. And Peruonto replied as before—

"If you would have me say the spell,
With figs and raisins feed me well!"

Then Vastolla quickly opened his lips, and scarcely had he spoken the words when he was changed, as it were from an owl to a nightingale, from an ogre to a beautiful youth, from a scarecrow to a fine gentleman. Vastolla, seeing such a transformation clasped him in her arms and was almost beside herself with joy. Then they were married and lived happily for years.

Meanwhile the King grew old and very sad, so that, one day, the courtiers persuaded him to go a-hunting to cheer him up. Night overtook him, and, seeing a light in a palace, he sent a servant to know if he could be entertained there; and he was answered that everything was at his disposal. So the King went to the palace and passing into a great guest-chamber he saw no living soul, but two little boys, who skipped around him crying, "Welcome, welcome!" The King, surprised and astonished, stood like one that was enchanted, and sitting down to rest himself at a table, to his amazement he saw invisibly spread on it a Flanders tablecloth, with dishes full of roast meats and all sorts of viands; so that, in truth, he feasted like a King, waited on by those beautiful children, and all the while he sat at table a concert of lutes and tambourines never ceased—such delicious music that it went to the tips of his fingers and toes. When he had done eating, a bed suddenly appeared all made of gold, and having his boots taken off, he went to rest and all his courtiers did the same, after having fed heartily at a hundred tables, which were laid out in the other rooms.

When morning came, the King wished to thank the two little children, but with them appeared Vastolla and her husband; and casting herself at his feet she asked his pardon and related the whole story. The King, seeing that he had found two grandsons who were two jewels and a son-in-law who was a fairy, embraced first one and then the other; and taking up the children in his arms, they all returned to the city where there was a great festival that lasted many days.

IV

VARDIELLO

If Nature had given to animals the necessity of clothing themselves, and of buying their food, the race of quadrupeds would inevitably be destroyed. Therefore it is that they find their food without trouble,—without gardener to gather it, purchaser to buy it, cook to prepare it, or carver to cut it up; whilst their skin defends them from the rain and snow, without the merchant giving them cloth, the tailor making the dress, or the errand-boy begging for a drink-penny. To man however, who has intelligence, Nature did not care to grant these indulgences, since he is able to procure for himself what he wants. This is the reason that we commonly see clever men poor, and blockheads rich; as you may gather from the story which I am going to tell you.

Grannonia of Aprano was a woman of a great sense and judgment, but she had a son named Vardiello, who was the greatest booby and simpleton in the whole country round about. Nevertheless, as a mother's eyes are bewitched and see what does not exist, she doted upon him so much, that she was for ever caressing and fondling him as if he were the handsomest creature in the world.

Now Grannonia kept a brood-hen, that was sitting upon a nest of eggs, in which she placed all her hope, expecting to have a fine brood of chickens, and to make a good profit of them. And having one day to go out on some business, she called her son, and said to him, "My pretty son of your own mother, listen to what I say: keep your eye upon the hen, and if she should get up to scratch and pick, look sharp and drive her back to the nest; for otherwise the eggs will grow cold, and then we shall have neither eggs nor chickens."

"Leave it to me," replied Vardiello, "you are not speaking to deaf ears."

"One thing more," said the mother; "look-ye, my blessed son, in yon cupboard is a pot full of certain poisonous things; take care that ugly Sin does not tempt you to touch them, for they would make you stretch your legs in a trice."

"Heaven forbid!" replied Vardiello, "poison indeed will not tempt me; but you have done wisely to give me the warning; for if I had got at it, I should certainly have eaten it all up."

Thereupon the mother went out, but Vardiello stayed behind; and, in order to lose no time, he went into the garden to dig holes, which he covered with boughs and earth, to catch the little thieves who come to steal the fruit. And as he was in the midst of his work, he saw the hen come running out of the room, whereupon he began to cry, "Hish, hish! this way, that way!" But the hen did not stir a foot; and Vardiello, seeing that she had something of the donkey in her, after crying "Hish, hish," began to stamp with his feet; and after stamping with his feet to throw his cap at her, and after the cap a cudgel which hit her just upon the pate, and made her quickly stretch her legs.

When Vardiello saw this sad accident, he bethought himself how to remedy the evil; and making a virtue of necessity, in order to prevent the eggs growing cold, he set himself down upon the nest; but in doing so, he gave the eggs an unlucky blow, and quickly made an omelet of them. In despair at what he had done, he was on the point of knocking his head against the wall; at last, however, as all grief turns to hunger, feeling his stomach begin to grumble, he resolved to eat up the hen. So he plucked her, and sticking her upon a spit, he made a great fire, and set to work to roast her. And when she was cooked, Vardiello, to do everything in due order, spread a clean cloth upon an old chest; and then, taking a flagon, he went down into the cellar to draw some wine. But just as he was in the midst of drawing the wine, he heard a noise, a disturbance, an uproar in the house, which seemed like the clattering of horses' hoofs. Whereat starting up in alarm and turning his eyes, he saw a big tom-cat, which had run off with the hen, spit and all; and another cat chasing after him, mewing, and crying out for a part.

Vardiello, in order to set this mishap to rights, darted upon the cat like an unchained lion, and in his haste he left the tap of the barrel running. And after chasing the cat through every hole and corner of the house, he recovered the hen; but the cask had meanwhile all run out; and when Vardiello returned, and saw the wine running about, he let the cask of his soul empty itself through the tap-holes of his eyes. But at last judgment came to his aid and he hit upon a plan to remedy the mischief, and prevent his mother's finding out what had happened; so, taking a sack of flour, filled full to the mouth, he sprinkled it over the wine on the floor.

But when he meanwhile reckoned up on his fingers all the disasters he had met with, and thought to himself that, from the number of fooleries he had committed, he must have lost the game in the good graces of Grannonia, he resolved in his heart not to let his mother see him again alive. So thrusting his hand into the jar of pickled walnuts which his mother had said contained poison, he never stopped eating until he came to the bottom; and when he had right well filled his stomach he went and hid himself in the oven.

In the meanwhile his mother returned, and stood knocking for a long time at the door; but at last, seeing that no one came, she gave it a kick; and going in, she called her son at the top of her voice. But as nobody answered, she imagined that some mischief must have happened, and with increased lamentation she went on crying louder and louder, "Vardiello! Vardiello! are you deaf, that you don't hear? Have you the cramp, that you don't run? Have you the pip, that you don't answer? Where are you, you rogue? Where are you hidden, you naughty fellow?"

Vardiello, on hearing all this hubbub and abuse, cried out at last with a piteous voice, "Here I am! here I am in the oven; but you will never see me again, mother!"

"Why so?" said the poor mother.

"Because I am poisoned," replied the son.

"Alas! alas!" cried Grannonia, "how came you to do that? What cause have you had to commit this homicide? And who has given you poison?" Then Vardiello told her, one after another, all the pretty things he had done; on which account he wished to die and not to remain any longer a laughing-stock in the world.

The poor woman, on hearing all this, was miserable and wretched, and she had enough to do and to say to drive this melancholy whimsey out of Vardiello's head. And being infatuated and dotingly fond of him, she gave him some nice sweetmeats, and so put the affair of the pickled walnuts out of his head, and convinced him that they were not poison, but good and comforting to the stomach. And having thus pacified him with cheering words, and showered on him a thousand caresses, she drew him out of the oven. Then giving him a fine piece of cloth, she bade him go and sell it, but cautioning him not to do business with folks of too many words.

"Tut, tut!" said Vardiello, "let me alone; I know what I'm about, never fear." So saying, he took the cloth, and went his way through the city of Naples, crying, "Cloth! cloth!" But whenever any one asked him, "What cloth have you there?" he replied, "You are no customer for me; you are a man of too many words." And when another said to him, "How do you sell your cloth?" he called him a chatterbox, who deafened him with his noise. At length he chanced to espy, in the courtyard of a house which was deserted on account of the Monaciello, a plaster statue; and being tired out, and wearied with going about and about, he sat himself down on a bench. But not seeing any one astir in the house, which looked like a sacked village, he was lost in amazement, and said to the statue: "Tell me, comrade, does no one live in this house?" Vardiello waited awhile; but as the statue gave no answer, he thought this surely was a man of few words. So he said, "Friend, will you buy my cloth? I'll sell it you cheap." And seeing that the statue still remained dumb, he exclaimed, "Faith, then, I've found my man at last! There, take the cloth, examine it, and give me what you will; to-morrow I'll return for the money."

So saying Vardiello left the cloth on the spot where he had been sitting, and the first mother's son who passed that way found the prize and carried it off.

When Vardiello returned home without the cloth, and told his mother all that had happened, she wellnigh swooned away, and said to him, "When will you put that headpiece of yours in order? See now what tricks you have played me—only think! But I am myself to blame, for being too tender-hearted, instead of having given you a good beating at first; and now I perceive that a pitiful doctor only makes the wound incurable. But you'll go on with your pranks until at last we come to a serious falling-out, and then there will be a long reckoning, my lad!"

"Softly, mother," replied Vardiello, "matters are not so bad as they seem; do you want more than crown-pieces brand new from the mint? Do you think me a fool, and that I don't know what I am about? To-morrow is not yet here. Wait awhile, and you shall see whether I know how to fit a handle to a shovel."

The next morning, as soon as the shades of Night, pursued by the constables of the Sun, had fled the country, Vardiello repaired to the courtyard where the statue stood, and said, "Good-day, friend! Can you give me those few pence you owe me? Come, quick, pay me for the cloth!" But when he saw that the statue remained speechless, he took up a stone and hurled it at its breast with such force that it burst a vein, which proved, indeed, the cure to his own malady; for some pieces of the statue falling off, he discovered a pot full of golden crown-pieces. Then taking it in both his hands, off he ran home, head over heels, as far as he could scamper, crying out, "Mother, mother! see here! what a lot of red lupins I've got. How many! how many!"

His mother, seeing the crown-pieces, and knowing very well that Vardiello would soon make the matter public, told him to stand at the door until the man with milk and new-made cheese came past, as she wanted to buy a pennyworth of milk. So Vardiello, who was a great glutton, went quickly and seated himself at the door; and his mother showered down from the window above raisins and dried figs for more than half an hour. Whereupon Vardiello, picking them up as fast as he could, cried aloud, "Mother, mother! bring out some baskets; give me some bowls! Here, quick with the tubs and buckets! for if it goes on to rain thus we shall be rich in a trice." And when he had eaten his fill Vardiello went up to sleep.

It happened one day that two countrymen—the food and life-blood of the law-courts—fell out, and went to law about a gold crown-piece which they had found on the ground. And Vardiello passing by said, "What jackasses you are to quarrel about a red lupin like this! For my part I don't value it at a pin's head, for I've found a whole potful of them."

When the judge heard this he opened wide his eyes and ears, and examined Vardiello closely, asking him how, when, and where he had found the crowns. And Vardiello replied, "I found them in a palace, inside a dumb man, when it rained raisins and dried figs." At this the judge stared with amazement; but instantly seeing how the matter stood, he decreed that Vardiello should be sent to a madhouse, as the most competent tribunal for him. Thus the stupidity of the son made the mother rich, and the mother's wit found a remedy for the foolishness of the son: whereby it is clearly seen that—

"A ship when steered by a skilful hand
Will seldom strike upon rock or sand."

V

THE FLEA

Resolutions taken without thought bring disasters without remedy. He who behaves like a fool repents like a wise man; as happened to the King of High-Hill, who through unexampled folly committed an act of madness putting in jeopardy both his daughter and his honour.

Once upon a time the King of High-Hill being bitten by a flea caught him by a wonderful feat of dexterity; and seeing how handsome and stately he was he had not the conscience to sentence him to death. So he put him into a bottle, and feeding him every day himself the little animal grew at such a rate that at the end of seven months it was necessary to shift his quarters, for he was grown bigger than a sheep. The King then had him flayed and his skin dressed. Then he issued a proclamation that whoever could tell what this skin was should marry the Princess.

As soon as this decree was made known the people flocked in crowds from all the ends of the world to try their luck. One said that it belonged to an ape, another to a lynx, a third to a crocodile, and in short some gave it to one animal and some to another; but they were all a hundred miles from the truth, and not one hit the nail on the head. At last there came to this trial an ogre who was the most ugly being in the world, the very sight of whom would make the boldest man tremble and quake with fear. But no sooner had he come and turned the skin round and smelt it than he instantly guessed the truth, saying, "This skin belongs to the king of fleas."

Now the King saw that the ogre had hit the mark; and not to break his word he ordered his daughter Porziella to be called. Porziella had a face like milk and roses, and was such a miracle of beauty that you would never be tired of looking at her. And the King said to her, "My daughter, you know who I am. I cannot go back from my promise whether a king or a beggar. My word is given, I must keep it though my heart should break. Who would ever have imagined that this prize would have fallen to an ogre! But it never does to judge hastily. Have patience then and do not oppose your father; for my heart tells me that you will be happy, for rich treasures are often found inside a rough earthen jar."

When Porziella heard this sad saying her eyes grew dim, her face turned pale, her lips fell, her knees shook; and at last, bursting into tears, she said to her father, "What crime have I committed that I should be punished thus! How have I ever behaved badly toward you that I should be given up to this monster. Is this, O Father, the affection you bear to your own child? Is this the love you show to her whom you used to call the joy of your soul? Do you drive from your sight her who is the apple of your eye? O Father, O cruel Father! Better had it been if my cradle had been my death-bed since I have lived to see this evil day."

Porziella was going on to say more when the King in a furious rage exclaimed, "Stay your anger! Fair and softly, for appearances deceive. Is it for a girl to teach her father, forsooth? Have done, I say, for if I lay these hands upon you I'll not leave a whole bone in your skin. Prithee, how long has a child hardly out of the nursery dared to oppose my will? Quick then, I say, take his hand and set off with him home this very instant, for I will not have that saucy face a minute longer in my sight."

Poor Porziella, seeing herself thus caught in the net, with the face of a person condemned to death, with the heart of one whose head is lying between the axe and the block, took the hand of the ogre, who dragged her off without any attendants to the wood where the trees made a palace for the meadow to prevent its being discovered by the sun, and the brooks murmured, having knocked against the stones in the dark, while the wild beasts wandered where they liked without paying toll, and went safely through the thicket whither no man ever came unless he had lost his way. Upon this spot, which was as black as an unswept chimney, stood the ogre's house ornamented all round with the bones of the men whom he had devoured. Think but for a moment of the horror of it to the poor girl.

But this was nothing at all in comparison with what was to come. Before dinner she had peas and after dinner parched beans. Then the ogre went out to hunt and returned home laden with the quarters of the men whom he had killed, saying, "Now, wife, you cannot complain that I don't take good care of you; here is a fine store of eatables, take and make merry and love me well, for the sky will fall before I will let you want for food."

Poor Porziella could not endure this horrible sight and turned her face away. But when the ogre saw this he cried, "Ha! this is throwing sweetmeats before swine; never mind, however, only have patience till to-morrow morning, for I have been invited to a wild boar hunt and will bring you home a couple of boars, and we'll make a grand feast with our kinsfolk and celebrate the wedding." So saying he went into the forest.

Now as Porziella stood weeping at the window it chanced that an old woman passed by who, being famished with hunger, begged some food. "Ah, my good woman," said Porziella, "Heaven knows I am in the power of the ogre who brings me home nothing but pieces of the men he has killed. I pass the most miserable life possible, and yet I am the daughter of a king and have been brought up in luxury." And so saying she began to cry like a little girl who sees her bread and butter taken away from her.

The old woman's heart was softened at this sight and she said to Porziella, "Be of good heart, my pretty girl, do not spoil your beauty with crying, for you have met with luck; I can help you to both saddle and trappings. Listen, now. I have seven sons who, you see, are seven giants, Mase, Nardo, Cola, Micco, Petrullo, Ascaddeo, and Ceccone, who have more virtues that rosemary, especially Mase, for every time he lays his ear to the ground he hears all that is passing within thirty miles round. Nardo, every time he washes his hands, makes a great sea of soapsuds. Every time that Cola throws a bit of iron on the ground he makes a field of sharp razors. Whenever Micco flings down a little stick a tangled wood springs up. If Petrullo lets fall a drop of water it makes a terrible river. When Ascaddeo wishes a strong tower to spring up he has only to throw a stone; and Ceccone shoots so straight with the cross-bow that he can hit a hen's eye a mile off. Now with the help of my sons, who are all courteous and friendly, and who will all take compassion on your condition, I will contrive to free you from the claws of the ogre."

"No time better than now," replied Porziella, "for that evil shadow of a husband of mine has gone out and will not return this evening, and we shall have time to slip off and run away."

"It cannot be this evening," replied the old woman, "for I live a long way off; but I promise you that to-morrow morning I and my sons will all come together and help you out of your trouble."

So saying, the old woman departed, and Porziella went to rest with a light heart and slept soundly all night. But as soon as the birds began to cry, "Long live the Sun," lo and behold, there was the old woman with her seven children; and placing Porziella in the midst of them they proceeded towards the city. But they had not gone above half a mile when Mase put his ear to the ground and cried: "Hallo, have a care; here's the fox. The ogre is come home. He has missed his wife and he is hastening after us with his cap under his arm."

No sooner did Nardo hear this than he washed his hands and made a sea of soap-suds; and when the ogre came and saw all the suds he ran home and fetching a sack of bran he strewed it about and worked away treading it down with his feet until at last he got over this obstacle, though with great difficulty.

But Mase put his ear once more to the ground and exclaimed, "Look sharp, comrade, here he comes!" Thereupon Cola flung a piece of iron on the ground and instantly a field of razors sprang up. When the ogre saw the path stopped he ran home again and clad himself in iron from head to foot and then returned and got over this peril.

Then Mase, again putting his ear to the ground, cried, "Up! up! to arms! to arms! For see here is the ogre coming at such a rate that he is actually flying." But Micco was ready with his little stick, and in an instant he caused a terrible wood to rise up, so thick that it was quite impenetrable. When the ogre came to this difficult pass he laid hold of a Carrara knife which he wore at his side, and began to cut down the poplars and oaks and pine trees and chestnut trees, right and left; so that with four or five strokes he had the whole forest on the ground and got clear of it. Presently, Mase who kept his ears on the alert like a hare, again raised his voice and cried, "Now we must be off, for the ogre is coming like the wind and here he is at our heels." As soon as Petrullo heard this he took water from a little fountain, sprinkled it on the ground, and in an twinkling of an eye a large river rose up on the spot. When the ogre saw this new obstacle, and that he could not make holes so fast as they found bungs to stop them, he stripped himself stark naked and swam across to the other side of the river with his clothes upon his head.

Mase, who put his ear to every chink, heard the ogre coming and exclaimed, "Alas! matters go ill with us now. I already hear the clatter of the ogre's heels. We must be on our guard and ready to meet the storm or else we are done for." "Never fear," said Ascaddeo, "I will soon settle this ugly ragamuffin." So saying, he flung a pebble on the ground and instantly up rose a tower in which they all took refuge without delay, and barred the door. But when the ogre came up and saw that they had got into so safe a place he ran home, got a vine-dresser's ladder, and carried it back on his shoulder to the tower.

Now Mase, who kept his ears hanging down, heard at a distance the approach of the ogre and cried, "We are now at the butt end of the Candle of Hope. Ceccone is our last resource, for the ogre is coming back in a terrible fury. Alas! how my heart beats, for I foresee an evil day." "You coward," answered Ceccone, "trust to me and I will hit him with a ball."

As Ceccone was speaking the ogre came, planted his ladder and began to climb up; but Ceccone, taking aim at him, shot out one of his eyes and laid him at full length on the ground, like a pear dropped from a tree. Then he went out of the tower and cut off the ogre's head with a big knife he carried about with him, just as if it had been new-made cheese. Thereupon they took the head with great joy to the King, who rejoiced at the recovery of his daughter, for he had repented a hundred times at having given her to an ogre. And not many days after Porziella was married to a handsome prince, and the seven sons and their mother who had delivered her from such a wretched life were rewarded with great riches.

VI

CENERENTOLA

In the sea of malice envy frequently gets out of her depth; and, while she is expecting to see another drowned, she is either drowned herself, or is dashed against a rock, as happened to some envious girls, about whom I will tell you a story.

There once lived a Prince, who was a widower. He had an only daughter, so dear to him that he saw with no other eyes than hers; and he kept a governess for her, who taught her chain-work and knitting, and to make point-lace, and showed her such affection as no words can tell. But she was very lonely, and many a time she said to the governess, "Oh, that you had been my mother, you who show me such kindness and love," and she said this so often that, at last, the governess, having a bee put into her bonnet, said to her one day, "If you will do as this foolish head of mine advises I shall be mother to you, and you will be as dear to me as the apple of my eye."

She was going to say more, when Zezolla, for that was the name of the Princess, said, "Pardon me if I stop the word upon your tongue. I know you wish me well, therefore, hush—enough. Only show me the way. Do you write and I will subscribe." "Well, then," answered the governess, "open your ears and listen, and you will get bread as white as the flowers. You know well enough that your father would even coin false money to please you, so do you entreat him when he is caressing you to marry me and make me Princess. Then, bless your stars! you shall be the mistress of my life."

When Zezolla heard this, every hour seemed to her a thousand years until she had done all that her governess had advised; and, as soon as the mourning for her mother's death was ended, she began to feel her father's pulse, and beg him to marry the governess. At first the Prince took it as a joke, but Zezolla went on shooting so long past the mark that at length she hit it, and he gave way to her entreaties. So he married the governess, and gave a great feast at the wedding.

Now, while the young folks were dancing, and Zezolla was standing at the window of her house, a dove came flying and perched upon a wall, and said to her, "Whenever you need anything send the request to the Dove of the Fairies in the Island of Sardinia, and you will instantly have what you wish."

For five or six days the new stepmother overwhelmed Zezolla with caresses, seating her at the best place at table, giving her the choicest morsels to eat, and clothing her in the richest apparel. But ere long, forgetting entirely the good service she had received (woe to him who has a bad master!), she began to bring forward six daughters of her own, for she had never before told any one that she was a widow with a bunch of girls; and she praised them so much, and talked her husband over in such a fashion, that at last the stepdaughters had all his favour, and the thought of his own child went entirely from his heart. In short, it fared so ill with the poor girl, bad to-day and worse to-morrow, that she was at last brought down from the royal chamber to the kitchen, from the canopy of state to the hearth, from splendid apparel of silks and gold to dishclouts, from the sceptre to the spit. And not only was her condition changed, but even her name, for, instead of Zezolla, she was now called Cenerentola.

It happened that the Prince had occasion to go to Sardinia upon affairs of state, and, calling the six stepdaughters, he asked them, one by one, what they would like him to bring them on his return. Then one wished for splendid dresses, another to have head-ornaments, another rouge for the face, another toys and trinkets: one wished for this and one for that. At last the Prince said to his own daughter, as if in mockery, "And what would you have, child?" "Nothing, father," she replied, "but that you commend me to the Dove of the Fairies, and bid her send me something; and if you forget my request, may you be unable to stir backwards or forwards; so remember what I tell you, for it will fare with you accordingly."

Then the Prince went his way and did his business in Sardinia, and procured all the things that his stepdaughters had asked for; but poor Zezolla was quite out of his thoughts. And going on board a ship he set sail to return, but the ship could not get out of the harbour; there it stuck fast just as if held by a sea-lamprey. The captain of the ship, who was almost in despair and fairly tired out, laid himself down to sleep, and in his dream he saw a fairy, who said to him, "Know you the reason why you cannot work the ship out of port? It is because the Prince who is on board with you has broken his promise to his daughter, remembering every one except his own child."

Then the captain awoke and told his dream to the Prince, who, in shame and confusion at the breach of his promise, went to the Grotto of the Fairies, and, commending his daughter to them, asked them to send her something. And behold, there stepped forth from the grotto a beautiful maiden, who told him that she thanked his daughter for her kind remembrances, and bade him tell her to be merry and of good heart out of love to her. And thereupon she gave him a date-tree, a hoe, and a little bucket all of gold, and a silken napkin, adding that the one was to hoe with and the other to water the plant.

The Prince, marvelling at this present, took leave of the fairy, and returned to his own country. And when he had given his stepdaughters all the things they had desired, he at last gave his own daughter the gift which the fairy had sent her. Then Zezolla, out of her wits with joy, took the date-tree and planted it in a pretty flower-pot, hoed the earth round it, watered it, and wiped its leaves morning and evening with the silken napkin. In a few days it had grown as tall as a woman, and out of it came a fairy, who said to Zezolla, "What do you wish for?" And Zezolla replied that she wished sometimes to leave the house without her sisters' knowledge. The fairy answered, "Whenever you desire this, come to the flower-pot and say:

My little Date-tree, my golden tree,
With a golden hoe I have hoed thee,
With a golden can I have watered thee,
With a silken cloth I have wiped thee dry,
Now strip thee and dress me speedily.

And when you wish to undress, change the last words and say, 'Strip me and dress thee.'"

When the time for the feast was come, and the stepmother's daughters appeared, dressed out so fine, all ribbons and flowers, and slippers and shoes, sweet smells and bells, and roses and posies, Zezolla ran quickly to the flower-pot, and no sooner had she repeated the words, as the fairy had told her, than she saw herself arrayed like a queen, seated upon a palfrey, and attended by twelve smart pages, all in their best clothes. Then she went to the ball, and made the sisters envious of this unknown beauty.

Even the young King himself was there, and as soon as he saw her he stood magic-bound with amazement, and ordered a trusty servant to find out who was that beautiful maiden, and where she lived. So the servant followed in her footsteps; but when Zezolla noticed the trick she threw on the ground a handful of crown-pieces which she had made the date-tree give her for this purpose. Then the servant lighted his lantern, and was so busy picking up all the crown-pieces that he forgot to follow the palfrey; and Zezolla came home quite safely, and had changed her clothes, as the fairy told her, before the wicked sisters arrived, and, to vex her and make her envious, told her of all the fine things they had seen. But the King was very angry with the servant, and warned him not to miss finding out next time who this beautiful maiden was, and where she dwelt.

Soon there was another feast, and again the sisters all went to it, leaving poor Zezolla at home on the kitchen hearth. Then she ran quickly to the date-tree, and repeated the spell, and instantly there appeared a number of damsels, one with a looking-glass, another with a bottle of rose-water, another with the curling-irons, another with combs, another with pins, another with dresses, and another with capes and collars. And they decked her out as glorious as the sun, and put her in a coach drawn by six white horses, and attended by footmen and pages in livery. And no sooner did she appear in the ball-room than the hearts of the sisters were filled with amazement, and the King was overcome with love.

When Zezolla went home the servant followed her again, but so that she should not be caught she threw down a handful of pearls and jewels, and the good fellow, seeing that they were not things to lose, stayed to pick them up. So she had time to slip away and take off her fine dress as before.

Meanwhile the servant had returned slowly to the King, who cried out when he saw him, "By the souls of my ancestors, if you do not find out who she is you shall have such a thrashing as was never before heard of, and as many kicks as you have hairs in your beard!"

When the next feast was held, and the sisters were safely out of the house, Zezolla went to the date-tree, and once again repeated the spell. In an instant she found herself splendidly arrayed and seated in a coach of gold, with ever so many servants around her, so that she looked just like a queen. Again the sisters were beside themselves with envy; but this time, when she left the ball-room, the King's servant kept close to the coach. Zezolla, seeing that the man was ever running by her side, cried, "Coachman, drive on quickly," and in a trice the coach set off at such a rattling pace that she lost one of her slippers, the prettiest thing that ever was seen. The servant being unable to catch the coach, which flew like a bird, picked up the slipper, and carrying it to the King told him all that happened. Whereupon the King, taking it in his hand, said, "If the basement, indeed, is so beautiful, what must the building be. You who until now were the prison of a white foot are now the fetter of an unhappy heart!"

Then he made a proclamation that all the women in the country should come to a banquet, for which the most splendid provision was made of pies and pastries, and stews and ragouts, macaroni and sweetmeats—enough to feed a whole army. And when all the women were assembled, noble and ignoble, rich and poor, beautiful and ugly, the King tried the slipper on each one of the guests to see whom it should fit to a hair, and thus be able to discover by the help of the slipper the maiden of whom he was in search, but not one foot could he find to fit it. So he examined them closely whether indeed every one was there; and the Prince confessed that he had left one daughter behind, "but," said he, "she is always on the hearth, and is such a graceless simpleton that she is unworthy to sit and eat at your table." But the King said, "Let her be the very first on the list, for so I will."

So all the guests departed—the very next day they assembled again, and with the wicked sisters came Zezolla. When the King saw her he had his suspicions, but said nothing. And after the feast came the trial of the slipper, which, as soon as ever it approached Zezolla's foot, it darted on to it of its own accord like iron flies to the magnet Seeing this, the King ran to her and took her in his arms, and seating her under the royal canopy, he set the crown upon her head, whereupon all made their obeisance and homage to her as their queen.

When the wicked sisters saw this they were full of venom and rage, and, not having patience to look upon the object of their hatred, they slipped quietly away on tip-toe and went home to their mother, confessing, in spite of themselves, that—

"He is a madman who resists the Stars."

VII

THE MERCHANT

Troubles are usually the brooms and shovels that smooth the road to a man's good fortune, of which he little dreams. Many a man curses the rain that falls upon his head, and knows not that it brings abundance to drive away hunger; as is seen in the person of a young man of whom I will tell you.

It is said that there was once a very rich merchant named Antoniello, who had a son called Cienzo. It happened that Cienzo was one day throwing stones on the sea-shore with the son of the King of Naples, and by chance broke his companion's head. When he told his father, Antoniello flew into a rage with fear of the consequences and abused his son; but Cienzo answered, "Sir, I have always heard say that better is the law court than the doctor in one's house. Would it not have been worse if he had broken my head? It was he who began and provoked me. We are but boys, and there are two sides to the quarrel. After all tis a first fault, and the King is a man of reason; but let the worst come to the worst, what great harm can he do me? The wide world is one's home; and let him who is afraid turn constable."

But Antoniello would not listen to reason. He made sure the King would kill Cienzo for his fault and said, "Don't stand here at risk of your life; but march off this very instant, so that nobody may hear a word, new or old, of what you have done. A bird in the bush is better than a bird in the cage. Here is money. Take one of the two enchanted horses I have in the stable, and the dog which is also enchanted, and tarry no longer here. It is better to scamper off and use your own heels than to be touched by another's; better to throw your legs over your back than to carry your head between two legs. If you don't take your knapsack and be off, none of the Saints can help you!"

Then begging his father's blessing, Cienzo mounted his horse, and tucking the enchanted dog under his arm, he went his way out of the city. Making a winter of tears with a summer of sighs he went his way until the evening, when he came to a wood that kept the Mule of the Sun outside its limits, while it was amusing itself with Silence and the Shades. An old house stood there, at the foot of a tower. Cienzo knocked at the door of the tower; but the master, being in fear of robbers, would not open to him, so the poor youth was obliged to remain in the ruined old house. He turned his horse out to graze in a meadow, and threw himself on some straw he found, with the dog by his side. But scarcely had he closed his eyes when he was awakened by the barking of the dog, and heard footsteps stirring in the house. Cienzo, who was bold and venturesome, seized his sword and began to lay about him in the dark; but perceiving that he was only striking the wind and hit no one, he turned round again to sleep. After a few minutes he felt himself pulled gently by the foot. He turned to lay hold again of his cutlass, and jumping up, exclaimed, "Hollo there! you are getting too troublesome; but leave off this sport and let's have a bout of it if you have any pluck, for you have found the last to your shoe!"

At these words he heard a shout of laughter and then a hollow voice saying, "Come down here and I will tell you who I am." Then Cienzo, without losing courage, answered, "Wait awhile, I'll come." So he groped about until at last he found a ladder which led to a cellar; and, going down, he saw a lighted lamp, and three ghost-looking figures who were making a piteous clamour, crying, "Alas, my beauteous treasure, I must lose thee!"

When Cienzo saw this he began himself to cry and lament, for company's sake; and after he had wept for some time, the Moon having now, with the axe of her rays broken the bar of the Sky, the three figures who were making the outcry said to Cienzo, "Take this treasure, which is destined for thee alone, but mind and take care of it." Then they vanished. And Cienzo, espying the sunlight through a hole in the wall, wished to climb up again, but could not find the ladder, whereat he set up such a cry that the master of the tower heard him and fetched a ladder, when they discovered a great treasure. He wished to give part of it to Cienzo, but the latter refused; and taking his dog and mounting once more on his horse set out again on his travels.

After a while he arrived at a wild and dreary forest, so dark that it made you shudder. There, upon the bank of a river, he found a fairy surrounded by a band of robbers. Cienzo, seeing the wicked intention of the robbers, seized his sword and soon made a slaughter of them. The fairy showered thanks upon him for this brave deed done for her sake, and invited him to her palace that she might reward him. But Cienzo replied, "It is nothing at all; thank you kindly. Another time I will accept the favour; but now I am in haste, on business of importance!"

So saying he took his leave; and travelling on a long way he came at last to the palace of a King, which was all hung with mourning, so that it made one's heart black to look at it. When Cienzo inquired the cause of the mourning the folks answered, "A dragon with seven heads has made his appearance in this country, the most terrible monster that ever was seen, with the crest of a cock, the head of a cat, eyes of fire, the mouth of a bulldog, the wings of a bat, the claws of a bear, and the tail of a serpent. Now this dragon swallows a maiden every day, and now the lot has fallen on Menechella, the daughter of the King. So there is great weeping and wailing in the royal palace, since the fairest creature in all the land is doomed to be devoured by this horrid beast."

When Cienzo heard this he stepped aside and saw Menechella pass by with the mourning train, accompanied by the ladies of the court and all the women of the land, wringing their hands and tearing out their hair by handfuls, and bewailing the sad fate of the poor girl. Then the dragon came out of the cave. But Cienzo laid hold of his sword and struck off a head in a trice; but the dragon went and rubbed his neck on a certain plant which grew not far off, and suddenly the head joined itself on again, like a lizard joining itself to its tail. Cienzo, seeing this, exclaimed, "He who dares not, wins not"; and, setting his teeth, he struck such a furious blow that he cut off all seven heads, which flew from the necks like peas from the pan. Whereupon he took out the tongues, and putting them in his pocket, he flung the heads a mile apart from the body, so that they might never come together again. Then he sent Menechella home to her father, and went himself to repose in a tavern.

When the King saw his daughter his delight is not to be told; and having heard the manner in which she had been freed, he ordered a proclamation to be instantly made, that whosoever had killed the dragon should come and marry the Princess. Now a rascal of a country fellow, hearing this proclamation, took the heads of the dragon, and said, "Menechella has been saved by me; these hands have freed the land from destruction; behold the dragon's heads, which are the proofs of my valour; therefore recollect, every promise is a debt." As soon as the King heard this, he lifted the crown from his own head and set it upon the countryman's poll, who looked like a thief on the gallows.

The news of this proclamation flew through the whole country, till at last it came to the ears of Cienzo, who said to himself, "Verily, I am a great blockhead! I had hold of Fortune by the forelock, and I let her escape out of my hand. Here's a man offers to give me the half of a treasure he finds, and I care no more for it than a German for cold water; the fairy wishes to entertain me in her palace, and I care as little for it as an ass for music; and now that I am called to the crown, here I stand and let a rascally thief cheat me out of my trump-card!" So saying he took an inkstand, seized a pen, and spreading out a sheet of paper, began to write:

"To the most beautiful jewel of women, Menechella—Having, by the favour of Sol in Leo, saved thy life, I hear that another plumes himself with my labours, that another claims the reward of the service which I rendered. Thou, therefore, who wast present at the dragon's death, canst assure the King of the truth, and prevent his allowing another to gain this reward while I have had all the toil. For it will be the right effect of thy fair royal grace and the merited recompense of this strong hero's fist. In conclusion, I kiss thy delicate little hands.

"From the Inn of the Flower-pot, Sunday."

Having written this letter, and sealed it with a wafer, he placed it in the mouth of the enchanted dog, saying, "Run off as fast as you can and take this to the King's daughter. Give it to no one else, but place it in the hand of that silver-faced maiden herself."

Away ran the dog to the palace as if he were flying, and going up the stairs he found the King, who was still paying compliments to the country clown. When the man saw the dog with the letter in his mouth, he ordered it to be taken from him; but the dog would not give it to any one, and bounding up to Menechella he placed it in her hand. Then Menechella rose from her seat, and, making a curtsey to the King, she gave him the letter to read; and when the King had read it he ordered that the dog should be followed to see where he went, and that his master should be brought before him. So two of the courtiers immediately followed the dog, until they came to the tavern, where they found Cienzo; and, delivering the message from the King, they conducted him to the palace, into the presence of the King. Then the King demanded how it was that he boasted of having killed the dragon, since the heads were brought by the man who was sitting crowned at his side. And Cienzo answered, "That fellow deserves a pasteboard mitre rather than a crown, since he has had the impudence to tell you a bouncing lie. But to prove to you that I have done the deed and not this rascal, order the heads to be produced. None of them can speak to the proof without a tongue, and these I have brought with me as witnesses to convince you of the truth."

So saying he pulled the tongues out of his pocket, while the countryman was struck all of a heap, not knowing what would be the end of it; and the more so when Menechella added, "This is the man! Ah, you dog of a countryman, a pretty trick you have played me!" When the King heard this, he took the crown from the head of that false loon and placed it on that of Cienzo; and he was on the point of sending the imposter to the galleys, but Cienzo begged the King to have mercy on him and to confound his wickedness with courtesy. Then he married Menechella, and the tables were spread and a royal banquet was set forth; and in the morning they sent for Antoniello with all his family; and Antoniello soon got into great favour with the King, and saw in the person of his son the saying verified—

"A straight port to a crooked ship."

VIII

GOAT-FACE

All the ill-deeds that a man commits have some colour of excuse—either contempt which provokes, need which compels, love which blinds, or anger which breaks the neck. But ingratitude is a thing that has no excuse, true or false, upon which it can fix; and it is therefore the worst of vices, since it dries up the fountain of compassion, extinguishes the fire of love, closes the road to benefits, and causes vexation and repentance to spring up in the hearts of the ungrateful. As you will see in the story which I am about to relate.

A peasant had twelve daughters, not one of whom was a head taller than the next; for every year their mother presented him with a little girl; so that the poor man, to support his family decently, went early every morning as a day labourer and dug hard the whole day long. With what his labour produced he just kept his little ones from dying of hunger.

He happened, one day, to be digging at the foot of a mountain, the spy of other mountains, that thrust its head above the clouds to see what they were doing up in the sky, and close to a cavern so deep and dark that the sun was afraid to enter it. Out of this cavern there came a green lizard as big as a crocodile; and the poor man was so terrified that he had not the power to run away, expecting every moment the end of his days from a gulp of that ugly animal. But the lizard, approaching him, said, "Be not afraid, my good man, for I am not come here to do you any harm, but to do you good."

When Masaniello (for that was the name of the labourer) heard this, he fell on his knees and said, "Mistress What's-your-name, I am wholly in your power. Act then worthily and have compassion on this poor trunk that has twelve branches to support."

"It is on this very account," said the lizard, "that I am disposed to serve you; so bring me, to-morrow morning the youngest of your daughters; for I will rear her up like my own child, and love her as my life."

At this the poor father was more confounded than a thief when the stolen goods are found on his back. For, hearing the lizard ask him for one of his daughters, and that too, the tenderest of them, he concluded that the cloak was not without wool on it, and that she wanted the child as a titbit to stay her appetite. Then he said to himself, "If I give her my daughter, I give her my soul. If I refuse her, she will take this body of mine. If I yield her, I am robbed of my heart; if I deny her she will suck out my blood. If I consent, she takes away part of myself; if I refuse, she takes the whole. What shall I resolve on? What course shall I take? What expedient shall I adopt? Oh, what an ill day's work have I made of it! What a misfortune has rained down from heaven upon me!"

While he was speaking thus, the lizard said, "Resolve quickly and do what I tell you; or you will leave only your rags here. For so I will have it, and so it will be." Masaniello, hearing this decree and having no one to whom he could appeal, returned home quite melancholy, as yellow in the face as if he had jaundice; and his wife, seeing him hanging his head like a sick bird and his shoulders like one that is wounded, said to him, "What has happened to you, husband? Have you had a quarrel with any one? Is there a warrant out against you? Or is the ass dead?"

"Nothing of that sort," said Masaniello, "but a horned lizard has put me into a fright, for she has threatened that if I do not bring her our youngest daughter, she will make me suffer for it. My head is turning like a reel. I know not what fish to take. On one side love constrains me; on the other the burden of my family. I love Renzolla dearly, I love my own life dearly. If I do not give the lizard this portion of my heart, she will take the whole compass of my unfortunate body. So now, dear wife, advise me, or I am ruined!"

When his wife heard this, she said, "Who knows, husband, but this may be a lizard with two tails, that will make our fortune? Who knows but this lizard may put an end to all our miseries? How often, when we should have an eagle's sight to discern the good luck that is running to meet us, we have a cloth before our eyes and the cramp in our hands, when we should lay hold on it. So go, take her away, for my heart tells me that some good fortune awaits the poor little thing!"

These words comforted Masaniello; and the next morning, as soon as the Sun with the brush of his rays whitewashed the Sky, which the shades of night had blackened, he took the little girl by the hand, and led her to the cave. Then the lizard came out, and taking the child gave the father a bag full of crowns, saying, "Go now, be happy, for Renzolla has found both father and mother."

Masaniello, overjoyed, thanked the lizard and went home to his wife. There was money enough for portions to all the other daughters when they married, and even then the old folks had sauce remaining for themselves to enable them to swallow with relish the toils of life.

Then the lizard made a most beautiful palace for Renzolla, and brought her up in such state and magnificence as would have dazzled the eyes of any queen. She wanted for nothing. Her food was fit for a count, her clothing for a princess. She had a hundred maidens to wait upon her, and with such good treatment she grew as sturdy as an oak-tree.

It happened, as the King was out hunting in those parts, that night overtook him, and as he stood looking round, not knowing where to lay his head, he saw a candle shining in the palace. So he sent one of his servants, to ask the owner to give him shelter. When the servant came to the palace, the lizard appeared before him in the shape of a beautiful lady; who, after hearing his message, said that his master should be a thousand times welcome, and that neither bread nor knife should there be wanting. The King, on hearing this reply, went to the palace and was received like a cavalier. A hundred pages went out to meet him, so that it looked like the funeral of a rich man. A hundred other pages brought the dishes to the table. A hundred others made a brave noise with musical instruments. But, above all, Renzolla served the King and handed him drink with such grace that he drank more love than wine.

When he had thus been so royally entertained, he felt he could not live without Renzolla; so, calling the fairy, he asked her for his wife. Whereupon the fairy, who wished for nothing but Renzolla's good, not only freely consented, but gave her a dowry of seven millions of gold.

The King, overjoyed at this piece of good fortune, departed with Renzolla, who, ill-mannered and ungrateful for all the fairy had done for her, went off with her husband without uttering one single word of thanks. Then the fairy, beholding such ingratitude, cursed her, and wished that her face should become like that of a she-goat; and hardly had she uttered the words, when Renzolla's mouth stretched out, with a beard a span long on it, her jaws shrunk, her skin hardened, her cheeks grew hairy, and her plaited tresses turned to pointed horns.

When the poor King saw this he was thunderstruck, not knowing what had happened that so great a beauty should be thus transformed; and, with sighs and tears he exclaimed, "Where are the locks that bound me? Where are the eyes that transfixed me? Must I then be the husband of a she-goat? No, no, my heart shall not break for such a goat-face!" So saying, as soon as they reached his palace, he put Renzolla into a kitchen, along with a chambermaid; and gave to each of them ten bundles of flax to spin, commanding them to have the thread ready at the end of a week.

The maid, in obedience to the King, set about carding the flax, preparing and putting it on the distaff, twirling her spindle, reeling it and working away without ceasing; so that on Saturday evening her thread was all done. But Renzolla, thinking she was still the same as in the fairy's house, not having looked at herself in the glass, threw the flax out of the window, saying, "A pretty thing indeed of the King to set me such work to do! If he wants shirts let him buy them, and not fancy that he picked me up out of the gutter. But let him remember that I brought him home seven millions of gold, and that I am his wife and not his servant. Methinks, too, that he is somewhat of a donkey to treat me this way!"

Nevertheless, when Saturday morning came, seeing that the maid had spun all her share of the flax, Renzolla was greatly afraid; so away she went to the palace of the fairy and told her misfortune. Then the fairy embraced her with great affection, and gave her a bag full of spun thread, to present to the King and show him what a notable and industrious housewife she was. Renzolla took the bag, and without saying one word of thanks, went to the royal palace; so again the fairy was quite angered at the conduct of the graceless girl.

When the King had taken the thread, he gave two little dogs, one to Renzolla and one to the maid, telling them to feed and rear them. The maid reared hers on bread crumbs and treated it like a child; but Renzolla grumbled, saying, "A pretty thing truly! As my grandfather used to say, Are we living under the Turks? Am I indeed to comb and wait upon dogs?" and she flung the dog out of the window!

Some months afterwards, the King asked for the dogs; whereat Renzolla, losing heart, ran off again to the fairy, and at the gate stood the old man who was the porter. "Who are you," said he, "and whom do you want?" Renzolla, hearing herself addressed in this off-hand way, replied, "Don't you know me, you old goat-beard?"

"Why do you miscall me?" said the porter. "This is the thief accusing the constable. I a goat-beard indeed! You are a goat-beard and a half, and you merit it and worse for your presumption. Wait awhile, you impudent woman; I'll enlighten you and you will see to what your airs and impertinence have brought you!"

So saying, he ran into his room, and taking a looking-glass, set it before Renzolla; who, when she saw her ugly, hairy visage, was like to have died with terror. Her dismay at seeing her face so altered that she did not know herself cannot be told. Whereupon the old man said to her, "You ought to recollect, Renzolla, that you are a daughter of a peasant and that it was the fairy that raised you to be a queen. But you, rude, unmannerly, and thankless as you are, having little gratitude for such high favours, have kept her waiting outside your heart, without showing the slightest mark of affection. You have brought the quarrel on yourself; see what a face you have got by it! See to what you are brought by your ingratitude; for through the fairy's spell you have not only changed face, but condition. But if you will do as this white-beard advises, go and look for the fairy; throw yourself at her feet, tear your beard, beat your breast, and ask pardon for the ill-treatment you have shown her. She is tender-hearted and she will be moved to pity by your misfortune."

Renzolla, who was touched to the quick, and felt that he had hit the nail on the head, followed the old man's advice. Then the fairy embraced and kissed her; and restoring her to her former appearance, she clad her in a robe that was quite heavy with gold; and placing her in a magnificent coach, accompanied with a crowd of servants, she brought her to the King. When the King beheld her, so beautiful and splendidly attired, he loved her as his own life; blaming himself for all the misery he had made her endure, but excusing himself on account of that odious goat-face which had been the cause of it. Thus Renzolla lived happy, loving her husband, honouring the fairy, and showing herself grateful to the old man, having learned to her cost that—

"It is always good to be mannerly."

IX

THE ENCHANTED DOE

Great is the power of friendship, which makes us willingly bear toils and perils to serve a friend. We value our wealth as a trifle and life as a straw, when we can give them for a friend's sake. Fables teach us this and history is full of instances of it; and I will give you an example which my grandmother used to relate to me. So open your ears and shut your mouths and hear what I shall tell you.

There was once a certain King of Long-Trellis named Giannone, who, desiring greatly to have children, continually made prayers to the gods that they would grant his wish; and, in order to incline them the more to his petition, he was so charitable to beggars and pilgrims that he shared with them all he possessed. But seeing, at last, that these things availed him nothing; and that there was no end to putting his hand into his pocket, he bolted fast his door, and shot with a cross-bow at all who came near.

Now it happened one day, that a long-bearded pilgrim was passing that way, and not knowing that the King had turned over a new leaf, or perhaps knowing it and wishing to make him change his mind again, he went to Giannone and begged for shelter in his house. But, with a fierce look and terrible growl, the King said to him, "If you have no other candle than this, you may go to bed in the dark. The kittens have their eyes open, and I am no longer a child." And when the old man asked what was the cause of this change, the King replied, "To further my desire for children, I have spent and lent to all who came and all who went, and have squandered all my treasure. At last, seeing the beard was gone, I stopped shaving and laid aside the razor."

"If that be all," replied the pilgrim, "you may set your mind at rest, for I promise that your wish shall forthwith be fulfilled, on pain of losing my ears."

"Be it so," said the King, "I pledge my word that I will give you one half of my kingdom." And the man answered, "Listen now to me—if you wish to hit the mark, you have only to get the heart of a sea-dragon, and have it cooked and eaten by the Queen, and you will see that what I say will speedily come to pass."

"That hardly seems possible," said the King, "but at the worst I lose nothing by the trial; so I must, this very moment, get the dragon's heart."

So he sent a hundred fishermen out; and they got ready all kinds of fishing-tackle, drag-nets, casting-nets, seine-nets, bow-nets, and fishing-lines; and they tacked and turned and cruised in all directions until at last they caught a dragon; then they took out its heart and brought it to the King, who gave it to the Queen to cook and eat. And when she had eaten it, there was great rejoicing, for the King's desire was fulfilled and he became the father of two sons, so like the other that nobody but the Queen could tell which was which. And the boys grew up together in such love for one another that they could not be parted for a moment. Their attachment was so great that the Queen began to be jealous, at seeing that the son whom she destined to be heir to his father, and whose name was Fonzo, testified more affection for his brother Canneloro than he did for herself. And she knew not in what way to remove this thorn from her eyes.

Now one day Fonzo wished to go a-hunting with his brother; so he had a fire lighted in his chamber and began to melt lead to make bullets; and being in want of I know not what, he went himself to look for it. Meanwhile the Queen came in, and finding no one there but Canneloro, she thought to put him out of the world. So stooping down, she flung the hot bullet-mould at his face, which hit him over the brow and made an ugly wound. She was just going to repeat the blow when Fonzo came in; so, pretending that she was only come in to see how he was, she gave him some caresses and went away.

Canneloro, pulling his hat down on his forehead, said nothing of his wound to Fonzo, but stood quite quiet though he was burning with the pain. But as soon as they had done making the balls, he told his brother that he must leave him. Fonzo, all in amazement at this new resolution, asked him the reason: but he replied, "Enquire no more, my dear Fonzo, let it suffice that I am obliged to go away and part with you, who are my heart and my soul and the breath of my body. Since it cannot be otherwise, farewell, and keep me in remembrance." Then after embracing one another and shedding many tears, Canneloro went to his own room. He put on a suit of armour and a sword and armed himself from top to toe; and, having taken a horse out of the stable, he was just putting his foot into the stirrup when Fonzo came weeping and said, "Since you are resolved to abandon me, you should, at least, leave me some token of your love, to diminish my anguish for your absence." Thereupon Canneloro struck his dagger into the ground, and instantly a fine fountain rose up. Then said he to his twin-brother, "This is the best memorial I can leave you. By the flowing of this fountain you will follow the course of my life. If you see it run clear, know that my life is likewise clear and tranquil. If it is turbid, think that I am passing through troubles; and if it is dry, depend on it that the oil of my life is all consumed and that I have paid the toll which belongs to Nature!"

Then he drove his sword into the ground, and immediately a myrtle-tree grew up, when he said, "As long as this myrtle is green, know that I too am green as a leek. If you see it wither, think that my fortunes are not the best in this world; but if it becomes quite dried up, you may mourn for your Canneloro."

So saying, after embracing one another again, Canneloro set out on his travels; journeying on and on, with many adventures which it would be too long to recount—he at length arrived at the Kingdom of Clear-Water, just at the time when they were holding a most splendid tournament, the hand of the King's daughter being promised to the victor. Here Canneloro presented himself and bore him so bravely that he overthrew all the knights who were come from divers parts to gain a name for themselves. Whereupon he married the Princess Fenicia, and a great feast was made.

When Canneloro had been there some months in peace and quiet, an unhappy fancy came into his head for going to the chase. He told it to the King, who said to him, "Take care, my son-in-law; do not be deluded. Be wise and keep open your eyes, for in these woods is a most wicked ogre who changes his form every day, one time appearing like a wolf, at another like a lion, now like a stag, now like an ass, like one thing and now like another. By a thousand stratagems he decoys those who are so unfortunate as to meet him into a cave, where he devours them. So, my son, do not put your safety into peril, or you will leave your rags there."

Canneloro, who did not know what fear was, paid no heed to the advice of his father-in-law. As soon as the Sun with the broom of his rays had cleared away the soot of the Night he set out for the chase; and, on his way, he came to a wood where, beneath the awning of the leaves, the Shades has assembled to maintain their sway, and to make a conspiracy against the Sun. The ogre, seeing him coming, turned himself into a handsome doe; which, as soon as Canneloro perceived he began to give chase to her. Then the doe doubled and turned, and led him about hither and thither at such a rate, that at last she brought him into the very heart of the wood, where she raised such a tremendous snow-storm that it looked as if the sky was going to fall. Canneloro, finding himself in front of a cave, went into it to seek for shelter; and being benumbed with the cold, he gathered some sticks which he found within it, and pulling his steel from his pocket, he kindled a large fire. As he was standing by the fire to dry his clothes, the doe came to the mouth of the cave, and said, "Sir Knight, pray give me leave to warm myself a little while, for I am shivering with the cold."

Canneloro, who was of a kindly disposition, said to her, "Draw near, and welcome."

"I would gladly," replied the doe, "but I am afraid you would kill me."

"Fear nothing," answered Canneloro, "trust to my word."

"If you wish me to enter," rejoined the doe, "tie up those dogs, that they may not hurt me, and tie up your horse that he may not kick me."

So Canneloro tied up his dogs and hobbled his horse, and the doe said, "I am now half assured, but unless you bind fast your sword, I dare not come in." Then Canneloro, who wished to become friends with the doe, bound his sword as a countryman does, when he carries it in the city for fear of the constables. As soon as the ogre saw Canneloro defenceless, he re-took his own form, and laying hold on him, flung him into a pit at the bottom of the cave, and covered it up with a stone—to keep him to eat.

But Fonzo, who, morning and evening visited the myrtle and the fountain, to learn news of the fate of Canneloro, finding the one withered and the other troubled, instantly thought that his brother was undergoing misfortunes. So, to help him, he mounted his horse without asking leave of his father or mother; and arming himself well and taking two enchanted dogs, he went rambling through the world. He roamed and rambled here, there, and everywhere until, at last, he came to Clear-Water, which he found all in mourning for the supposed death of Canneloro. And scarcely was he come to the court, when every one, thinking, from the likeness he bore him, that it was Canneloro, hastened to tell Fenicia the good news, who ran leaping down the stairs, and embracing Fonzo cried, "My husband! my heart! where have you been all this time?"

Fonzo immediately perceived that Canneloro had come to this country and had left it again; so he resolved to examine the matter adroitly, to learn from the Princess's discourse where his brother might be found. And, hearing her say that he had put himself in great danger by that accursed hunting, especially if the cruel ogre should meet him, he at once concluded that Canneloro must be there.

The next morning, as soon as the Sun had gone forth to give the gilded frills to the Sky, he jumped out of bed, and neither the prayers of Fenicia, nor the commands of the King could keep him back, but he would go to the chase. So, mounting his horse, he went with the enchanted dogs to the wood, where the same thing befell him that had befallen Canneloro; and, entering the cave, he saw his brother's arms and dogs and horse fast bound, by which he became assured of the nature of the snare. Then the doe told him in like manner to tie his arms, dogs, and horse, but he instantly set them upon her and they tore her to pieces. And as he was looking about for some traces of his brother, he heard his voice down in the pit; so, lifting up the stone, he drew out Canneloro, with all the others whom the ogre had buried alive to fatten. Then embracing each other with great joy, the twin-brothers went home, where Fenicia, seeing them so much alike, did not know which to choose for her husband, until Canneloro took off his cap and she saw the mark of the old wound and recognised him. Fonzo stayed there a month, taking his pleasure, and then wished to return to his own country, and Canneloro wrote by him to his mother, bidding her lay aside her enmity and come and visit him and partake of his greatness, which she did. But from that time forward, he never would hear of dogs or of hunting, recollecting the saying—

"Unhappy is he who corrects himself at his own cost."

X

PARSLEY

This is one of the stories which that good soul, my uncle's grandmother (whom Heaven take to glory), used to tell; and, unless I have put on my spectacles upside down, I fancy it will give you pleasure.

There was, once upon a time, a woman named Pascadozzia, and one day, when she was standing at her window, which looked into the garden of an ogress, she saw such a fine bed of parsley that she almost fainted away with desire for some. So when the ogress went out she could not restrain herself any longer, but plucked a handful of it. The ogress came home and was going to cook her pottage when she found that some one had been stealing the parsley, and said, "Ill luck to me, but I'll catch this long-fingered rogue and make him repent it; I'll teach him to his cost that every one should eat off his own platter and not meddle with other folks' cups."

The poor woman went again and again down into the garden, until one morning the ogress met her, and in a furious rage exclaimed, "Have I caught you at last, you thief, you rogue; prithee, do you pay the rent of the garden that you come in this impudent way and steal my plants? By my faith, I'll make you do penance without sending you to Rome."

Poor Pascadozzia, in a terrible fright, began to make excuses, saying that neither from gluttony nor the craving of hunger had she been tempted by the devil to commit this fault, but from her fear lest her child should be born with a crop of parsley on its face.

"Words are but wind," answered the ogress, "I am not to be caught with such prattle; you have closed the balance-sheet of life, unless you promise to give me the child, girl or boy, whichever it may be."

The poor woman, in order to escape the peril in which she found herself, swore, with one hand upon the other, to keep the promise, and so the ogress let her go free. But when the baby came it was a little girl, so beautiful that she was a joy to look upon, who was named Parsley. The little girl grew from day to day until, when she was seven years old, her mother sent her to school, and every time she went along the street and met the ogress the old woman said to her, "Tell your mother to remember her promise." And she went on repeating this message so often that the poor mother, having no longer patience to listen to the refrain, said one day to Parsley, "If you meet the old woman as usual, and she reminds you of the hateful promise, answer her, Take it.'"

When Parsley, who dreamt of no ill, met the ogress again, and heard her repeat the same words, she answered innocently as her mother had told her, whereupon the ogress, seizing her by her hair, carried her off to a wood which the horses of the Sun never entered, not having paid the toll to the pastures of those Shades. Then she put the poor girl into a tower which she caused to arise by her art, having neither gate nor ladder, but only a little window through which she ascended and descended by means of Parsley's hair, which was very long, just as sailors climb up and down the mast of a ship.

Now it happened one day, when the ogress had left the tower, that Parsley put her head out of the little window and let loose her tresses in the sun, and the son of a Prince passing by saw those two golden banners which invited all souls to enlist under the standard of Beauty, and, beholding with amazement, in the midst of those gleaming waves, a face that enchanted all hearts, he fell desperately in love with such wonderful beauty; and, sending her a memorial of sighs, she decreed to receive him into favour. She told him her troubles, and implored him to rescue her. But a gossip of the ogress, who was for ever prying into things that did not concern her, and poking her nose into every corner, overheard the secret, and told the wicked woman to be on the look-out, for Parsley had been seen talking with a certain youth, and she had her suspicions. The ogress thanked the gossip for the information, and said that she would take good care to stop up the road. As to Parsley, it was, moreover, impossible for her to escape, as she had laid a spell upon her, so that unless she had in her hand the three gall-nuts which were in a rafter in the kitchen it would be labour lost to attempt to get away.

Whilst they were thus talking together, Parsley, who stood with her ears wide open and had some suspicion of the gossip, overheard all that had passed. And when Night had spread out her black garments to keep them from the moth, and the Prince had come as they had appointed, she let fall her hair; he seized it with both hands, and cried, "Draw up." When he was drawn up she made him first climb on to the rafters and find the gall-nuts, knowing well what effect they would have, as she had been enchanted by the ogress. Then, having made a rope-ladder, they both descended to the ground, took to their heels, and ran off towards the city. But the gossip, happening to see them come out, set up a loud "Halloo," and began to shout and make such a noise that the ogress awoke, and, seeing that Parsley had run away, she descended by the same ladder, which was still fastened to the window, and set off after the couple, who, when they saw her coming at their heels faster than a horse let loose, gave themselves up for lost. But Parsley, recollecting the gall-nuts, quickly threw one of the ground, and lo, instantly a Corsican bulldog started up—O, mother, such a terrible beast!—which, with open jaws and barking loud, flew at the ogress as if to swallow her at a mouthful. But the old woman, who was more cunning and spiteful than ever, put her hand into her pocket, and pulling out a piece of bread gave it to the dog, which made him hang his tail and allay his fury.

Then she turned to run after the fugitives again, but Parsley, seeing her approach, threw the second gall-nut on the ground, and lo, a fierce lion arose, who, lashing the earth with his tail, and shaking his mane and opening wide his jaws a yard apart, was just preparing to make a slaughter of the ogress, when, turning quickly back, she stripped the skin off an ass which was grazing in the middle of a meadow and ran at the lion, who, fancying it a real jackass, was so frightened that he bounded away as fast as he could.

The ogress having leaped over this second ditch turned again to pursue the poor lovers, who, hearing the clatter of her heels, and seeing clouds of dust that rose up to the sky, knew that she was coming again. But the old woman, who was every moment in dread lest the lion should pursue her, had not taken off the ass's skin, and when Parsley now threw down the third gall-nut there sprang up a wolf, who, without giving the ogress time to play any new trick, gobbled her up just as she was in the shape of a jackass. So Parsley and the Prince, now freed from danger, went their way leisurely and quietly to the Prince's kingdom, where, with his father's free consent, they were married. Thus, after all these storms of fate, they experienced the truth that—

"One hour in port, the sailor, freed from fears,
Forgets the tempests of a hundred years."

XI

THE THREE SISTERS

It is a great truth that from the same wood are formed the statues of idols and the rafters of gallows, kings' thrones and cobblers' stalls; and another strange thing is that from the same rags are made the paper on which the wisdom of sages is recorded, and the crown which is placed on the head of a fool. The same, too, may be said of children: one daughter is good and another bad; one idle, another a good housewife; one fair, another ugly; one spiteful, another kind; one unfortunate, another born to good luck, and who being all of one family ought to be of one nature. But leaving this subject to those who know more about it, I will merely give you an example in the story of the three daughters of the same mother, wherein you will see the difference of manners which brought the wicked daughters into the ditch and the good daughter to the top of the Wheel of Fortune.

There was at one time a woman who had three daughters, two of whom were so unlucky that nothing ever succeeded with them, all their projects went wrong, all their hopes were turned to chaff. But the youngest, who was named Nella, was born to good luck, and I verily believe that at her birth all things conspired to bestow on her the best and choicest gifts in their power. The Sky gave her the perfection of its light; Venus, matchless beauty of form; Love, the first dart of his power; Nature, the flower of manners. She never set about any work that it did not go off to a nicety; she never took anything in hand that it did not succeed to a hair; she never stood up to dance, that she did not sit down with applause. On which account she was envied by her jealous sisters and yet not so much as she was loved and wished well to by all others; as greatly as her sisters desired to put her underground, so much more did other folks carry her on the palms of their hands.

Now there was in that country an enchanted Prince who was so attracted by her beauty that he secretly married her. And in order that they might enjoy one another's company without exciting the suspicion of the mother, who was a wicked woman, the Prince made a crystal passage which led from the royal palace directly into Nella's apartment, although it was eight miles distant. Then he gave her a certain powder saying, "Every time you wish to see me throw a little of this powder into the fire, and instantly I will come through this passage as quick as a bird, running along the crystal road to gaze upon this face of silver."

Having arranged it thus, not a night passed that the Prince did not go in and out, backwards and forwards, along the crystal passage, until at last the sisters, who were spying the actions of Nella, found out the secret and laid a plan to put a stop to the sport. And in order to cut the thread at once, they went and broke the passage here and there; so that, when the unhappy girl threw the powder into the fire, to give the signal to her husband, the Prince, who used always to come running in furious haste, hurt himself in such a manner against the broken crystal that it was truly a pitiable sight to see. And being unable to pass further on he turned back all cut and slashed like a Dutchman's breeches. Then he sent for all the doctors in the town; but as the crystal was enchanted the wounds were mortal, and no human remedy availed. When the King saw this, despairing of his son's condition, he sent out a proclamation that whoever would cure the wounds of the Prince—if a woman she should have him for a husband—if a man he should have half his kingdom.

Now when Nella, who was pining away from the loss of the Prince, heard this she dyed her face, disguised herself, and unknown to her sisters she left home to go to see him before his death. But as by this time the Sun's gilded ball with which he plays in the Fields of Heaven, was running towards the west, night overtook her in a wood close to the house of an ogre, where, in order to get out of the way of danger, she climbed up into a tree. Meanwhile the ogre and his wife were sitting at table with the windows open in order to enjoy the fresh air while they ate; as soon as they had emptied their cups and put out the lamps they began to chat of one thing and another, so that Nella, who was as near to them as the mouth to the nose, heard every word they spoke.

Among other things the ogress said to her husband, "My pretty Hairy-Hide, tell me what news; what do they say abroad in the world?" And he answered, "Trust me, there is no hand's breadth clean; everything's going topsy-turvy and awry." "But what is it?" replied his wife. "Why I could tell pretty stories of all the confusion that is going on," replied the ogre, "for one hears things that are enough to drive one mad, such as buffoons rewarded with gifts, rogues esteemed, cowards honoured, robbers protected, and honest men little thought of. But, as these things only vex one, I will merely tell you what has befallen the King's son. He had made a crystal path along which he used to go to visit a pretty lass; but by some means or other, I know not how, all the road has been broken; and as he was going along the passage as usual, he has wounded himself in such a manner that before he can stop the leak the whole conduit of his life will run out. The King has indeed issued a proclamation with great promises to whoever cures his son; but it is all labour lost, and the best he can do is quickly to get ready mourning and prepare the funeral."

When Nella heard the cause of the Prince's illness she sobbed and wept bitterly and said to herself, "Who is the wicked soul who has broken the passage and caused so much sorrow?" But as the ogress now went on speaking Nella was as silent as a mouse and listened.

"And is it possible," said the ogress, "that the world is lost to this poor Prince, and that no remedy can be found for his malady?"

"Hark-ye, Granny," replied the ogre, "the doctors are not called upon to find remedies that may pass the bounds of nature. This is not a fever that will yield to medicine and diet, much less are these ordinary wounds which require lint and oil; for the charm that was on the broken glass produces the same effect as onion juice does on the iron heads of arrows, which makes the wound incurable. There is one thing only that could save his life, but don't ask me to tell it to you, for it is a thing of importance."

"Do tell me, dear old Long-tusk," cried the ogress; "tell me, if you would not see me die."

"Well then," said the ogre, "I will tell you provided you promise me not to confide it to any living soul, for it would be the ruin of our house and the destruction of our lives."

"Fear nothing, my dear, sweet little husband," replied the ogress; "for you shall sooner see pigs with horns, apes with tails, moles with eyes, than a single word shall pass my lips." And so saying, she put one hand upon the other and swore to it.

"You must know then," said the ogre, "that there is nothing under the sky nor above the ground that can save the Prince from the snares of death, but our fat. If his wounds are anointed with this his soul will be arrested which is just at the point of leaving the dwelling of his body."

Nella, who overheard all that passed, gave time to Time to let them finish their chat; and then, getting down from the tree and taking heart, she knocked at the ogre's door crying, "Ah! my good masters, I pray you for charity, alms, some sign of compassion. Have a little pity on a poor, miserable, wretched creature who is banished by fate far from her own country and deprived of all human aid, who has been overtaken by night in this wood and is dying of cold and hunger." And crying thus, she went on knocking and knocking at the door.

Upon hearing this deafening noise, the ogress was going to throw her half a loaf and send her away. But the ogre, who was more greedy of flesh than the squirrel is of nuts, the bear of honey, the cat of fish, the sheep of salt, or the ass of bran, said to his wife, "Let the poor creature come in, for if she sleeps in the fields, who knows but she may be eaten up by some wolf." In short, he talked so much that his wife at length opened the door for Nella; whilst with all his pretended charity he was all the time reckoning on making four mouthfuls of her. But the glutton counts one way and the host another; for the ogre and his wife drank till they were fairly tipsy. When they lay down to sleep Nella took a knife from a cupboard and made a hash of them in a trice. Then she put all the fat into a phial, went straight to the court, where, presenting herself before the King, she offered to cure the Prince. At this the King was overjoyed and led her to the chamber of his son, and no sooner had she anointed him well with the fat than the wound closed in a moment just as if she had thrown water on the fire, and he became sound as a fish.

When the King saw this, he said to his son, "This good woman deserves the reward promised by the proclamation and that you should marry her." But the Prince replied, "It is hopeless, for I have no store-room full of hearts in my body to share among so many; my heart is already disposed of, and another woman is already the mistress of it." Nella, hearing this, replied, "You should no longer think of her who has been the cause of all your misfortune." "My misfortune has been brought on me by her sisters," replied the Prince, "and they shall repent it." "Then do you really love her?" said Nella. And the Prince replied, "More than my own life." "Embrace me then," said Nella, "for I am the fire of your heart." But the Prince seeing the dark hue of her face answered, "I would sooner take you for the coal than the fire, so keep off—don't blacken me." Whereupon Nella, perceiving that he did not know her, called for a basin of clean water and washed her face. As soon as the cloud of soot was removed the sun shone forth; and the Prince, recognising her, pressed her to his heart and acknowledged her for his wife. Then he had her sisters thrown into an oven, thus proving the truth of the old saying—

"No evil ever went without punishment."

XII

VIOLET

Envy is a wind which blows with such violence, that it throws down the props of the reputation of good men, and levels with the ground the crops of good fortune. But, very often, as a punishment from Heaven, when this envious blast seems as if it would cast a person flat on the ground, it aids him instead of attain the happiness he is expecting sooner even than he expected: as you will hear in the story which I shall now tell you.

There was once upon a time a good sort of man named Cola Aniello, who had three daughters, Rose, Pink, and Violet, the last of whom was so beautiful that her very look was a syrup of love, which cured the hearts of beholders of all unhappiness. The King's son was burning with love of her, and every time he passed by the little cottage where these three sisters sat at work, he took off his cap and said, "Good-day, good-day, Violet," and she replied, "Good-day, King's son! I know more than you." At these words her sisters grumbled and murmured, saying, "You are an ill-bred creature and will make the Prince in a fine rage." But as Violet paid no heed to what they said, they made a spiteful complaint of her to her father, telling him that she was too bold and forward; and that she answered the Prince without any respect, as if she were just as good as he; and that, some day or other, she would get into trouble and suffer the just punishment of her offence. So Cola Aniello, who was a prudent man, in order to prevent any mischief, sent Violet to stay with an aunt, to be set to work.

Now the Prince, when he passed by the house as usual, no longer seeing the object of his love, was for some days like a nightingale that has lost her young ones from her nest, and goes from branch to branch wailing and lamenting her loss; but he put his ear so often to the chink that at last he discovered where Violet lived. Then he went to the aunt, and said to her, "Madam, you know who I am, and what power I have; so, between ourselves, do me a favour and then ask for whatever you wish." "If I can do anything to serve you," replied the old woman, "I am entirely at your command." "I ask nothing of you," said the Prince, "but to let me give Violet a kiss." "If that's all," answered the old woman, "go and hide yourself in the room downstairs in the garden, and I will find some pretence or another for sending Violet to you."

As soon as the Prince heard this, he stole into the room without loss of time; and the old woman, pretending that she wanted to cut a piece of cloth, said to her niece, "Violet, if you love me, go down and fetch me the yard-measure." So Violet went, as her aunt bade her, but when she came to the room she perceived the ambush, and, taking the yard-measure, she slipped out of the room as nimbly as a cat, leaving the Prince with his nose made long out of pure shame and bursting with vexation.

When the old woman saw Violet come running so fast, she suspected that the trick had not succeeded; so presently after, she said to the girl, "Go downstairs, niece, and fetch me the ball of thread that is on the top shelf in the cupboard." So Violet ran, and taking the thread slipped like an eel out of the hands of the Prince. But after a little while the old woman said again, "Violet, my dear, if you do not go downstairs and fetch me the scissors, I cannot get on at all." Then Violet went down again, but she sprang as vigorously as a dog out of the trap, and when she came upstairs she took the scissors and cut off one of her aunt's ears, saying, "Take that, madam, as a reward for your pains—every deed deserves its need. If I don't cut off your nose, it is only that you may smell the bad odour of your reputation." So saying, she went her way home with a hop, skip, and jump, leaving her aunt eased of one ear and the Prince full of Let-me-alone.

Not long afterwards, the Prince again passed by the house of Violet's father; and, seeing her at the window where she used to stand, he began his old tune, "Good-day, good-day, Violet!" Whereupon she answered as quickly as a good parish-clerk, "Good-day, King's son! I know more than you." But Violet's sisters could no longer bear this behaviour, and they plotted together how to get rid of her. Now, one of the windows looked into the garden of an ogre, so they proposed to drive the poor girl away through this; and letting fall from it a skein of thread with which they were working a door-curtain for the queen, they cried, "Alas! alas! we are ruined and shall not be able to finish the work in time, if Violet, who is the smallest and lightest of us, does not let herself down by a cord and pick up the thread that has fallen."

Violet could not endure to see her sisters grieving thus, and instantly offered to go down; so, tying a cord to her, they lowered her into the garden. But no sooner did she reach the ground than they let go the rope. It happened that just at that time the ogre came out to look at his garden, and having caught cold from the dampness of the ground, he gave such a tremendous sneeze, with such a noise and explosion, that Violet screamed out with terror, "Oh, mother, help me!" Thereupon the ogre looked round and seeing the beautiful maiden behind him, he received her with the greatest care and affection; and treating her as his own daughter, he gave her in charge of three fairies, bidding them take care of her, and rear her up on cherries.

The Prince no longer seeing Violet, and hearing no news of her, good or bad, fell into such grief that his eyes became swollen, his face became pale as ashes, his lips livid; and he neither ate a morsel to get flesh on his body, nor slept a wink to get any rest to his mind. But trying all possible means and offering large rewards, he went about spying and inquiring everywhere until, at last, he discovered where Violet was. Then he sent for the ogre and told him that, finding himself ill (as he might see was the case) he begged of him permission to spend a single day and night in his garden, adding that a small chamber would suffice for him to repose in. Now, as the ogre was a subject of the Prince's father he could not refuse him this trifling pleasure; so he offered him all the rooms in his house; if one was not enough, and his very life itself. The Prince thanked him, and chose a room which by good luck was near to Violet's; and, as soon as Night came out to play games with the Stars, the Prince, finding that Violet had left her door open, as it was summertime and the place was safe, stole softly into her room, and taking Violet's arm he gave her two pinches. Then she awoke and exclaimed, "Oh, father, father, what a quantity of fleas!" So she went to another bed and the Prince did the same again and she cried out as before. Then she changed first the mattress and then the sheet; and so the sport went on the whole night long, until the Dawn, having brought the news that the Sun was alive, the mourning that was hung round the sky was all removed.

As soon as it was day, the Prince, passing by that house, and seeing the maiden at the door, said, as he was wont to do, "Good-day, good-day, Violet!" and when Violet replied, "Good-day, King's son! I know more than you!" the Prince answered, "Oh, father, father, what a quantity of fleas!"

The instant Violet felt this shot she guessed at once that the Prince had been the cause of her annoyance in the past night; so off she ran and told it to the fairies. "If it be he," said the fairies, "we will soon give him tit for tat and as good in return. If this dog has bitten you, we will manage to get a hair from him. He has give you one, we will give him back one and a half. Only get the ogre to make you a pair of slippers covered with little bells, and leave the rest to us. We will pay him in good coin."

Violet, who was eager to be revenged, instantly got the ogre to make the slippers for her; and, waiting till the Sky, like a Genoese woman, had wrapped the black taffety round her face, they went, all four together, to the house of the Prince, where the fairies and Violet hid themselves in the chamber. And as soon as ever the Prince had closed his eyes the fairies made a great noise and racket, and Violet began to stamp with her feet at such a rate that, what with the clatter of her heels and the jingling of her bells, the Prince awoke in great terror and cried out, "Oh, mother, mother, help me!" And after repeating this two or three times, they slipped away home.

The next morning the Prince went to take a walk in the garden, for he could not live a moment without the sight of Violet, who was a pink of pinks. And seeing her standing at the door, he said, "Good-day, good-day, Violet!" And Violet answered, "Good-day, King's son! I know more than you!" Then the Prince said, "Oh, father, father, what a quantity of fleas!" But Violet replied, "Oh, mother, mother, help me!"

When the Prince heard this, he said to Violet, "You have won—your wits are better than mine. I yield—you have conquered. And now that I see you really know more than I do, I will marry you without more ado." So he called the ogre and asked her of him for his wife; but the ogre said it was not his affair, for he had learned that very morning that Violet was the daughter of Cola Aniello. So the Prince ordered her father to be called and told him of the good fortune that was in store for his daughter; whereupon the marriage feast was celebrated with great joy, and the truth of the saying was seen that—

"A fair maiden soon gets wed."

XIII

PIPPO

Ingratitude is a nail, which, driven into the tree of courtesy, causes it to wither. It is a broken channel by which the foundations of affection are undermined; and a lump of soot, which, falling into the dish of friendship, destroys its scent and savour—as is seen in daily instances, and, amongst others, in the story which I will now tell you.

There was one time in my dear city of Naples an old man who was as poor as poor could be. He was so wretched, so bare, so light, and with not a farthing in his pocket, that he went naked as a flea. And being about to shake out the bags of life, he called to him his sons, Oratiello and Pippo, and said to them, "I am now called upon by the tenor of my bill to pay the debt I owe to Nature. Believe me, I should feel great pleasure in quitting this abode of misery, this den of woes, but that I leave you here behind me—a pair of miserable fellows, as big as a church, without a stitch upon your backs, as clean as a barber's basin, as nimble as a serjeant, as dry as a plum-stone, without so much as a fly can carry upon its foot; so that, were you to run a hundred miles, not a farthing would drop from you. My ill-fortune has indeed brought me to such beggary that I lead the life of a dog, for I have all along, as well you know, gaped with hunger and gone to bed without a candle. Nevertheless, now that I am a-dying, I wish to leave you some token of my love. So do you, Oratiello, who are my first-born, take the sieve that hangs yonder against the wall, with which you can earn your bread; and do you, little fellow, take the cat and remember your daddy!" So saying, he began to whimper; and presently after said, "God be with you—for it is night!"

Oratiello had his father buried by charity; and then took the sieve and went riddling here, there, and everywhere to gain a livelihood; and the more he riddled, the more he earned. But Pippo, taking the cat, said, "Only see now what a pretty legacy my father has left me! I, who am not able to support myself, must now provide for two. Whoever beheld so miserable an inheritance?" Then the cat, who overheard this lamentation, said to him, "You are grieving without need, and have more luck than sense. You little know the good fortune in store for you; and that I am able to make you rich if I set about it." When Pippo had heard this, he thanked Her Pussyship, stroked her three or four times on the back, and commended himself warmly to her. So the cat took compassion on poor Pippo; and, every morning, when the Sun, with the bait of light on his golden hook, fishes for the shakes of Night, she betook herself to the shore, and catching a goodly grey mullet or a fine dory, she carried it to the King and said, "My Lord Pippo, your Majesty's most humble slave, sends you this fish with all reverence, and says, A small present to a great lord.'" Then the King, with a joyful face, as one usually shows to those who bring a gift, answered the cat, "Tell this lord, whom I do not know, that I thank him heartily."

Again, the cat would run to the marshes or the fields, and when the fowlers had brought down a blackbird, a snipe, or a lark, she caught it up and presented it to the King with the same message. She repeated this trick again and again, until one morning the King said to her, "I feel infinitely obliged to this Lord Pippo, and am desirous of knowing him, that I may make a return for the kindness he has shown me." And the cat replied, "The desire of my Lord Pippo is to give his life for your Majesty's crown; and tomorrow morning, without fail, as soon as the Sun has set fire to the stubble of the fields of air, he will come and pay his respects to you."

So when the morning came, the cat went to the King, and said to him: "Sire, my Lord Pippo sends to excuse himself for not coming, as last night some of his servants robbed him and ran off, and have not left him a single shirt to his back." When the King heard this, he instantly commanded his retainers to take out of his own wardrobe a quantity of clothes and linen, and sent them to Pippo; and, before two hours had passed, Pippo went to the palace, conducted by the cat, where he received a thousand compliments from the King, who made him sit beside himself, and gave him a banquet that would amaze you.

While they were eating, Pippo from time to time turned to the cat and said to her, "My pretty puss, pray take care that those rags don't slip through our fingers." Then the cat answered, "Be quiet, be quiet; don't be talking of these beggarly things." The King, wishing to know the subject of their talk, the cat made answer that Pippo had taken a fancy to a small lemon; whereupon the King instantly sent out to the garden for a basketful. But Pippo returned to the same tune about the old coats and shirts, and the cat again told him to hold his tongue. Then the King once more asked what was the matter, and the cat had another excuse to make amends for Pippo's rudeness.

At last, when they had eaten and conversed for some time about one thing and another, Pippo took his leave; and the cat stayed with the King, describing the worth, the wisdom, and the judgment of Pippo; and, above all, the great wealth he had in the plains of Rome and Lombardy, which well entitled him to marry even into the family of a crowned King. Then the King asked what might be his fortune; and the cat replied that no one could ever count the moveables, the fixtures, and the household furniture of this rich man, who did not even know what he possessed. If the King wished to be informed of it, he had only to send messengers with the cat, and she would prove to him that there was no wealth in the world equal to his.

Then the King called some trusty persons, and commanded them to inform themselves minutely of the truth; so they followed in the footsteps of the cat, who, as soon as they had passed the frontier of the kingdom, from time to time ran on before, under the pretext of providing refreshments for them on the road. Whenever she met a flock of sheep, a herd of cows, a troop of horses, or a drove of pigs, she would say to the herdsmen and keepers, "Ho! have a care! A troop of robbers is coming to carry off everything in the country. So if you wish to escape their fury, and to have your things respected, say that they all belong to the Lord Pippo, and not a hair will be touched."

She said the same at all the farmhouses, so that wherever the King's people came they found the pipe tuned; for everything they met with, they were told, belonged to the Lord Pippo. At last they were tired of asking, and returned to the King, telling seas and mountains of the riches of Lord Pippo. The King, hearing this report, promised the cat a good drink if she should manage to bring about the match; and the cat, playing the shuttle between them, at last concluded the marriage. So Pippo came, and the King gave him his daughter and a large portion.

At the end of a month of festivities, Pippo wished to take his bride to his estates, so the King accompanied them as far as the frontiers; and he went on to Lombardy, where, by the cat's advice, he purchased a large estate and became a baron.

Pippo, seeing himself now so rich, thanked the cat more than words can express, saying that he owed his life and his greatness to her good offices; and that the ingenuity of a cat had done more for him that the wit of his father. Therefore, said he, she might dispose of his life and his property as she pleased; and he gave her his word that when she died, which he prayed might not be for a hundred years, he would have her embalmed and put into a golden coffin, and set in his own chamber, that he might keep her memory always before his eyes.

The cat listened to these lavish professions; and before three days she pretended to be dead, and stretched herself at full length in the garden. When Pippo's wife saw her, she cried out, "Oh, husband, what a sad misfortune! The cat is dead!" "Devil die with her!" said Pippo. "Better her than we!" "What shall we do with her?" replied the wife. "Take her by the leg," said he, "and fling her out of the window!"

Then the cat, who heard this fine reward when she least expected it, began to say, "Is this the return you make for my taking you from beggary? Are these the thanks I get for freeing you from rags that you might have hung distaffs with? Is this my reward for having put good clothes on your back when you were a poor, starved, miserable, tattershod ragamuffin? But such is the fate of him who washes an ass's head! Go! A curse upon all I have done for you! A fine gold coffin you had prepared for me! A fine funeral you were going to give me! Go, now! serve, labour, toil, sweat to get this fine reward! Unhappy is he who does a good deed in hope of a return. Well was it said by the philosopher, He who lies down an ass, an ass he finds himself.' But let him who does most, expect least; smooth words and ill deeds deceive alike both fools and wise!"

So saying, she drew her cloak about her and went her way. All that Pippo, with the utmost humility, could do to soothe her was of no avail. She would not return; but ran on and on without ever turning her head about, saying—

"Heaven keep me from the rich grown poor,
And from the beggar who of wealth gains store."

XIV

THE SERPENT

It always happens that he who is over-curious in prying into the affairs of other people, strikes his own foot with the axe; and the King of Long-Furrow is a proof of this, who, by poking his nose into secrets, brought his daughter into trouble and ruined his unhappy son-in-law—who, in attempting to make a thrust with his head was left with it broken.

There was once on a time a gardener's wife, who longed to have a son more than a man in a fever for cold water, or the innkeeper for the arrival of the mail-coach.

It chanced one day that the poor man went to the mountain to get a faggot, and when he came home and opened it he found a pretty little serpent among the twigs. At the sight of this, Sapatella (for that was the name of the gardener's wife) heaved a deep sigh, and said, "Alas! even the serpents have their little serpents; but I brought ill-luck with me into this world." At these words, the little serpent spoke, and said, "Well, then, since you cannot have children, take me for a child, and you will make a good bargain, for I shall love you better than my mother." Sapatella, hearing a serpent speak thus, nearly fainted; but, plucking up courage, she said, "If it were for nothing else than the affection which you offer, I am content to take you, and treat you as if you were really my own child." So saying, she assigned him a hole in a corner of the house for a cradle, and gave him for food a share of what she had with the greatest goodwill in the world.

The serpent increased in size from day to day; and when he had grown pretty big, he said to Cola Matteo, the gardener, whom he looked on as his father, "Daddy, I want to get married." "With all my heart," said Cola Matteo. "We must look out for another serpent like yourself, and try to make up a match between you." "What serpent are you talking of?" said the little serpent. "I suppose, forsooth, we are all the same with vipers and adders! It is easy to see you are nothing but a country bumpkin, and make a nosegay of every plant. I want the King's daughter; so go this very instant and ask the King for her, and tell him it is a serpent who demands her." Cola Matteo, who was a plain, straightforward kind of man, and knew nothing about matters of this sort, went innocently to the King and delivered his message, saying—

"The messenger should not be beaten more
Than are the sands upon the shore!"

"Know then that a serpent wants your daughter for his wife, and I am come to try if we can make a match between a serpent and a dove!" The King, who saw at a glance that he was a blockhead, to get rid of him, said, "Go and tell the serpent that I will give him my daughter if he turns all the fruit of this orchard into gold." And so saying, he burst out a-laughing, and dismissed him.

When Cola Matteo went home and delivered the answer to the serpent, he said, "Go to-morrow morning and gather up all the fruit-stones you can find in the city, and sow them in the orchard, and you will see pearls strung on rushes!" Cola Mateo, who was no conjurer, neither knew how to comply nor refuse; so next morning, as soon as the Sun with his golden broom had swept away the dirt of the Night from the fields watered by the dawn, he took a basket on his arm and went from street to street, picking up all the stones of peaches, plums, nectarines, apricots, and cherries that he could find. He then went to the orchard of the palace and sowed them, as the serpent had desired. In an instant the trees shot up, and stems and branches, leaves, flowers, and fruit were all of glittering gold—at the sight of which the King was in an ecstasy of amazement, and cried aloud with joy.

But when Cola Matteo was sent by the serpent to the King, to demand the performance of his promise, the King said, "Fair and easy, I must first have something else if he would have my daughter; and it is that he make all the walls and the ground of the orchard to be of precious stones."

When the gardener told this to the serpent, he made answer, "Go to-morrow morning and gather up all the bits of broken crockery-ware you can find, and throw them on the walks and on the walls of the orchard; for we will not let this small difficulty stand in our way." As soon, therefore, as the Night, having aided the robbers, is banished from the sky, and goes about collecting the faggots of twilight, Cola Matteo took a basket under his arm, and went about collecting bits of tiles, lids and bottoms of pipkins, pieces of plate and dishes, handles of jugs, spouts of pitchers. He picked up all the spoiled, broken, cracked lamps and all the fragments of pottery he could find in his way. And when he had done all that the serpent had told him, you could see the whole orchard mantled with emeralds and chalcedonies, and coated with rubies and carbuncles, so that the lustre dazzled your eyes. The King was struck all of a heap by the sight, and knew not what had befallen him. But when the serpent sent again to let him know that he was expecting the performance of his promise, the King answered, "Oh, all that has been done is nothing, if he does not turn this palace into gold."

When Cola Matteo told the serpent this new fancy of the King's, the serpent said, "Go and get a bundle of herbs and rub the bottom of the palace walls with them. We shall see if we cannot satisfy this whim!" Away went Cola that very moment, and made a great broom of cabbages, radishes, leeks, parsley, turnips, and carrots; and when he had rubbed the lower part of the palace with it, instantly you might see it shining like a golden ball on a weather-vane. And when the gardener came again to demand the hand of the Princess, the King, seeing all his retreat cut off, called his daughter, and said to her, "My dear Grannonia, I have tried to get rid of a suitor who asked to marry you, by making such conditions as seemed to me impossible. But as I am beaten, and obliged to consent, I pray you, as you are a dutiful daughter, to enable me to keep my word, and to be content with what Fate wills and I am obliged to do."

"Do as you please, father," said Grannonia; "I shall not oppose a single jot of your will!" The King, hearing this, bade Cola Matteo tell the serpent to come.

The serpent then set out for the palace, mounted on a car all of gold and drawn by four golden elephants. But wherever he came the people fled away in terror, seeing such a large and frightful serpent making his progress through the city; and when he arrived at the palace, the courtiers all trembled like rushes and ran away; and even the very scullions did not dare to stay in the place. The King and Queen, also, shivering with fear, crept into a chamber. Only Grannonia stood her ground; for though her father and her mother cried continually, "Fly, fly, Grannonia, save yourself," she would not stir from the spot, saying, "Why should I fly from the husband you have given me?" And when the serpent came into the room, he took Grannonia by the waist, in his tail, and gave her such a shower of kisses that the King writhed like a worm, and went as pale as Death. Then the serpent carried her into another room and fastened the door; and shaking off his skin on the floor, he became a most beautiful youth, with a head all covered with ringlets of gold, and with eyes that would enchant you!

When the King saw the serpent go into the room with his daughter and shut the door after him, he said to his wife, "Heaven have mercy on that good soul, my daughter! for she is dead to a certainty, and that accursed serpent has doubtless swallowed her down like the yolk of an egg." Then he put his eye to the key-hole to see what had become of her; but when he saw the exceeding beauty of the youth, and the skin of the serpent that he had left lying on the ground, he gave the door a kick, then in they rushed, and, taking the skin, flung it into the fire and burned it.

When the youth saw this, he cried, "Ah, fools, what have you done!" and instantly he was turned into a dove and flew at the window, where, as he struck his head through the panes, he cut himself sorely.

Grannonia, who thus saw herself at the same moment happy and unhappy, joyful and miserable, rich and poor, tore her hair and bewailed her fate, reproaching her father and mother; but they excused themselves, declaring that they had not meant to do harm. But she went on weeping and wailing until Night came forth to drape the canopy of the sky for the funeral of the Sun; and when they were all in bed, she took her jewels, which were in a writing-desk, and went out by the back-door, to search everywhere for the treasure she had lost.

She went out of the city, guided by the light of the moon; and on her way she met a fox, who asked her if she wished for company. "Of all things, my friend," replied Grannonia. "I should be delighted; for I am not over well acquainted with the country." So they travelled along together till they came to a wood, where the trees, at play like children, were making baby-houses for the shadows to lie in. And as they were now tired and wished to rest, they sheltered under the leaves where a fountain was playing tricks with the grass, throwing water on it by the dishful. There they stretched themselves on a mattress of tender soft grass, and paid the duty of repose which they owed to Nature for the merchandise of life.

They did not awake till the Sun, with his usual fire, gave the signal to sailors and travellers to set out on their road; and, after they awoke, they still stayed for some time listening to the songs of the birds, in which Grannonia took great delight. The fox, seeing this, said to her, "You would feel twice as much pleasure if, like me, you understood what they are saying." At these words Grannonia—for women are by nature as curious as they are talkative—begged the fox to tell her what he had heard the birds saying. So, after having let her entreat him for a long time, to raise her curiosity about what he was going to relate, he told her that the birds were talking to each other about what had lately befallen the King's son, who was as beautiful as a jay. Because he had offended a wicked ogress, she had laid him under a spell to pass seven years in the form of a serpent; and when he had nearly ended the seven years, he fell in love with the daughter of a King, and being one day in a room with the maiden, he had cast his skin on the ground, when her father and mother rushed in and burned it. Then, when the Prince was flying away in the shape of a dove, he broke a pane in the window to escape, and hurt his head so severely that he was given over by the doctors.

Grannonia, who thus heard her own onions spoken of, asked if there was any cure for this injury. The fox replied that there was none other than by anointing his wounds with the blood of those very birds that had been telling the story. When Grannonia heard this, she fell down on her knees to the fox, entreating him to catch those birds for her, that she might get their blood; adding that, like honest comrades, they would share the gain. "Fair and softly," said the fox; "let us wait till night, and when the birds are gone to bed, trust me to climb the tree and capture them, one after the other."

So they waited till Day was gone, and Earth had spread out her great black board to catch the wax that might drop from the tapers of Night. Then the fox, as soon as he saw all the birds fast asleep on the branches, stole up quite softly, and one after another, throttled all the linnets, larks, tomtits, blackbirds, woodpeckers, thrushes, jays, fly-catchers, little owls, goldfinches, bullfinches, chaffinches, and redbreasts that were on the trees. And when he had killed them all they put the blood in a little bottle, which the fox carried with him, to refresh himself on the road.

Grannonia was so overjoyed that she hardly touched the ground; but the fox said to her, "What fine joy in a dream is this, my daughter! You have done nothing, unless you mix my blood also with that of the birds"; and so saying he set off to run away. Grannonia, who saw all her hopes likely to be destroyed, had recourse to woman's art—flattery; and she said to him, "Gossip fox, there would be some reason for your saving your hide if I were not under so many obligations to you, and if there were no other foxes in the world.

But you know how much I owe you, and that there is no scarcity of the likes of you on these plains. Rely on my good faith. Don't act like the cow that kicks over the pail which she has just filled with milk. You have done the chief part, and now you fail at the last. Do stop! Believe me, and come with me to the city of this King, where you may sell me for a slave if you will!"

The fox never dreamed that he could be out-forced by a woman; so he agreed to travel on with her. But they had hardly gone fifty paces, when she lifted up the stick she carried and gave him such a neat rap that he forthwith stretched his legs. Then she put his blood into the little bottle; and setting off again she stayed not till she came to Big Valley, where she went straightway to the royal palace, and sent word that she was come to cure the Prince.

Then the King ordered her to be brought before him, and he was astonished at seeing a girl undertake a thing which the best doctors in his kingdom had failed to do. However, a trial could do no harm; and so he said he wished greatly to see the experiment made. But Grannonia answered, "If I succeed, you must promise to give him to me for a husband." The King, who looked on his son to be even as already dead, answered her, "If you give him to me safe and sound, I will give him to you sound and safe; for it is no great matter to give a husband to her that gives me a son."

So they went to the chamber of the Prince, and hardly had she anointed him with the blood, when he found himself just as if nothing had ever ailed him. Grannonia, when she saw the Prince stout and hearty, bade the King keep his word; whereupon he, turning to his son, said, "My son, a moment ago you were all but dead, and now I see you alive, and can hardly believe it. Therefore, as I have promised this maiden that if she cured you she should have you for a husband, now enable me to perform my promise, by all the love you bear me, since gratitude obliges me to pay this debt."

When the Prince heard these words, he said, "Sir, I would that I was free to prove to you the love I bear you. But as I have already pledged my faith to another woman, you would not consent that I should break my word, nor would this maiden wish that I should do such a wrong to her whom I love; nor can I, indeed, alter my mind!"

Grannonia, hearing this, felt a secret pleasure not to be described at finding herself still alive in the memory of the Prince. Her whole face became crimson as she said, "If I could induce this maiden to resign her claims, would you then consent to my wish?" "Never," replied the Prince, "will I banish from this breast the fair image of her whom I love. I shall ever remain of the same mind and will; and I would sooner see myself in danger of losing my place at the table of life than play so mean a trick!"

Grannonia could no longer disguise herself, and discovered to the Prince who she was; for, the chamber having been darkened on account of the wound in his head, he had not known her. But the Prince, now that he recognised her, embraced her with a joy that would amaze you, telling his father what he had done and suffered for her. Then they sent to invite her parents, the King and Queen of Long Field; and they celebrated the wedding with wonderful festivity, making great sport of the great ninny of a fox, and concluding at the last of the last that—

"Pain doth indeed a seasoning prove
Unto the joys of constant love."

XV

THE SHE-BEAR

Truly the wise man said well that a command of gall cannot be obeyed like one of sugar. A man must require just and reasonable things if he would see the scales of obedience properly trimmed.

From orders which are improper springs resistance which is not easily overcome, as happened to the King of Rough-Rock, who, by asking what he ought not of his daughter, caused her to run away from him, at the risk of losing both honour and life.

There lived, it is said, once upon a time a King of Rough-Rock, who had a wife the very mother of beauty, but in the full career of her years she fell from the horse of health and broke her life. Before the candle of life went out at the auction of her years she called her husband and said to him, "I know you have always loved me tenderly; show me, therefore, at the close of my days the completion of your love by promising me never to marry again, unless you find a woman as beautiful as I have been, otherwise I leave you my curse, and shall bear you hatred even in the other world."

The King, who loved his wife beyond measure, hearing this her last wish, burst into tears, and for some time could not answer a single word. At last, when he had done weeping, he said to her, "Sooner than take another wife may the gout lay hold of me; may I have my head cut off like a mackerel! My dearest love, drive such a thought from your mind; do not believe in dreams, or that I could love any other woman; you were the first new coat of my love, and you shall carry away with you the last rags of my affection."

As he said these words the poor young Queen, who was at the point of death, turned up her eyes and stretched out her feet. When the King saw her life thus running out he unstopped the channels of his eyes, and made such a howling and beating and outcry that all the Court came running up, calling on the name of the dear soul, and upbraiding Fortune for taking her from him, and plucking out his beard, he cursed the stars that had sent him such a misfortune. But bearing in mind the maxim, "Pain in one's elbow and pain for one's wife are alike hard to bear, but are soon over," ere the Night had gone forth into the place-of-arms in the sky to muster the bats he began to count upon his fingers and to reflect thus to himself, "Here is my wife dead, and I am left a wretched widower, with no hope of seeing any one but this poor daughter whom she has left me. I must therefore try to discover some means or other of having a son and heir. But where shall I look? Where shall I find a woman equal in beauty to my wife? Every one appears a witch in comparison with her; where, then, shall I find another with a bit of stick, or seek another with the bell, if Nature made Nardella (may she be in glory), and then broke the mould? Alas, in what a labyrinth has she put me, in what a perplexity has the promise I made her left me! But what do I say? I am running away before I have seen the wolf; let me open my eyes and ears and look about; may there not be some other as beautiful? Is it possible that the world should be lost to me? Is there such a dearth of women, or is the race extinct?"

So saying he forthwith issued a proclamation and command that all the handsome women in the world should come to the touch-stone of beauty, for he would take the most beautiful to wife and endow her with a kingdom. Now, when this news was spread abroad, there was not a woman in the universe who did not come to try her luck—not a witch, however ugly, who stayed behind; for when it is a question of beauty, no scullion-wench will acknowledge herself surpassed; every one piques herself on being the handsomest; and if the looking-glass tells her the truth she blames the glass for being untrue, and the quicksilver for being put on badly.

When the town was thus filled with women the King had them all drawn up in a line, and he walked up and down from top to bottom, and as he examined and measured each from head to foot one appeared to him wry-browed, another long-nosed, another broad-mouthed, another thick-lipped, another tall as a may-pole, another short and dumpy, another too stout, another too slender; the Spaniard did not please him on account of her dark colour, the Neopolitan was not to his fancy on account of her gait, the German appeared cold and icy, the Frenchwoman frivolous and giddy, the Venetian with her light hair looked like a distaff of flax. At the end of the end, one for this cause and another for that, he sent them all away, with one hand before and the other behind; and, seeing that so many fair faces were all show and no wool, he turned his thoughts to his own daughter, saying, "Why do I go seeking the impossible when my daughter Preziosa is formed in the same mould of beauty as her mother? I have this fair face here in my house, and yet go looking for it at the fag-end of the world. She shall marry whom I will, and so I shall have an heir."

When Preziosa heard this she retired to her chamber, and bewailing her ill-fortune as if she would not leave a hair upon her head; and, whilst she was lamenting thus, an old woman came to her, who was her confidant. As soon as she saw Preziosa, who seemed to belong more to the other world than to this, and heard the cause of her grief, the old woman said to her, "Cheer up, my daughter, do not despair; there is a remedy for every evil save death. Now listen; if your father speaks to you thus once again put this bit of wood into your mouth, and instantly you will be changed into a she-bear; then off with you! for in his fright he will let you depart, and go straight to the wood, where Heaven has kept good-fortune in store for you since the day you were born, and whenever you wish to appear a woman, as you are and will remain, only take the piece of wood out of your mouth and you will return to your true form." Then Preziosa embraced the old woman, and, giving her a good apronful of meal, and ham and bacon, sent her away.

As soon as the Sun began to change his quarters, the King ordered the musicians to come, and, inviting all his lords and vassals, he held a great feast. And after dancing for five or six hours, they all sat down to table, and ate and drank beyond measure. Then the King asked his courtiers to whom he should marry Preziosa, as she was the picture of his dead wife. But the instant Preziosa heard this, she slipped the bit of wood into her mouth, and took the figure of a terrible she-bear, at the sight of which all present were frightened out of their wits, and ran off as fast as they could scamper.

Meanwhile Preziosa went out, and took her way to a wood, where the Shades were holding a consultation how they might do some mischief to the Sun at the close of day. And there she stayed, in the pleasant companionship of the other animals, until the son of the King of Running-Water came to hunt in that part of the country, who, at the sight of the bear, had like to have died on the spot. But when he saw the beast come gently up to him, wagging her tail like a little dog and rubbing her sides against him, he took courage, and patted her, and said, "Good bear, good bear! there, there! poor beast, poor beast!" Then he led her home and ordered that she should be taken great care of; and he had her put into a garden close to the royal palace, that he might see her from the window whenever he wished.

One day, when all the people of the house were gone out, and the Prince was left alone, he went to the window to look out at the bear; and there he beheld Preziosa, who had taken the piece of wood out of her mouth, combing her golden tresses. At the sight of this beauty, which was beyond the beyonds, he had like to have lost his senses with amazement, and tumbling down the stairs he ran out into the garden. But Preziosa, who was on the watch and observed him, popped the piece of wood into her mouth, and was instantly changed into a bear again.

When the Prince came down and looked about in vain for Preziosa, whom he had seen from the window above, he was so amazed at the trick that a deep melancholy came over him, and in four days he fell sick, crying continually, "My bear, my bear!" His mother, hearing him wailing thus, imagined that the bear had done him some hurt, and gave orders that she should be killed. But the servants, enamoured of the tameness of the bear, who made herself beloved by the very stones in the road, took pity on her, and, instead of killing her, they led her to the wood, and told the queen that they had put an end to her.

When this came to the ears of the Prince, he acted in a way to pass belief. Ill or well he jumped out of bed, and was going at once to make mincemeat of the servants. But when they told him the truth of the affair, he jumped on horseback, half-dead as he was, and went rambling about and seeking everywhere, until at length he found the bear. Then he took her home again, and putting her into a chamber, said to her, "O lovely morsel for a King, who art shut up in this skin! O candle of love, who art enclosed within this hairy lanthorn! Wherefore all this trifling? Do you wish to see me pine and pant, and die by inches? I am wasting away; without hope, and tormented by thy beauty. And you see clearly the proof, for I am shrunk two-thirds in size, like wine boiled down, and am nothing but skin and bone, for the fever is double-stitched to my veins. So lift up the curtain of this hairy hide, and let me gaze upon the spectacle of thy beauty! Raise, O raise the leaves off this basket, and let me get a sight of the fine fruit beneath! Lift up that curtain, and let my eyes pass in to behold the pomp of wonders! Who has shut up so smooth a creature in a prison woven of hair? Who has locked up so rich a treasure in a leathern chest? Let me behold this display of graces, and take in payment all my love; for nothing else can cure the troubles I endure."

But when he had said, again and again, this and a great deal more, and still saw that all his words were thrown away, he took to his bed, and had such a desperate fit that the doctors prognosticated badly of his case. Then his mother, who had no other joy in the world, sat down by his bedside, and said to him, "My son, whence comes all this grief? What melancholy humour has seized you? You are young, you are loved, you are great, you are rich—what then is it you want, my son? Speak; a bashful beggar carries an empty bag. If you want a wife, only choose, and I will bring the match about; do you take, and I'll pay. Do you not see that your illness is an illness to me? Your pulse beats with fever in your veins, and my heart beats with illness in my brain, for I have no other support of my old age than you. So be cheerful now, and cheer up my heart, and do not see the whole kingdom thrown into mourning, this house into lamentation, and your mother forlorn and heart-broken."

When the Prince heard these words, he said, "Nothing can console me but the sight of the bear. Therefore, if you wish to see me well again, let her be brought into this chamber; I will have no one else to attend me, and make my bed, and cook for me, but she herself; and you may be sure that this pleasure will make me well in a trice."

Thereupon his mother, although she thought it ridiculous enough for the bear to act as cook and chambermaid, and feared that her son was not in his right mind, yet, in order to gratify him, had the bear fetched. And when the bear came up to the Prince's bed, she raised her paw and felt the patient's pulse, which made the Queen laugh outright, for she thought every moment that the bear would scratch his nose. Then the Prince said, "My dear bear, will you not cook for me, and give me my food, and wait upon me?" and the bear nodded her head, to show that she accepted the office. Then his mother had some fowls brought, and a fire lighted on the hearth in the same chamber, and some water set to boil; whereupon the bear, laying hold on a fowl, scalded and plucked it handily, and drew it, and then stuck one portion of it on the spit, and with the other part she made such a delicious hash that the Prince, who could not relish even sugar, licked his fingers at the taste. And when he had done eating, the bear handed him drink with such grace that the Queen was ready to kiss her on the forehead. Thereupon the Prince arose, and the bear quickly set about making the bed; and running into the garden, she gathered a clothful of roses and citron-flowers and strewed them over it, so that the queen said the bear was worth her weight in gold, and that her son had good reason to be fond of her.

But when the Prince saw these pretty offices they only added fuel to the fire; and if before he wasted by ounces, he now melted away by pounds, and he said to the Queen, "My lady mother, if I do not give this bear a kiss, the breath will leave my body." Whereupon the Queen, seeing him fainting away, said, "Kiss him, kiss him, my beautiful beast! Let me not see my poor son die of longing!" Then the bear went up to the Prince, and taking him by the cheeks, kissed him again and again. Meanwhile (I know not how it was) the piece of wood slipped out of Preziosa's mouth, and she remained in the arms of the Prince, the most beautiful creature in the world; and pressing her to his heart, he said, "I have caught you, my little rogue! You shall not escape from me again without a good reason." At these words Preziosa, adding the colour of modesty to the picture of her natural beauty, said to him, "I am indeed in your hands—only guard me safely, and marry me when you will."

Then the Queen inquired who the beautiful maiden was, and what had brought her to this savage life; and Preziosa related the whole story of her misfortunes, at which the Queen, praising her as a good and virtuous girl, told her son that she was content that Preziosa should be his wife. Then the Prince, who desired nothing else in life, forthwith pledged her his faith; and the mother giving them her blessing, this happy marriage was celebrated with great feasting and illuminations, and Preziosa experienced the truth of the saying that—

"One who acts well may always expect good."

XVI

THE DOVE

He who is born a prince should not act like a beggar boy. The man who is high in rank ought not to set a bad example to those below him; for the little donkey learns from the big one to eat straw. It is no wonder, therefore, that Heaven sends him troubles by bushels—as happened to a prince who was brought into great difficulties for ill-treating and tormenting a poor woman, so that he was near losing his life miserably.

About eight miles from Naples there was once a deep wood of fig-trees and poplars. In this wood stood a half-ruined cottage, wherein dwelt an old woman, who was as light of teeth as she was burdened with years. She had a hundred wrinkles in her face, and a great many more in her purse, and all her silver covered her head, so that she went from one thatched cottage to another, begging alms to keep life in her. But as folks nowadays much rather give a purseful of crowns to a crafty spy than a farthing to a poor needy man, she had to toil a whole day to get a dish of kidney-beans, and that at a time when they were very plentiful. Now one day the poor old woman, after having washed the beans, put them in a pot, placed it outside the window, and went on her way to the wood to gather sticks for the fire. But while she was away, Nardo Aniello, the King's son, passed by the cottage on his way to the chase; and, seeing the pot at the window, he took a great fancy to have a fling at it; and he made a bet with his attendants to see who should fling the straightest and hit in the middle with a stone. Then they began to throw at the innocent pot; and in three or four casts the prince hit it to a hair and won the bet.

The old woman returned just after they had gone away, and seeing the sad disaster, she began to act as if she were beside herself, crying, "Ay, let him stretch out his arm and go about boasting how he has broken this pot! The villainous rascal who has sown my beans out of season. If he had no compassion for my misery, he should have had some regard for his own interest; for I pray Heaven, on my bare knees and from the bottom of my soul, that he may fall in love with the daughter of some ogress, who may plague and torment him in every way. May his mother-in-law lay on him such a curse that he may see himself living and yet bewail himself as dead; and being spellbound by the beauty of the daughter, and the arts of the mother, may he never be able to escape, but be obliged to remain. May she order him about with a cudgel in her hand, and give him bread with a little fork, that he may have good cause to lament over my beans which he has spilt on the ground." The old woman's curses took wing and flew up to Heaven in a trice; so that, notwithstanding what a proverb says, "for a woman's curse you are never the worse, and the coat of a horse that has been cursed always shines," she rated the Prince so soundly that he well-nigh jumped out of his skin.

Scarcely had two hours passed when the Prince, losing himself in the wood and parted from his attendants, met a beautiful maiden, who was going along picking up snails and saying with a laugh—

"Snail, snail, put out your horn,
Your mother is laughing you to scorn,
For she has a little son just born."

When the Prince saw this beautiful apparition he knew not what had befallen him; and, as the beams from the eyes of that crystal face fell upon the tinder of his heart, he was all in a flame, so that he became a lime-kiln wherein the stones of designs were burnt to build the houses of hopes.

Now Filadoro (for so the maiden was named) was no wiser than other people; and the Prince, being a smart young fellow with handsome moustachios, pierced her heart through and through, so that they stood looking at one another for compassion with their eyes, which proclaimed aloud the secret of their souls. After they had both remained thus for a long time, unable to utter a single word, the Prince at last, finding his voice, addressed Filadoro thus, "From what meadow has this flower of beauty sprung? From what mine has this treasure of beauteous things come to light? O happy woods, O fortunate groves, which this nobility inhabits, which this illumination of the festivals of love irradiates."

"Kiss this hand, my lord," answered Filadoro, "not so much modesty; for all the praise that you have bestowed on me belongs to your virtues, not to my merits. Such as I am, handsome or ugly, fat or thin, a witch or a fairy, I am wholly at your command; for your manly form has captivated my heart, your princely mien has pierced me through from side to side, and from this moment I give myself up to you for ever as a chained slave."

At these words the Prince seized at once her hand, kissing the ivory hook that had caught his heart. At this ceremony of the prince, Filadoro's face grew as red as scarlet. But the more Nardo Aniello wished to continue speaking, the more his tongue seemed tied; for in this wretched life there is no wine of enjoyment without dregs of vexation. And just at this moment Filadoro's mother suddenly appeared, who was such an ugly ogress that Nature seemed to have formed her as a model of horrors. Her hair was like a besom of holly; her forehead like a rough stone; her eyes were comets that predicted all sorts of evils; her mouth had tusks like a boar's—in short, from head to foot she was ugly beyond imagination. Now she seized Nardo Aniello by the nape of his neck, saying, "Hollo! what now, you thief! you rogue!"

"Yourself the rogue," replied the Prince, "back with you, old hag!" And he was just going to draw his sword, when all at once he stood fixed like a sheep that has seen the wolf and can neither stir nor utter a sound, so that the ogress led him like an ass by the halter to her house. And when they came there she said to him, "Mind, now, and work like a dog, unless you wish to die like a dog. For your first task to-day you must have this acre of land dug and sown level as this room; and recollect that if I return in the evening and do not find the work finished, I shall eat you up." Then, bidding her daughter take care of the house, she went to a meeting of the other ogresses in the wood.

Nardo Aniello, seeing himself in this dilemma, began to bathe his breast with tears, cursing his fate which brought him to this pass. But Filadoro comforted him, bidding him be of good heart, for she would ever risk her life to assist him. She said that she ought not to lament his fate which had led him to the house where she lived, who loved him so dearly, and that he showed little return for her love by being so despairing at what had happened. The Prince replied: "I am not grieved at having exchanged the royal palace for this hovel; splendid banquets for a crust of bread; a sceptre for a spade; not at seeing myself, who have terrified armies, now frightened by this hideous scarecrow; for I should deem all my disasters good fortune to be with you and to gaze upon you with these eyes. But what pains me to the heart is that I have to dig till my hands are covered with hard skin—I whose fingers are so delicate and soft as Barbary wool; and, what is still worse, I have to do more than two oxen could get through in a day. If I do not finish the task this evening your mother will eat me up; yet I should not grieve so much to quit this wretched body as to be parted from so beautiful a creature."

So saying he heaved sighs by bushels, and shed many tears. But Filadoro, drying his eyes, said to him, "Fear not that my mother will touch a hair of your head. Trust to me and do not be afraid; for you must know that I possess magical powers, and am able to make cream set on water and to darken the sun. Be of good heart, for by the evening the piece of land will be dug and sown without any one stirring a hand."

When Nardo Aniello heard this, he answered, "If you have magic power, as you say, O beauty of the world, why do we not fly from this country? For you shall live like a queen in my father's house." And Filadoro replied, "A certain conjunction of the stars prevents this, but the trouble will soon pass and we shall be happy."

With these and a thousand other pleasant discourses the day passed, and when the ogress came back she called to her daughter from the road and said, "Filadoro, let down your hair," for as the house had no staircase she always ascended by her daughter's tresses. As soon as Filadoro heard her mother's voice she unbound her hair and let fall her tresses, making a golden ladder to an iron heart. Whereupon the old woman mounted up quickly, and ran into the garden; but when she found it all dug and sown, she was beside herself with amazement; for it seemed to her impossible that a delicate lad should have accomplished such hard labour.

But the next morning, hardly had the Sun gone out to warm himself on account of the cold he had caught in the river of India, than the ogress went down again, bidding Nardo Aniello take care that in the evening she should find ready split six stacks of wood which were in the cellar, with every log cleft into four pieces, or otherwise she would cut him up like bacon and make a fry of him for supper.

On hearing this decree the poor Prince had liked to have died of terror, and Filadoro, seeing him half dead and pale as ashes, said, "Why! What a coward you are to be frightened at such a trifle." "Do you think it a trifle," replied Nardo Aniello, "to split six stacks of wood, with every log cleft into four pieces, between this time and the evening? Alas, I shall sooner be cleft in halves myself to fill the mouth of this horrid old woman." "Fear not," answered Filadoro, "for without giving yourself any trouble the wood shall all be split in good time. But meanwhile cheer up, if you love me, and do not split my heart with such lamentations."

Now when the Sun had shut up the shop of his rays, in order not to sell light to the Shades, the old woman returned; and, bidding Filadoro let down the usual ladder, she ascended, and finding the wood already split she began to suspect it was her own daughter who had given her this check. At the third day, in order to make a third trial, she told the Prince to clean out for her a cistern which held a thousand casks of water, for she wished to fill it anew, adding that if the task were not finished by the evening she would make mincemeat of him. When the old woman went away Nardo Aniello began again to weep and wail; and Filadoro, seeing that the labours increased, and that the old woman had something of the brute in her to burden the poor fellow with such tasks and troubles, said to him, "Be quiet, and as soon as the moment has passed that interrupts my art, before the Sun says I am off,' we will say good-bye to this house; sure enough, this evening my mother shall find the land cleared, and I will go off with you, alive or dead." The Prince, on hearing this news, embraced Filadoro and said, "Thou art the pole-star of this storm-tossed bark, my soul! Thou art the prop of my hopes."

Now, when the evening drew nigh, Filadoro having dug a hole in the garden into a large underground passage, they went out and took the way to Naples. But when they arrived at the grotto of Pozzuolo, Nardo Aniello said to Filadoro, "It will never do for me to take you to the palace on foot and dressed in this manner. Therefore wait at this inn and I will soon return with horses, carriages, servants, and clothes." So Filadoro stayed behind and the Prince went on his way to the city. Meantime the ogress returned home, and as Filadoro did not answer to her usual summons, she grew suspicious, ran into the wood, and cutting a great, long pole, placed it against the window and climbed up like a cat. Then she went into the house and hunted everywhere inside and out, high and low, but found no one. At last she perceived the hole, and seeing that it led into the open air, in her rage she did not leave a hair upon her head, cursing her daughter and the Prince, and praying that at the first kiss Filadoro's lover should receive he might forget her.

But let us leave the old woman to say her wicked curses and return to the Prince, who on arriving at the palace, where he was thought to be dead, put the whole house in an uproar, every one running to meet him and crying, "Welcome! welcome! Here he is, safe and sound, how happy we are to see him back in this country," with a thousand other words of affection. But as he was going up the stairs his mother met him half-way and embraced and kissed him, saying, "My son, my jewel, the apple of my eye, where have you been and why have you stayed away so long to make us all die with anxiety?" The Prince knew not what to answer, for he did not wish to tell her of his misfortunes; but no sooner had his mother kissed him than, owing to the curse, all that had passed went from his memory. Then the Queen told her son that to put an end to his going hunting and wasting his time in the woods, she wished him to get married. "Well and good," replied the Prince, "I am ready and prepared to do what you desire." So it was settled that within four days they should lead home to him the bride who had just arrived from the country of Flanders; and thereupon a great feasting and banquets were held.

But meanwhile Filadoro, seeing that her husband stayed away so long and hearing (I know not how) of the feast, waited in the evening till the servant-lad of the inn had gone to bed, and taking his clothes from the head of the bed, she left her own in their place, and disguising herself like a man, went to the court of the king, where the cooks, being in want of help, took her as kitchen boy. When the tables were set out and the guests all took their seats, and the dishes were set down and the carver was cutting up a large English pie which Filadoro had made with her own hands, lo, out flew such a beautiful dove that the guests in their astonishment, forgetting to eat, fell to admiring the pretty bird, which said to the Prince in a piteous voice, "Have you so soon forgotten the love of

Filadoro, and have all the services you received from her, ungrateful man, gone from your memory? Is it thus you repay the benefits she has done you: she who took you out of the claws of the ogress and gave you life and herself too? Woe to the woman who trusts too much to the words of man, who ever requites kindness with ingratitude, and pays debts with forgetfulness. But go, forget your promises, false man. And may the curses follow you which the unhappy maiden sends you from the bottom of her heart. But if the gods have not locked up their ears they will witness the wrong you have done her, and when you least expect it the lightning and thunder, fever and illness, will come to you. Enough, eat and drink, take your sports, for unhappy Filadoro, deceived and forsaken, will leave you the field open to make merry with your new wife." So saying, the dove flew away quickly and vanished like the wind. The Prince, hearing the murmuring of the dove, stood for a while stupefied. At length, he inquired whence the pie came, and when the carver told him that a scullion boy who had been taken to assist in the kitchen had made it, he ordered him to be brought into the room. Then Filadoro, throwing herself at the feet of Nardo Aniello, shedding a torrent of tears, said merely, "What have I done to you?" Whereupon the Prince at once recalled to mind the engagement he had made with her; and, instantly raising her up, seated her by his side, and when he related to his mother the great obligation he was under to this beautiful maiden and all that she had done for him, and how it was necessary that the promise he had given should be fulfilled, his mother, who had no other joy in life than her son, said to him, "Do as you please, so that you offend not this lady whom I have given you to wife." "Be not troubled," said the lady, "for, to tell the truth, I am very loth to remain in this country; with your kind permission I wish to return to my dear Flanders." Thereupon the Prince with great joy offered her a vessel and attendants; and, ordering Filadoro to be dressed like a Princess, when the tables were removed, the musicians came and they began the ball which lasted until evening.

So the feast being now ended, they all betook themselves to rest, and the Prince and Filadoro lived happily ever after, proving the truth of the proverb that—

"He who stumbles and does not fall,
Is helped on his way like a rolling ball."

XVII

CANNETELLA

It is an evil thing to seek for better than wheaten bread, for a man comes at last to desire what others throw away, and must content himself with honesty. He who loses all and walks on the tops of the trees has as much madness in his head as danger under his feet, as was the case with the daughter of a King whose story I have now to tell you.

There was once on a time a King of High-Hill who longed for children more than the porters do for a funeral that they may gather wax. And at last his wife presented him with a little girl, to whom he gave the name Cannetella.

The child grew by hands, and when she was as tall as a pole the King said to her, "My daughter, you are now grown as big as an oak, and it is full time to provide you with a husband worthy of that pretty face. Since, therefore, I love you as my own life and desire to please you, tell me, I pray, what sort of a husband you would like, what kind of a man would suit your fancy? Will you have him a scholar or a dunce? a boy, or man in years?

brown or fair or ruddy? tall as a maypole or short as a peg? small in the waist or round as an ox? Do you choose, and I am satisfied."

Cannetella thanked her father for these generous offers, but told him that she would on no account encumber herself with a husband. However, being urged by the King again and again, she said, "Not to show myself ungrateful for so much love I am willing to comply with your wish, provided I have such a husband that he has no like in the world."

Her father, delighted beyond measure at hearing this, took his station at the window from morning till evening, looking out and surveying, measuring and examining every one that passed along the street. And one day, seeing a good-looking man go by, the King said to his daughter, "Run, Cannetella! see if yon man comes up to the measure of your wishes." Then she desired him to be brought up, and they made a most splendid banquet for him, at which there was everything he could desire. And as they were feasting an almond fell out of the youth's mouth, whereupon, stooping down, he picked it up dexterously from the ground and put it under the cloth, and when they had done eating he went away. Then the King said to Cannetella, "Well, my life, how does this youth please you?" "Take the fellow away," said she; "a man so tall and so big as he should never have let an almond drop out of his mouth."

When the King heard this he returned to his place at the window, and presently, seeing another well-shaped youth pass by, he called his daughter to hear whether this one pleased her. Then Cannetella desired him to be shown up; so he was called, and another entertainment made. And when they had done eating, and the man had gone away, the King asked his daughter whether he had pleased her, whereupon she replied, "What in the world should I do with such a miserable fellow who wants at least a couple of servants with him to take off his cloak?"

"If that be the case," said the King, "it is plain that these are merely excuses, and that you are only looking for pretexts to refuse me this pleasure. So resolve quickly, for I am determined to have you married." To these angry words Cannetella replied, "To tell you the truth plainly, dear father, I really feel that you are digging in the sea and making a wrong reckoning on your fingers. I will never subject myself to any man who has not a golden head and teeth." The poor King, seeing his daughter's head thus turned, issued a proclamation, bidding any one in his kingdom who should answer to Cannetella's wishes to appear, and he would give him his daughter and the kingdom.

Now this King had a mortal enemy named Fioravante, whom he could not bear to see so much as painted on a wall. He, when he heard of this proclamation, being a cunning magician, called a parcel of that evil brood to him, and commanded them forthwith to make his head and teeth of gold. So they did as he desired, and when he saw himself with a head and teeth of pure gold he walked past under the window of the King, who, when he saw the very man he was looking for, called his daughter. As soon as Cannetella set eyes upon him she cried out, "Ay, that is he! he could not be better if I had kneaded him with my own hands."

When Fioravante was getting up to go away the King said to him, "Wait a little, brother; why in such a hurry! One would think you had quicksilver in your body! Fair and softly, I will give you my daughter and baggage and servants to accompany you, for I wish her to be your wife."

"I thank you," said Fioravante, "but there is no necessity; a single horse is enough if the beast will carry double, for at home I have servants and goods as many as the sands on the sea-shore." So, after arguing awhile, Fioravante at last prevailed, and, placing Cannetella behind him on a horse, he set out.

In the evening, when the red horses are taken away from the corn-mill of the sky and white oxen are yoked in their place, they came to a stable where some horses were feeding. Fioravante led Cannetella into it and said, "Listen! I have to make a journey to my own house, and it will take me seven years to get there. Mind, therefore, and wait for me in this stable and do not stir out, nor let yourself be seen by any living person, or else I will make you remember it as long as you live." Cannetella replied, "You are my lord and master, and I will carry out your commands exactly, but tell me what you will leave me to live upon in the meantime." And Fioravante answered, "What the horses leave of their own corn will be enough for you."

Only conceive how poor Cannetella now felt, and guess whether she did not curse the hour and moment she was born! Cold and frozen, she made up in tears what she wanted in food, bewailing her fate which had brought her down from a royal palace to a stable, from mattresses of Barbary wool to straw, from nice, delicate morsels to the leavings of horses. And she led this miserable life for several months, during which time corn was given to the horses by an unseen hand, and what they left supported her.

But at the end of this time, as she was standing one day looking through a hole, she saw a most beautiful garden, in which there were so many espaliers of lemons, and grottoes of citron, beds of flowers and fruit-trees and trellises of vines, that it was a joy to behold. At this sight a great longing seized her for a great bunch of grapes that caught her eye, and she said to herself, "Come what will and if the sky fall, I will go out silently and softly and pluck it. What will it matter a hundred years hence? Who is there to tell my husband? And should he by chance hear of it, what will he do to me? Moreover, these grapes are none of the common sort." So saying, she went out and refreshed her spirits, which were weakened by hunger.

A little while after, and before the appointed time, her husband came back, and one of his horses accused Cannetella of having taken the grapes. Whereat, Fioravante in a rage, drawing his knife, was about to kill her, but, falling on her knees, she besought him to stay his hand, since hunger drives the wolf from the wood. And she begged so hard that Fioravante replied, "I forgive you this time, and grant you your life out of charity, but if ever again you are tempted to disobey me, and I find that you have let the sun see you, I will make mincemeat of you. Now, mind me; I am going away once more, and shall be gone seven years. So take care and plough straight, for you will not escape so easily again, but I shall pay you off the new and the old scores together."

So saying, he departed, and Cannetella shed a river of tears, and, wringing her hands, beating her breast, and tearing her hair, she cried, "Oh, that ever I was born into the world to be destined to this wretched fate! Oh, father, why have you ruined me? But why do I complain of my father when I have brought this ill upon myself? I alone am the cause of my misfortunes. I wished for a head of gold, only to come to grief and die by iron! This is the punishment of Fate, for I ought to have done my father's will, and not have had such whims and fancies. He who minds not what his father and mother say goes a road he does not know." And so she lamented every day, until her eyes became two fountains, and her face was so thin and sallow, that her own father would not have known her.

At the end of a year the King's locksmith, whom Cannetella knew, happening to pass by the stable, she called to him and went out. The smith heard his name, but did not recognise the poor girl, who was so much altered; but when he knew who she was, and how she had become thus changed, partly out of pity and partly to gain the King's favour, he put her into an empty cask he had with him on a pack-horse, and, trotting off towards High-Hill, he arrived at midnight at the King's palace. Then he knocked at the door, and at first the servants would not let him in, but roundly abused him for coming at such an hour to disturb the sleep of the whole house. The King, however, hearing the uproar, and being told by a chamberlain what was the matter, ordered the smith to be instantly admitted, for he knew that something unusual must have made him come at that hour. Then the smith, unloading his beast, knocked out the head of the cask, and forth came

Cannetella, who needed more than words to make her father recognise her, and had it not been for a mole on her arm she might well have been dismissed. But as soon as he was assured of the truth he embraced and kissed her a thousand times. Then he instantly commanded a warm bath to be got ready; when she was washed from head to foot, and had dressed herself, he ordered food to be brought, for she was faint with hunger. Then her father said to her, "Who would ever have told me, my child, that I should see you in this plight? Who has brought you to this sad condition?" And she answered, "Alas, my dear sire, that Barbary Turk has made me lead the life of a dog, so that I was nearly at death's door again and again. I cannot tell you what I have suffered, but, now that I am here, never more will I stir from your feet. Rather will I be a servant in your house than a queen in another. Rather will I wear sackcloth where you are than a golden mantle away from you. Rather will I turn a spit in your kitchen than hold a sceptre under the canopy of another."

Meanwhile Fioravante, returning home, was told by the horses that the locksmith had carried off Cannetella in the cask, on hearing which, burning with shame, and all on fire with rage, off he ran towards High-Hill, and, meeting an old woman who lived opposite to the palace, he said to her, "What will you charge, good mother, to let me see the King's daughter?" Then she asked a hundred ducats, and Fioravante, putting his hand in his purse, instantly counted them out, one a-top of the other. Thereupon the old woman took him up on the roof, where he saw Cannetella drying her hair on a balcony. But—just as if her heart had whispered to her—the maiden turned that way and saw the knave. She rushed downstairs and ran to her father, crying out, "My lord, if you do not this very instant make me a chamber with seven iron doors I am lost and undone!"

"I will not lose you for such a trifle," said her father; "I would pluck out an eye to gratify such a dear daughter!" So, no sooner said than done, the doors were instantly made.

When Fioravante heard of this he went again to the old woman and said to her, "What shall I give you now? Go to the King's house, under pretext of selling pots of rouge, and make your way to the chamber of the King's daughter. When you are there contrive to slip this little piece of paper between the bed-clothes, saying, in an undertone, as you place it there—

Let every one now soundly sleep,
But Cannetella awake shall keep."

So the old woman agreed for another hundred ducats, and she served him faithfully.

Now, as soon as she had done this trick, such a sound sleep fell on the people of the house that they seemed as if they all were dead. Cannetella alone remained awake, and when she heard the doors bursting open she began to cry aloud as if she were burnt, but no one heard her, and there was no one to run to her aid. So Fioravante threw down all the seven doors, and, entering her room, seized up Cannetella, bed-clothes and all, to carry her off. But, as luck would have it, the paper the old woman had put there fell on the ground, and the spell was broken. All the people of the house awoke, and, hearing Cannetella's cries, they ran—cats, dogs, and all—and, laying hold on the ogre, quickly cut him in pieces like a pickled tunny. Thus he was caught in the trap he had laid for poor Cannetella, learning to his cost that—

"No one suffereth greater pain
Than he who by his own sword is slain."

XVIII

CORVETTO

I once heard say that Juno went to Candia to find Falsehood. But if any one were to ask me where fraud and hypocrisy might truly be found, I should know of no other place to name than the Court, where detraction always wears the mask of amusement; where, at the same time, people cut and sew up, wound and heal, break and glue together—of which I will give you one instance in the story that I am going to tell you.

There was once upon a time in the service of the King of Wide-River an excellent youth named Corvetto, who, for his good conduct, was beloved by his master; and for this very cause was disliked and hated by all the courtiers. These courtiers were filled with spite and malice, and bursting with envy at the kindness which the King showed to Corvetto; so that all day long, in every corner of the palace, they did nothing but tattle and whisper, murmur and grumble at the poor lad, saying, "What sorcery has this fellow practised on the King that he takes such a fancy to him? How comes he by this luck that not a day passes that he receives some new favours, whilst we are for ever going backward like a rope-maker, and getting from bad to worse, though we slave like dogs, toil like field-labourers, and run about like deer to hit the King's pleasure to a hair? Truly one must be born to good fortune in this world, and he who has not luck might as well be thrown into the sea. What is to be done? We can only look on and envy." These and other words fell from their mouths like poisoned arrows aimed at the ruin of Corvetto as at a target. Alas for him who is condemned to that den the Court, where flattery is sold by the kilderkin, malignity and ill-offices are measured out in bushels, deceit and treachery are weighed by the ton! But who can count all the attempts these courtiers made to bring him to grief, or the false tales that they told to the King to destroy his reputation! But Corvetto, who was enchanted, and perceived the traps, and discovered the tricks, was aware of all the intrigues and the ambuscades, the plots and conspiracies of his enemies. He kept his ears always on the alert and his eyes open in order not to take a false step, well knowing that the fortune of courtiers is as glass. But the higher the lad continued to rise the lower the others fell; till at last, being puzzled to know how to take him off his feet, as their slander was not believed, they thought of leading him to disaster by the path of flattery, which they attempted in the following manner.

Ten miles distant from Scotland, where the seat of this King was, there dwelt an ogre, the most inhuman and savage that had ever been in Ogreland, who, being persecuted by the King, had fortified himself in a lonesome wood on the top of a mountain, where no bird ever flew, and was so thick and tangled that one could never see the sun there. This ogre had a most beautiful horse, which looked as if it were formed with a pencil; and amongst other wonderful things, it could speak like any man. Now the courtiers, who knew how wicked the ogre was, how thick the wood, how high the mountain, and how difficult it was to get at the horse, went to the King, and telling him minutely the perfections of the animal, which was a thing worthy of a King, added that he ought to endeavour by all means to get it out of the ogre's claws, and that Corvetto was just the lad to do this, as he was expert and clever at escaping out of the fire. The King, who knew not that under the flowers of these words a serpent was concealed, instantly called Corvetto, and said to him, "If you love me, see that in some way or another you obtain for me the horse of my enemy the ogre, and you shall have no cause to regret having done me this service."

Corvetto knew well that this drum was sounded by those who wished him ill; nevertheless, to obey the King, he set out and took the road to the mountain. Then going very quietly to the ogre's stable, he saddled and mounted the horse, and fixing his feet firmly in the stirrup, took his way back. But as soon as the horse saw himself spurred out of the palace, he cried aloud, "Hollo! be on your guard! Corvetto is riding off with me."

At this alarm the ogre instantly set out, with all the animals that served him, to cut Corvetto in pieces. From this side jumped an ape, from that was seen a large bear; here sprang forth a lion, there came running a wolf. But the youth, by the aid of bridle and spur, distanced the mountain, and galloping without stop to the city, arrived at the Court, where he presented the horse to the King.

Then the King embraced him more than a son, and pulling out his purse, filled his hands with crown-pieces. At this the rage of the courtiers knew no bounds; and whereas at first they were puffed up with a little pipe, they were now bursting with the blasts of a smith's bellows, seeing that the crowbars with which they thought to lay Corvetto's good fortune in ruins only served to smooth the road to his prosperity. Knowing, however, that walls are not levelled by the first attack of the battering-ram, they resolved to try their luck a second time, and said to the King, "We wish you joy of the beautiful horse! It will indeed be an ornament to the royal stable. But what a pity you have not the ogre's tapestry, which is a thing more beautiful than words can tell, and would spread your fame far and wide! There is no one, however, able to procure this treasure but Corvetto, who is just the lad to do such a kind of service."

Then the King, who danced to every tune, and ate only the peel of this bitter but sugared fruit, called Corvetto, and begged him to procure for him the ogre's tapestry. Off went Corvetto and in four seconds was on the top of the mountain where the ogre lived; then passing unseen into the chamber in which he slept, he hid himself under the bed, and waited as still as a mouse, until Night, to make the Stars laugh, puts a carnival-mask on the face of the Sky. And as soon as the ogre and his wife were gone to bed, Corvetto stripped the walls of the chamber very quietly, and wishing to steal the counterpane of the bed likewise, he began to pull it gently. Thereupon the ogre, suddenly starting up, told his wife not to pull so, for she was dragging all the clothes off him, and would give him his death of cold.

"Why you are uncovering me!" answered the ogress.

"Where is the counterpane?" replied the ogre; and stretching out his hand to the floor he touched Corvetto's face; whereupon he set up a loud cry,—"The imp! the imp! Hollo, here, lights! Run quickly!"—till the whole house was turned topsy-turvy with the noise. But Corvetto, after throwing the clothes out of the window, let himself drop down upon them. Then making up a good bundle, he set out on the road to the city, where the reception he met with from the King, and the vexation of the courtiers, who were bursting with spite, are not to be told. Nevertheless they laid a plan to fall upon Corvetto with the rear-guard of their roguery, and went again to the King, who was almost beside himself with delight at the tapestry—which was not only of silk embroidered with gold, but had besides more than a thousand devices and thoughts worked on it. And amongst the rest, if I remember right, there was a cock in the act of crowing at daybreak, and out of its mouth was seen coming a motto in Tuscan: IF I ONLY SEE YOU. And in another part a drooping heliotrope with a Tuscan motto: AT SUNSET—with so many other pretty things that it would require a better memory and more time than I have to relate them.

When the courtiers came to the King, who was thus transported with joy, they said to him, "As Corvetto has done so much to serve you, it would be no great matter for him, in order to give you a signal pleasure, to get the ogre's palace, which is fit for an emperor to live in; for it has so many rooms and chambers, inside and out, that it can hold an army. And you would never believe all the courtyards, porticoes, colonnades, balconies, and spiral chimneys which there are—built with such marvellous architecture that Art prides herself upon them, Nature is abashed, and Stupor is in delight."

The King, who had a fruitful brain which conceived quickly, called Corvetto again, and telling him the great longing that had seized him for the ogre's palace, begged him to add this service to all the others he had done him, promising to score it up with the chalk of gratitude at the tavern of memory. So Corvetto instantly set out heels over head; and arriving at the ogre's palace, he found that the ogress, whilst her husband was gone to invite the kinsfolk, was busying herself with preparing the feast. Then Corvetto entering, with a look of compassion, said, "Good-day, my good woman! Truly, you are a brave housewife! But why do you torment the very life out of you in this way? Only yesterday you were ill in bed, and now you are slaving thus, and have no pity on your own flesh."

"What would you have me do?" replied the ogress. "I have no one to help me."

"I am here," answered Corvetto, "ready to help you tooth and nail."

"Welcome, then!" said the ogress; "and as you proffer me so much kindness, just help me to split four logs of wood."

"With all my heart," answered Corvetto, "but if four logs are not enow, let me split five." And taking up a newly-ground axe, instead of striking the wood, he struck the ogress on the neck, and made her fall to the ground like a pear. Then running quickly to the gate, he dug a deep hole before the entrance, and covering it over with bushes and earth, he hid himself behind the gate.

As soon as Corvetto saw the ogre coming with his kinsfolk, he set up a loud cry in the courtyard, "Stop, stop! I've caught him!" and "Long live the King of Wide-River." When the ogre heard this challenge, he ran like mad at Corvetto, to make a hash of him. But rushing furiously towards the gate, down he tumbled with all his companions, head over heels to the bottom of the pit, where Corvetto speedily stoned them to death. Then he shut the door, and took the keys to the King, who, seeing the valour and cleverness of the lad, in spite of ill-fortune and the envy and annoyance of the courtiers, gave him his daughter to wife; so that the crosses of envy had proved rollers to launch Corvetto's bark of life on the sea of greatness; whilst his enemies remained confounded and bursting with rage, and went to bed without a candle; for—

"The punishment of ill deeds past,
Though long delay'd, yet comes at last."

XIX

THE BOOBY

An ignorant man who associates with clever people has always been more praised than a wise man who keeps the company of fools; for as much profit and fame as one may gain from the former, so much wealth and honour one may lose by the fault of the latter; and as the proof of the pudding is in the eating, you will know from the story which I am going to tell you whether my proposition be true.

There was once a man who was as rich as the sea, but as there can never be any perfect happiness in this world, he had a son so idle and good-for-nothing that he could not tell a bean from a cucumber. So being unable any longer to put up with his folly, he gave him a good handful of crowns, and sent him to trade in the Levant; for he well knew that seeing various countries and mixing with divers people awaken the genius and sharpen the judgment, and make men expert.

Moscione (for that was the name of the son) got on horseback, and began his journey towards Venice, the arsenal of the wonders of the world, to embark on board some vessel bound for Cairo; and when he had travelled a good day's journey, he met with a person who was standing fixed at the foot of a poplar, to whom he said, "What is your name, my lad? Whence are you, and what is your trade?" And the lad replied, "My name is Lightning; I am from Arrowland, and I can run like the wind." "I should like to see a proof of it," said Moscione; and Lightning answered, "Wait a moment, and you will see whether it is dust or flour."

When they had stood waiting a little while, a doe came bounding over the plain, and Lightning, letting her pass on some way, to give her the more law, darted after her so rapidly and light of foot, that he would have gone over a place covered with flour without leaving the mark of his shoe, and in four bounds he came up with her. Moscione, amazed at this exploit, asked if he would come and live with him, and promised to pay him royally.

So Lightning consented, and they went on their way together; but they had not journeyed many miles when they met another youth, to whom Moscione said, "What is your name, comrade? What country are you from? And what is your trade?" "My name," replied the lad, "is Quick-ear; I am from Vale-Curious; and when I put my ear the ground I hear all that is passing in the world without stirring from the spot. I perceive the monopolies and agreements of tradespeople to raise the prices of things, the ill-offices of courtiers, the appointments of lovers, the plots of robbers, the reports of spies, the complaints of servants, the gossiping of old women, and the oaths of sailors; so that no one has ever been able to discover so much as my ears can."

"If that be true," said Moscione, "tell me what they are now saying at my home."

So the lad put his ear to the ground, and replied, "An old man is talking to his wife, and saying, 'Praised be Sol in Leo! I have got rid from my sight of that fellow Moscione, that face of old-fashioned crockery, that nail in my heart. By travelling through the world he will at least become a man, and no longer be such a stupid ass, such a simpleton, such a lose-the-day fellow, such a——'"

"Stop, stop!" cried Moscione, "you tell the truth and I believe you. So come along with me, for you have found the road to good-luck."

"Well and good!" said the youth. So they all went on together and travelled ten miles farther, when they met another man, to whom Moscione said, "What is your name, my brave fellow? Where were you born? And what can you do in the world?" And the man answered, "My name is Shoot-straight; I am from Castle Aimwell; and I can shoot with a crossbow so point-blank as to hit a crab-apple in the middle."

"I should like to see the proof," said Moscione. So the lad charged his crossbow, took aim, and made a pea leap from the top of a stone; whereupon Moscione took him also like the others into his company. And they travelled on another day's journey, till they came to some people who were building a large pier in the scorching heat of the sun, and who might well say, "Boy, put water to the wine, for my heart is burning." So Moscione had compassion on them, and said, "My masters, how is it you have the head to stand in this furnace, which is fit to roast a buffalo?" And one of them answered, "Oh, we are as cool as a rose; for we have a young man here who blows upon us from behind in such a manner that it seems just as if the west wind were blowing." "Let me see him, I pray," cried Moscione. So the mason called the lad, and Moscione said to him, "Tell me, by the life of your father, what is your name? what country are you from? and what is your profession!" And the lad replied, "My name is Blow-blast; I am from Windy-land; and I can make all the winds with my mouth. If you wish for a zephyr, I will breathe one that will send you in transports; if you wish for a squall, I will throw down houses."

"Seeing is believing," said Moscione. Whereupon Blow-blast breathed at first quite gently, so that it seemed to be the wind that blows at Posilippo towards evening; then turning suddenly to some trees, he sent forth such a furious blast that it uprooted a row of oaks.

When Moscione saw this he took him for a companion; and travelling on as far again, he met another lad, to whom he said, "What is your name, if I may make so bold? Whence are you, if one may ask? And what is your trade, if it is a fair question?" And the lad answered, "My name is Strong-back; I am from Valentino; and I have such strength that I can take a mountain on my back, and it seems to me only a feather."

"If that be the case," said Moscione, "you deserve to be the king of the custom-house, and you should be chosen for standard-bearer on the first of May. But I should like to see a proof of what you say."

Then Strong-back began to load himself with masses of rock, trunks of trees, and so many other weights that a thousand large waggons could not have carried them; which, when Moscione saw, he agreed with the lad to join him.

So they travelled on till they came to Fair-Flower, the King of which place had a daughter who ran like the wind, and could pass over the waving corn without bending an ear; and the King had issued a proclamation that whoever could over-take her in running should have her to wife, but whoever was left behind should lose his head.

When Moscione arrived in this country and heard the proclamation, he went straight to the King, and offered to run with his daughter, making the wise agreement either to win the race or leave his noddle there. But in the morning he sent to inform the King that he was taken ill, and being unable to run himself he would send another young man in his place. "Come who will!" said Ciannetella (for that was the King's daughter), "I care not a fig—it is all one to me."

So when the great square was filled with people, come to see the race, insomuch that the men swarmed like ants, and the windows and roofs were all as full as an egg, Lightning came out and took his station at the top of the square, waiting for the signal. And lo! forth came Ciannetella, dressed in a little gown, tucked half-way up her legs, and a neat and pretty little shoe with a single sole. Then they placed themselves shoulder to shoulder, and as soon as the tarantara and too-too of the trumpets was heard, off they darted, running at such a rate that their heels touched their shoulders, and in truth they seemed just like hares with the grey-hounds after them, horses broken loose from the stable, or dogs with kettles tied to their tails. But Lightning (as he was both by name and nature) left the princess more than a hand's-breadth behind him, and came first to the goal. Then you should have heard the huzzaing and shouting, the cries and the uproar, the whistling and clapping of hands of all the people, bawling out, "Hurra! Long life to the stranger!" Whereat Ciannetella's face turned as red as a schoolboy's who is going to be whipped, and she stood lost in shame and confusion at seeing herself vanquished. But as there were to be two heats to the race, she fell to planning how to be revenged for this affront; and going home, she put a charm into a ring of such power that if any one had it upon his finger his legs would totter so that he would not be able to walk, much less run; then she sent it as a present to Lightning, begging him to wear it on his finger for love of her.

Quick-ear, who heard this trick plotted between the father and daughter, said nothing, and waited to see the upshot of the affair. And when, at the trumpeting of the birds, the Sun whipped on the Night, who sat mounted on the jackass of the Shades, they returned to the field, where at the usual signal they fell to plying their heels. But if Ciannetella was like another Atalanta, Lightning had become no less like an old donkey and a foundered horse, for he could not stir a step. But Shoot-straight, who saw his comrade's danger, and heard from Quick-ear how matters stood, laid hold of his crossbow and shot a bolt so exactly that it hit Lightning's finger, and out flew the stone from the ring, in which the virtue of the charm lay; whereupon his legs, that had been tied, were set free, and with four goat-leaps he passed Ciannetella and won the race.

The King seeing this victory of a blockhead, the palm thus carried off by a simpleton, the triumph of a fool, bethought himself seriously whether or no he should give him his daughter; and taking counsel with the wiseacres of his court, they replied that Ciannetella was not a mouthful for the tooth of such a miserable dog and lose-the-day bird, and that, without breaking his word, he might commute the promise of his daughter for a gift of crowns, which would be more to the taste of a poor beggar like Moscione than all the women in the world.

This advice pleased the King, and he asked Moscione how much money he would take instead of the wife who had been promised him. Then Moscione, after consulting with the others, answered, "I will take as much gold and silver as one of my comrades can carry on his back." The king consented; whereupon they brought Strong-back, on whom they began to load bales of ducats, sacks of patacas, large purses full of crowns, barrels of copper money, chests full of chains and rings; but the more they loaded him the firmer he stood, just like a tower, so that the treasury, the banks, the usurers, and the money-dealers of the city did not suffice, and he sent to all the great people in every direction to borrow their silver candlesticks, basins, jugs, plates, trays, and baskets; and yet all was not enough to make up the full load. At length they went away, not laden but tired and satisfied.

When the councillors saw what heaps and stores these six miserable dogs were carrying off, they said to the King that it was a great piece of assery to load them with all the sinews of his kingdom, and that it would be well to send people after them to lessen the load of that Atlas who was carrying on his shoulders a heaven of treasure. The King gave ear to this advice, and immediately despatched a party of armed men, foot and horse, to overtake Moscione and his friends. But Quick-ear, who had heard this counsel, informed his comrades; and while the dust was rising to the sky from the trampling of those who were coming to unload the rich cargo, Blow-blast, seeing that things were come to a bad pass, began to blow at such a rate that he not only made the enemies fall flat on the ground, but he sent them flying more than a mile distant, as the north wind does the folks who pass through that country. So without meeting any more hindrance, Moscione arrived at his father's house, where he shared the booty with his companions, since, as the saying goes, a good deed deserves a good meed. So he sent them away content and happy; but he stayed with his father, rich beyond measure, and saw himself a simpleton laden with gold, not giving the lie to the saying—

"Heaven sends biscuits to him who has no teeth."

XX

THE STONE IN THE COCK'S HEAD

The robber's wife does not always laugh; he who weaves fraud works his own ruin; there is no deceit which is not at last discovered, no treachery that does not come to light; walls have ears, and are spies to rogues; the earth gapes and discovers theft, as I will prove to you if you pay attention.

There was once in the city of Dark-Grotto a certain man named Minecco Aniello, who was so persecuted by fortune that all his fixtures and moveables consisted only of a short-legged cock, which he had reared upon bread-crumbs. But one morning, being pinched with appetite (for hunger drives the wolf from the thicket), he took it into his head to sell the cock, and, taking it to the market, he met two thievish magicians, with whom he made a bargain, and sold it for half-a-crown. So they told him to take it to their house, and they would count him out the money. Then the magicians went their way, and, Minecco Aniello following them, overheard them talking gibberish together and saying, "Who would have told us that we should meet with such a piece of good luck, Jennarone? This cock will make our fortune to a certainty by the stone which, you know, he has in his pate. We will quickly have it set in a ring, and then we shall have everything we can ask for."

"Be quiet, Jacovuccio," answered Jennarone; "I see myself rich and can hardly believe it, and I am longing to twist the cock's neck and give a kick in the face of beggary, for in this world virtue without money goes for nothing, and a man is judged of by his coat."

When Minecco Aniello, who had travelled about in the world and eaten bread from more than one oven, heard this gibberish he turned on his heel and scampered off. And, running home, he twisted the cock's neck, and opening its head found the stone, which he had instantly set in a brass ring. Then, to make a trial of its virtue, he said, "I wish to become a youth eighteen years old."

Hardly had he uttered the words when his blood began to flow more quickly, his nerves became stronger, his limbs firmer, his flesh fresher, his eyes more fiery, his silver hairs were turned into gold, his mouth, which was a sacked village, became peopled with teeth; his beard, which was as thick as a wood, became like a nursery garden—in short, he was changed to a most beautiful youth. Then he said again, "I wish for a splendid palace, and to marry the King's daughter." And lo! there instantly appeared a palace of incredible magnificence, in which were apartments that would amaze you, columns to astound you, pictures to fill you with wonder; silver glittered around, and gold was trodden underfoot; the jewels dazzled your eyes; the servants swarmed like ants, the horses and carriages were not to be counted—in short, there was such a display of riches that the King stared at the sight, and willingly gave him his daughter Natalizia.

Meanwhile the magicians, having discovered Minecco Aniello's great wealth, laid a plan to rob him of his good fortune, so they made a pretty little doll which played and danced by means of clockwork; and, dressing themselves like merchants, they went to Pentella, the daughter of Minecco Aniello, under pretext of selling it to her. When Pentella saw the beautiful little thing she asked them what price they put upon it, and they replied that it was not to be bought with money, but that she might have it and welcome if she would only do them a favour, which was to let them see the make of the ring which her father possessed, in order to take the model and make another like it, then they would give her the doll without any payment at all.

Pentella, who had never heard the proverb, "Think well before you buy anything cheap," instantly accepted this offer, and, bidding them return the next morning, she promised to ask her father to lend her the ring. So the magicians went away, and when her father returned home Pentella coaxed and caressed him, until at last she persuaded him to give her the ring, making the excuse that she was sad at heart, and wished to divert her mind a little.

When the next day came, as soon as the scavenger of the Sun sweeps the last traces of the Shades from the streets and squares of Heaven, the magicians returned, and no sooner had they the ring in their hands than they instantly vanished, and not a trace of them was to be seen, so that poor Pentella had like to have died with terror.

But when the magicians came to a wood, where the branches of some of the trees were dancing the sword-dance, and the boughs of the others were playing together at hot-cockles, they desired the ring to destroy the spell by which the old man had become young again. And instantly Minecco Aniello, who was just at that moment in the presence of the King, was suddenly seen to grow hoary, his hairs to whiten, his forehead to wrinkle, his eyebrows to grow bristly, his eyes to sink in, his face to be furrowed, his mouth to become toothless, his beard to grow bushy, his back to be humped, his legs to tremble, and, above all, his glittering garments to turn to rags and tatters.

The King, seeing the miserable beggar seated beside him at table, ordered him to be instantly driven away with blows and hard words, whereupon Aniello, thus suddenly fallen from his good luck, went weeping to his daughter, and asked for the ring in order to set matters to rights again. But when he heard the fatal trick played by the false merchants he was ready to throw himself out of the window, cursing a thousand times the ignorance of his daughter, who, for the sake of a silly doll had turned him into a miserable scarecrow, and for a paltry thing of rags had brought him to rags himself, adding that he was resolved to go wandering about the world like a bad shilling, until he should get tidings of those merchants. So saying he threw a cloak about his neck and a wallet on his back, drew his sandals on his feet, took a staff in his hand, and, leaving his daughter all chilled and frozen, he set out walking desperately on and on until he arrived at the kingdom of Deep-Hole, inhabited by the mice, where, being taken for a big spy of the cats, he was instantly led before Rosecone, the King. Then the King asked him who he was, whence he came, and what he was about in that country; and Minecco Aniello, after first giving the King a cheese-paring, in sign of tribute, related to him all his misfortunes one by one, and concluded by saying that he was resolved to continue his toil and travel, until he should get tidings of those thievish villains who had robbed him of so precious a jewel, taking from him at once the flower of his youth, the source of his wealth, and the prop of his honour.

At these words Rosecone felt pity nibbling at his heart, and, wishing to comfort the poor man, he summoned the eldest mice to a council, and asked their opinions on the misfortunes of Minecco Aniello, commanding them to use all diligence and endeavour to obtain some tidings of these false merchants. Now, among the rest, it happened that Rudolo and Saltariello were present—mice who were well used to the ways of the world, and had lived for six years at a tavern of great resort hard by; and they said to Aniello, "Be of good heart, comrade! matters will turn out better than you imagine. You must know that one day, when we were in a room in the hostelry of the Horn,' where the most famous men in the world lodge and make merry, two persons from Hook Castle came in, who, after they had eaten their fill and had seen the bottom of their flagon, fell to talking of a trick they had played a certain old man of Dark-Grotto, and how they had cheated him out of a stone of great value, which one of them, named Jennarone, said he would never take from his finger, that he might not run the risk of losing it as the old man's daughter had done."

When Minecco Aniello heard this, he told the two mice that if they would trust themselves to accompany him to the country where these rogues lived and recover the ring for him, he would give them a good lot of cheese and salt meat, which they might eat and enjoy with his majesty the King. Then the two mice, after bargaining for a reward, offered to go over sea and mountain, and, taking leave of his mousy majesty, they set out.

After journeying a long way they arrived at Hook Castle, where the mice told Minecco Aniello to remain under some trees on the brink of a river, which like a leech drew the moisture from the land and discharged it into the sea. Then they went to seek the house of the magicians, and, observing that Jennarone never took the ring from his finger, they sought to gain the victory by stratagem. So, waiting till Night had dyed with purple grape-juice the sunburnt face of Heaven, and the magicians had gone to bed and were fast asleep, Rudolo began to nibble the finger on which the ring was, whereupon Jennarone, feeling the smart, took the ring off and laid it on a table at the head of the bed. But as soon as Saltariello saw this, he popped the ring into his mouth, and in four skips he was off to find Minecco Aniello, who, with even greater joy than a man at the gallows feels when a pardon arrives, instantly turned the magicians into two jackasses; and, turning his mantle over one of them, he bestrode him like a noble count, then he loaded the other with cheese and bacon, and set off toward Deep-Hole, where, having given presents to the King and his councillors, he thanked them for all the good fortune he had received by their assistance, praying Heaven that no mouse-trap might ever lay hold of them, that no cat might ever harm them, and that no arsenic might ever poison them.

Then, leaving that country, Minecco Aniello returned to Dark-Grotto even more handsome than before, and was received by the King and his daughter with the greatest affection in the world. And, having ordered the two asses to be cast down from a rock, he lived happily with his wife, never more taking the ring from his finger that he might not again commit such a folly, for—

"The cat who has been burnt with fire ever after fears the cold hearthstone."

XXI

THE THREE ENCHANTED PRINCES

Once upon a time the King of Green-Bank had three daughters, who were perfect jewels, with whom three sons of the King of Fair-Meadow were desperately in love. But these Princes having been changed into animals by the spell of a fairy, the King of Green-Bank disdained to give them his daughters to wife. Whereupon the first, who was a beautiful Falcon, called together all the birds to a council; and there came the chaffinches, tomtits, woodpeckers, fly-catchers, jays, blackbirds, cuckoos, thrushes, and every other kind of bird. And when they were all assembled at his summons, he ordered them to destroy all the blossoms on the trees of Green-Bank, so that not a flower or leaf should remain. The second Prince, who was a Stag, summoning all the goats, rabbits, hares, hedgehogs, and other animals of that country, laid waste all the corn-fields so that there was not a single blade of grass or corn left. The third Prince, who was a Dolphin, consulting together with a hundred monsters of the sea, made such a tempest arise upon the coast that not a boat escaped.

Now the King saw that matters were going from bad to worse, and that he could not remedy the mischief which these three wild lovers were causing; so he resolved to get out of his trouble, and made up his mind to give them his daughters to wife; and thereupon, without wanting either feasts or songs, they carried their brides off and out of the kingdom.

On parting from her daughters, Granzolla the Queen gave each of them a ring, one exactly like the other, telling them that if they happened to be separated, and after a while to meet again, or to see any of their kinsfolk, they would recognise one another by means of these rings. So taking their leave they departed. And the Falcon carried Fabiella, who was the eldest of the sisters, to the top of a mountain, which was so high that, passing the confines of the clouds, it reached with a dry head to a region where it never rains; and there, leading her to a most beautiful palace, she lived like a Queen.

The Stag carried Vasta, the second sister, into a wood, which was so thick that the Shades, when summoned by the Night, could not find their way out to escort her. There he placed her, as befitted her rank, in a wonderfully splendid house with a garden.

The Dolphin swam with Rita, the third sister, on his back into the middle of the sea, where, upon a large rock, he showed her a mansion in which three crowned Kings might live.

Meanwhile Granzolla gave birth to a fine little boy, whom they named Tittone. And when he was fifteen years old, hearing his mother lamenting continually that she never heard any tidings of her three daughters, who were married to three animals; he took it into his head to travel through the world until he should obtain some news of them. So after begging and entreating his father and mother for a long time, they granted him permission, bidding him take for his journey attendants and everything needful and befitting a Prince; and the Queen also gave him another ring similar to those she had given to her daughters.

Tittone went his way, and left no corner of Italy, not a nook of France, nor any part of Spain unsearched. Then he passed through England, and traversed Slavonia, and visited Poland, and, in short, travelled both east and west. At length, leaving all his servants, some at the taverns and some at the hospitals, he set out without a farthing in his pocket, and came to the top of the mountain where dwelt the Falcon and Fabiella. And as he stood there, beside himself with amazement, contemplating the beauty of the palace—the corner-stones of which were of porphyry, the walls of alabaster, the windows of gold, and the tiles of silver—his sister observed him, and ordering him to be called, she demanded who he was, whence he came, and what chance had brought him to that country. When Tittone told her his country, his father and mother, and his name, Fabiella knew him to be her brother, and the more when she compared the ring upon his finger with that which her mother had given her; and embracing him with great joy, she concealed him, fearing that her husband would be angry when he returned home.

As soon as the Falcon came home, Fabiella began to tell him that a great longing had come over her to see her parents. And the Falcon answered, "Let the wish pass, wife; for that cannot be unless the humour takes me."

"Let us at least," said Fabiella, "send to fetch one of my kinsfolk to keep my company."

"And, pray, who will come so far to see you?" replied the Falcon.

"Nay, but if any one should come," added Fabiella, "would you be displeased?"

"Why should I be displeased?" said the Falcon, "it would be enough that he were one of your kinsfolk to make me take him to my heart."

When Fabiella heard this she took courage, and calling to her brother to come forth, she presented him to the Falcon, who exclaimed, "Five and five are ten; love passes through the glove, and water through the boot. A hearty welcome to you! you are master in this house; command, and do just as you like." Then he gave orders that Tittone should be served and treated with the same honour as himself.

Now when Tittone had stayed a fortnight on the mountain, it came into his head to go forth and seek his other sisters. So taking leave of Fabiella and his brother-in-law, the Falcon gave him one of his feathers, saying, "Take this and prize it, my dear Tittone; for you may one day be in trouble, and you will then esteem it a treasure. Enough—take good care of it; and if ever you meet with any mishap, throw it on the ground, and say, Come hither, come hither!' and you shall have cause to thank me."

Tittone wrapped the feather up in a sheet of paper, and, putting it in his pocket, after a thousand ceremonies departed. And travelling on and on a very long way, he arrived at last at the wood where the Stag lived with Vasta; and going, half-dead with hunger, into the garden to pluck some fruit, his sister saw him, and recognised him in the same manner as Fabiella had done. Then she presented Tittone to her husband, who received him with the greatest friendship, and treated him truly like a Prince.

At the end of a fortnight, when Tittone wished to depart, and go in search of his other sister, the Stag gave him one of his hairs, repeating the same words as the Falcon had spoken about the feather. And setting out on his way, with a bagful of crown-pieces which the Falcon had given him, and as many more which the Stag gave him, he walked on and on, until he came to the end of the earth, where, being stopped by the sea and unable to walk any further, he took ship, intending to seek through all the islands for tidings of his sister. So setting sail, he went about and about, until at length he was carried to an island, where lived the Dolphin with Rita. And no sooner had he landed, than his sister saw and recognised him in the same manner as the others had done, and he was received by her husband with all possible affection.

Now after a while Tittone wished to set out again to go and visit his father and mother, whom he had not seen for so long a time. So the Dolphin gave him one of his scales, telling him the same as the others had; and Tittone, mounting a horse, set out on his travels. But he had hardly proceeded half a mile from the seashore, when entering a wood—the abode of Fear and the Shades, where a continual fair of darkness and terror was kept up—he found a great tower in the middle of a lake, whose waters were kissing the feet of the trees, and entreating them not to let the Sun witness their pranks. At a window in the tower Tittone saw a most beautiful maiden sitting at the feet of a hideous dragon, who was asleep. When the damsel saw Tittone, she said in a low and piteous voice, "O noble youth, sent perchance by heaven to comfort me in my miseries in this place, where the face of a Christian is never seen, release me from the power of this tyrannical serpent, who has carried me off from my father, the King of Bright-Valley, and shut me up in this frightful tower, where I must die a miserable death."

"Alas, my beauteous lady!" replied Tittone, "what can I do to serve thee? Who can pass this lake? Who can climb this tower? Who can approach yon horrid dragon, that carries terror in his look, sows fear, and causes dismay to spring up? But softly, wait a minute, and we'll find a way with another's help to drive this serpent away. Step by step—the more haste, the worse speed: we shall soon see whether tis egg or wind." And so saying he threw the feather, the hair, and the scale, which his brothers-in-law had given him, on the ground, exclaiming, "Come hither, come hither!" And falling on the earth like drops of summer rain, which makes the frogs spring up, suddenly there appeared the Falcon, the Stag, and the Dolphin, who cried out all together, "Behold us here! what are your commands?"

When Tittone saw this, he said with great joy, "I wish for nothing but to release this poor damsel from the claws of yon dragon, to take her away from this tower, to lay it all in ruins, and to carry this beautiful lady home with me as my wife."

"Hush!" answered the Falcon, "for the bean springs up where you least expect it. We'll soon make him dance upon a sixpence, and take good care that he shall have little ground enough."

"Let us lose no time," said the Stag, "troubles and macaroni are swallowed hot."

So the Falcon summoned a large flock of griffins, who, flying to the window of the tower, carried off the damsel, bearing her over the lake to where Tittone was standing with his three brothers-in-law; and if from afar she appeared a moon, believe me, when near she looked truly like a sun, she was so beautiful.

Whilst Tittone was embracing her and telling her how he loved her, the dragon awoke; and, rushing out of the window, he came swimming across the lake to devour Tittone. But the Stag instantly called up a squadron of lions, tigers, panthers, bears, and wild-cats, who, falling upon the dragon, tore him in pieces with their claws. Then Tittone wishing to depart, the Dolphin said, "I likewise desire to do something to serve you." And in order that no trace should remain of the frightful and accursed place, he made the sea rise so high that, overflowing its bounds, it attacked the tower furiously, and overthrew it to its foundations.

When Tittone saw these things, he thanked the animals in the best manner he could, telling the damsel at the same time that she ought to do so too, as it was by their aid she had escaped from peril. But the animals answered, "Nay, we ought rather to thank this beauteous lady, since she is the means of restoring us to our proper shapes; for a spell was laid upon us at our birth, caused by our mother's having offended a fairy, and we were compelled to remain in the form of animals until we should have freed the daughter of a King from some great trouble. And now behold the time is arrived which we have longed for; the fruit is ripe, and we already feel new spirit in our breasts, new blood in our veins." So saying, they were changed into three handsome youths, and one after another they embraced their brother-in-law, and shook hands with the lady, who was in an ecstasy of joy.

When Tittone saw this, he was on the point of fainting away; and heaving a deep sigh, he said, "O Heavens! why have not my mother and father a share in this happiness? They would be out of their wits with joy were they to see such graceful and handsome sons-in-law before their eyes."

"Nay," answered the Princes, "'tis not yet night; the shame at seeing ourselves so transformed obliged us to flee from the sight of men; but now that, thank Heaven! we can appear in the world again, we will all go and live with our wives under one roof, and spend our lives merrily. Let us, therefore, set out instantly, and before the Sun to-morrow morning unpacks the bales of his rays at the custom-house of the East, our wives shall be with you."

So saying, in order that they might not have to go on foot—for there was only an old broken-down mare which Tittone had brought—the brothers caused a most beautiful coach to appear, drawn by six lions, in which they all five seated themselves; and having travelled the whole day, they came in the evening to a tavern, where, whilst the supper was being prepared, they passed the time in reading all the proofs of men's ignorance which were scribbled upon the walls. At length, when all had eaten their fill and retired to rest, the three youths, feigning to go to bed, went out and walked about the whole night long, till in the morning, when the Stars, like bashful maidens, retire from the gaze of the Sun, they found themselves in the same inn with their wives, whereupon there was a great embracing, and a joy beyond the beyonds. Then they all eight seated themselves in the same coach, and after a long journey arrived at Green-Bank, where they were received with incredible affection by the King and Queen, who had not only regained the capital of four children, whom they had considered lost, but likewise the interest of three sons-in-law and a daughter-in-law, who were verily four columns of the Temple of Beauty. And when the news of the adventures of their children was brought to the Kings of Fair-Meadow and Bright-Valley, they both came to the feasts which were made, adding the rich ingredient of joy to the porridge of their satisfaction, and receiving a full recompense for all their past misfortunes; for—

"One hour of joy dispels the cares
And sufferings of a thousand years."

XXII

THE DRAGON

He who seeks the injury of another finds his own hurt; and he who spreads the snares of treachery and deceit often falls into them himself; as you shall hear in the story of a queen, who with her own hands constructed the trap in which she was caught by the foot.

There was one time a King of High-Shore, who practised such tyranny and cruelty that, whilst he was once gone on a visit of pleasure to a castle at a distance from the city, his royal seat was usurped by a certain sorceress. Whereupon, having consulted a wooden statue which used to give oracular responses, it answered that he would recover his dominions when the sorceress should lose her sight. But seeing that the sorceress, besides being well guarded, knew at a glance the people whom he sent to annoy her, and did dog's justice upon them, he became quite desperate, and out of spite to her he killed all the women of that place whom he could get into his hands.

Now after hundreds and hundreds had been led thither by their ill-luck, only to lose their lives, there chanced, among others, to come a maiden named Porziella, the most beautiful creature that could be seen on the whole earth, and the King could not help falling in love with her and making her his wife. But he was so cruel and spiteful to women that, after a while, he was going to kill her like the rest; but just as he was raising the dagger a bird let fall a certain root upon his arm, and he was seized with such a trembling that the weapon fell from his hand. This bird was a fairy, who, a few days before, having gone to sleep in a wood, where beneath the tent of the Shades Fear kept watch and defied the Sun's heat, a certain satyr was about to rob her when she was awakened by Porziella, and for this kindness she continually followed her steps in order to make her a return.

When the King saw this, he thought that the beauty of Porziella's face had arrested his arm and bewitched the dagger to prevent its piercing her as it had done so many others. He resolved, therefore, not to make the attempt a second time, but that she should die built up in a garret of his palace. No sooner said than done: the unhappy creature was enclosed within four walls, without having anything to eat or drink, and left to waste away and die little by little.

The bird, seeing her in this wretched state, consoled her with kind words, bidding her be of good cheer, and promising, in return for the great kindness she had done for her, to aid her if necessary with her very life. In spite, however, of all the entreaties of Porziella, the bird would never tell her who she was, but only said that she was under obligations to her, and would leave nothing undone to serve her. And seeing that the poor girl was famished with hunger, she flew out and speedily returned with a pointed knife which she had taken from the king's pantry, and told her to make a hole in the corner of the floor just over the kitchen, through which she would regularly bring her food to sustain her life. So Porziella bored away until she had made a passage for the bird, who, watching till the cook was gone out to fetch a pitcher of water from the well, went down through the hole, and taking a fine fowl that was cooking at the fire, brought it to Porziella; then to relieve her thirst, not knowing how to carry her any drink, she flew to the pantry, where there was a quantity of grapes hanging, and brought her a fine bunch; and this she did regularly for many days.

Meanwhile Porziella gave birth to a fine little boy, whom she suckled and reared with the constant aid of the bird. And when he was grown big, the fairy advised his mother to make the hole larger, and to raise so many boards of the floor as would allow Miuccio (for so the child was called) to pass through; and then, after letting him down with some cords which the bird brought, to put the boards back into their place, that it might not be seen where he came from. So Porziella did as the bird directed her; and as soon as the cook was gone out, she let down her son, desiring him never to tell whence he came nor whose son he was.

When the cook returned and saw such a fine little boy, he asked him who he was, whence he came, and what he wanted; whereupon, the child, remembering his mother's advice, said that he was a poor forlorn boy who was looking about for a master. As they were talking, the butler came in, and seeing the spritely little fellow, he thought he would make a pretty page for the King. So he led him to the royal apartments; and when the King saw him look so handsome and lovely that he appeared a very jewel, he was vastly pleased with him, and took him into his service as a page and to his heart as a son, and had him taught all the exercises befitting a cavalier, so that Miuccio grew up the most accomplished one in the court, and the King loved him much better than his stepson. Now the King's stepmother, who was really the queen, on this account began to take a dislike to him, and to hold him in aversion; and her envy and malice gained ground just in proportion as the favours and kindness which the King bestowed on Miuccio cleared the way for them; so she resolved to soap the ladder of his fortune in order that he should tumble down from top to bottom.

Accordingly one evening, when the King and his stepmother had tuned their instruments together and were making music of their discourse, the Queen told the King that Miuccio had boasted he would build three castles in the air. So the next morning, at the time when the Moon, the school-mistress of the Shades, gives a holiday to her scholars for the festival of the Sun, the King, either from surprise or to gratify the old Queen, ordered Miuccio to be called, and commanded him forthwith to build the three castles in the air as he had promised, or else he would make him dance a jig in the air.

When Miuccio heard this he went to his chamber and began to lament bitterly, seeing what glass the favour of princes is, and how short a time it lasts. And while he was weeping thus, lo! the bird came, and said to him, "Take heart, Miuccio, and fear not while you have me by your side, for I am able to draw you out of the fire." Then she directed him to take pasteboard and glue and make three large castles; and calling up three large griffins, she tied a castle to each, and away they flew up into the air. Thereupon Miuccio called the King, who came running with all his court to see the sight; and when he saw the ingenuity of Miuccio he had a still greater affection for him, and lavished on him caresses of the other world, which added snow to the envy of the Queen and fire to her rage, seeing that all her plans failed; insomuch that, both sleeping and waking, she was for ever thinking of some way to remove this thorn from her eyes. So at last, after some days, she said to the King, "Son, the time is now come for us to return to our former greatness and the pleasures of past times, since Miuccio has offered to blind the sorceress, and by the disbursement of her eyes to make you recover your lost kingdom."

The King, who felt himself touched in the sore place, called for Miuccio that very instant, and said to him, "I am greatly surprised that, notwithstanding all my love for you, and that you have the power to restore me to the seat from which I have fallen, you remain thus careless, instead of endeavouring to relieve me from the misery I am in— reduced thus from a kingdom to a wood, from a city to a paltry castle, and from commanding so great a people to be hardly waited on by a parcel of half-starved menials. If, therefore, you do not wish me ill, run now at once and blind the eyes of the fairy who has possession of my property, for by putting out her lanterns you will light the lamps of my honour that are now dark and dismal."

When Miuccio heard this proposal he was about to reply that the King was ill-informed and had mistaken him, as he was neither a raven to pick out eyes nor an auger to bore holes; but the King said, "No more words—so I will have it, so let it be done! Remember now, that in the mint of this brain of mine I have the balance ready; in one scale the reward, if you do what I tell you; in the other the punishment, if you neglect doing what I command."

Miuccio, who could not butt against a rock, and had to do with a man who was not to be moved, went into a corner to bemoan himself; and the bird came to him and said, "Is it possible, Miuccio, that you will always be drowning yourself in a tumbler of water? If I were dead indeed you could not make more fuss. Do you not know that I have more regard for your life than for my own? Therefore don't lose courage; come with me, and you shall see what I can do." So saying off she flew, and alighted in the wood, where as soon as she began to chirp, there came a large flock of birds about her, to whom she told the story, assuring them that whoever would venture to deprive the sorceress of sight should have from her a safeguard against the talons of the hawks and kites, and a letter of protection against the guns, crossbows, longbows, and bird-lime of the fowlers.

There was among them a swallow who had made her nest against a beam of the royal palace, and who hated the sorceress, because, when making her accursed conjurations, she had several times driven her out of the chamber with her fumigations; for which reason, partly out of a desire of revenge, and partly to gain the reward that the bird promised, she offered herself to perform the service. So away she flew like lightning to the city, and entering the palace, found the fairy lying on a couch, with two damsels fanning her. Then the swallow came, and alighting directly over the fairy, pecked out her eyes. Whereupon the fairy, thus seeing night at midday, knew that by this closing of the custom-house the merchandise of the kingdom was all lost; and uttering yells, as of a condemned soul, she abandoned the sceptre and went off to hide herself in a certain cave, where she knocked her head continually against the wall, until at length she ended her days.

When the sorceress was gone, the councillors sent ambassadors to the King, praying him to come back to his castle, since the blinding of the sorceress had caused him to see this happy day. And at the same time they arrived came also Miuccio, who, by the bird's direction, said to the King, "I have served you to the best of my power; the sorceress is blinded, the kingdom is yours. Wherefore, if I deserve recompense for this service, I wish for no other than to be left to my ill-fortune, without being again exposed to these dangers."

But the King, embracing him with great affection, bade him put on his cap and sit beside him; and how the Queen was enraged at this, Heaven knows, for by the bow of many colours that appeared in her face might be known the wind of the storm that was brewing in her heart against poor Miuccio.

Not far from this castle lived a most ferocious dragon, who was born the same hour with the Queen; and the astrologers being called by her father to astrologise on this event, said that his daughter would be safe as long as the dragon was safe, and that when one died, the other would of necessity die also. One thing alone could bring back the Queen to life, and that was to anoint her temples, chest, nostrils, and pulse with the blood of the same dragon.

Now the Queen, knowing the strength and fury of this animal, resolved to send Miuccio into his claws, well assured that the beast would make but a mouthful of him, and that he would be like a strawberry in the throat of a bear. So turning to the King, she said, "Upon my word, this Miuccio is the treasure of your house, and you would be ungrateful indeed if you did not love him, especially as he had expressed his desire to kill the dragon, who, though he is my brother, is nevertheless your enemy; and I care more for a hair of your head than for a hundred brothers."

The King, who hated the dragon mortally, and knew not how to remove him out of his sight, instantly called Miuccio, and said to him, "I know that you can put your hand to whatever you will; therefore, as you have done so much, grant me yet another pleasure, and then turn me whithersoever you will. Go this very instant and kill the dragon; for you will do me a singular service, and I will reward you well for it."

Miuccio at these words was near losing his senses, and as soon as he was able to speak, he said to the King, "Alas, what a headache have you given me by your continual teasing! Is my life a black goat-skin rug that you are for ever wearing it away thus? This is not a pared pear ready to drop into one's mouth, but a dragon, that tears with his claws, breaks to pieces with his head, crunches with his tail, poisons with his teeth, poisons with his eyes, and kills with his breath. Wherefore do you want to send me to death? Is this the sinecure you give me for having given you a kingdom? Who is the wicked soul that has set this die on the table? What son of perdition has taught you these capers and put these words into your mouth?" Then the King, who, although he let himself be tossed to and fro as light as a ball, was firmer than a rock in keeping to what he had once said, stamped with his feet, and exclaimed, "After all you have done, do you fail at the last? But no more words; go, rid my kingdom of this plague, unless you would have me rid you of life."

Poor Miuccio, who thus received one minute a favour, at another a threat, now a pat on the face, and now a kick, now a kind word, now a cruel one, reflected how mutable court fortune is, and would fain have been without the acquaintance of the King. But knowing that to reply to great men is a folly, and like plucking a lion by the beard, he withdrew, cursing his fate, which had led him to the court only to curtail the days of his life. And as he was sitting on one of the door-steps, with his head between his knees, washing his shoes with his tears and warming the ground with his sighs, behold the bird came flying with a plant in her beak, and throwing it to him, said, "Get up, Miuccio, and take courage! for you are not going to play at unload the ass' with your days, but at backgammon with the life of the dragon. Take this plant, and when you come to the cave of that horrid animal, throw it in, and instantly such a drowsiness will come over him that he will fall fast asleep; whereupon, nicking and sticking him with a good knife, you may soon make an end of him. Then come away, for things will turn out better than you think."

"Enough!" cried Miuccio, "I know what I carry under my belt; we have more time than money, and he who has time has life." So saying, he got up, and sticking a pruning-knife in his belt and taking the plant, he went his way to the dragon's cave, which was under a mountain of such goodly growth, that the three mountains that were steps to the Giants would not have reached up to its waist. When he came there, he threw the plant into the cave, and instantly a deep sleep laid hold on the dragon, and Miuccio began to cut him in pieces.

Now just at the time that he was busied thus, the Queen felt a cutting pain at her heart; and seeing herself brought to a bad pass, she perceived her error in having purchased death with ready money. So she called her stepson and told him what the astrologers had predicted—how her life depended on that of the dragon, and how she feared that Miuccio had killed him, for she felt herself gradually sliding away. Then the King replied, "If you knew that the life of the dragon was the prop of your life and the root of your days, why did you make me send Miuccio? Who is in fault? You must have done yourself the mischief, and you must suffer for it; you have broken the glass, and you may pay the cost." And the Queen answered, "I never thought that such a stripling could have the skill and strength to overthrow an animal which made nothing of an army, and I expected that he would have left his rags there. But since I reckoned without my host, and the bark of my projects is gone out of its course, do me one kindness if you love me. When I am dead, take a sponge dipped in the blood of this dragon and anoint with it all the extremities of my body before you bury me."

"That is but a small thing for the love I bear you," replied the King; "and if the blood of the dragon is not enough, I will add my own to give you satisfaction." The Queen was about to thank him, but the breath left her with the speech; for just then Miuccio had made an end of scoring the dragon.

No sooner had Miuccio come into the King's presence with the news of what he had done than the King ordered him to go back for the dragon's blood; but being curious to see the deed done by Miuccio's hand, he followed him. And as Miuccio was going out of the palace gate, the bird met him, and said, "Whither are you going?" and Miuccio answered, "I am going whither the King sends me; he makes me fly backwards and forwards like a shuttle, and never lets me rest an hour." "What to do?" said the bird. "To fetch the blood of the dragon," said Miuccio. And the bird replied, "Ah, wretched youth! this dragon's blood will be bull's blood to you, and make you burst; for this blood will cause to spring up again the evil seed of all your misfortunes. The Queen is continually exposing you to new dangers that you may lose your life; and the King, who lets this odious creature put the pack-saddle on him, orders you, like a castaway, to endanger your person, which is his own flesh and blood and a shoot of his stem. But the wretched man does not know you, though the inborn affection he bears you should have betrayed your kindred. Moreover, the services you have rendered the King, and the gain to himself of so handsome a son and heir, ought to obtain favour for unhappy Porziella, your mother, who has now for fourteen years been buried alive in a garret, where is seen a temple of beauty built up within a little chamber."

While the fairy was thus speaking, the King, who had heard every word, stepped forward to learn the truth of the matter better; and finding that Miuccio was his own and Porziella's son, and that Porziella was still alive in the garret, he instantly gave orders that she should be set free and brought before him. And when he saw her looking more beautiful than ever, owing to the care taken of her by the bird, he embraced her with the greatest affection, and was never satisfied with pressing to his heart first the mother and then the son, praying forgiveness of Porziella for his ill-treatment of her, and of his son for all the dangers to which he had exposed him. Then he ordered her to be clothed in the richest robes, and had her crowned Queen before all the people. And when the King heard that her preservation, and the escape of his son from so many dangers were entirely owing to the bird, which had given food to the one and counsel to the other, he offered her his kingdom and his life. But the bird said she desired no other reward for her services than to have Miuccio for a husband; and as she uttered the words she was changed into a beautiful maiden, and, to the great joy and satisfaction of the King and Porziella, she was given to Miuccio to wife. Then the newly-married couple, to give still greater festivals, went their way to their own kingdom, where they were anxiously expected, every one ascribing this good fortune to the fairy, for the kindness that Porziella had done her; for at the end of the end—

"A good deed is never lost."

XXIII

THE TWO CAKES

I have always heard say, that he who gives pleasure finds it: the bell of Manfredonia says, "Give me, I give thee": he who does not bait the hook of the affections with courtesy never catches the fish of kindness; and if you wish to hear the proof of this, listen to my story, and then say whether the covetous man does not always lose more than the liberal one.

There were once two sisters, named Luceta and Troccola, who had two daughters, Marziella and Puccia. Marziella was as fair to look upon as she was good at heart; whilst, on the contrary, Puccia by the same rule had a face of ugliness and a heart of pestilence, but the girl resembled her parent, for Troccola was a harpy within and a very scare-crow without.

Now it happened that Luceta had occasion to boil some parsnips, in order to fry them with green sauce; so she said to her daughter, "Marziella, my dear, go to the well and fetch me a pitcher of water."

"With all my heart, mother," replied the girl, "but if you love me give me a cake, for I should like to eat it with a draught of the fresh water."

"By all means," said the mother; so she took from a basket that hung upon a hook a beautiful cake (for she had baked a batch the day before), and gave it to Marziella, who set the pitcher on a pad upon her head, and went to the fountain, which like a charlatan upon a marble bench, to the music of the falling water, was selling secrets to drive away thirst. And as she was stooping down to fill her pitcher, up came a hump-backed old woman, and seeing the beautiful cake, which Marziella was just going to bite, she said to her, "My pretty girl, give me a little piece of your cake, and may Heaven send you good fortune!"

Marziella, who was as generous as a queen, replied, "Take it all, my good woman, and I am only sorry that it is not made of sugar and almonds, for I would equally give it you with all my heart."

The old woman, seeing Marziella's kindness, said to her, "Go, and may Heaven reward you for the goodness you have shown me! and I pray all the stars that you may ever be content and happy; that when you breathe roses and jessamines may fall from your mouth; that when you comb your locks pearls and garnets may fall from them, and when you set your foot on the ground lilies and violets may spring up."

Marziella thanked the old woman, and went her way home, where her mother, having cooked a bit of supper, they paid the natural debt to the body, and thus ended the day. And the next morning, when the Sun displayed in the market-place of the celestial fields the merchandise of light which he had brought from the East, as Marziella was combing her hair, she saw a shower of pearls and garnets fall from it into her lap; whereupon calling her mother with great joy, they put them all into a basket, and Luceta went to sell a great part of them to a usurer, who was a friend of hers. Meanwhile Troccola came to see her sister, and finding Marziella in great delight and busied with the pearls, she asked her how, when, and where she had gotten them. But the maiden, who did not understand the ways of the world, and had perhaps never heard the proverb, "Do not all you are able, eat not all you wish, spend not all you have, and tell not all you know," related the whole affair to her aunt, who no longer cared to await her sister's return, for every hour seemed to her a thousand years until she got home again. Then giving a cake to her daughter, she sent her for water to the fountain, where Puccia found the same old woman. And when the old woman asked her for a little piece of cake she answered gruffly, "Have I nothing to do, forsooth, but to give you cake? Do you take me to be so foolish as to give you what belongs to me? Look ye, charity begins at home." And so saying she swallowed the cake in four pieces, making the old woman's mouth water, who when she saw the last morsel disappear and her hopes buried with the cake, exclaimed in a rage, "Begone! and whenever you breathe may you foam at the mouth like a doctor's mule, may toads drop from your lips, and every time you set foot to the ground may there spring up ferns and thistles!"

Puccia took the pitcher of water and returned home, where her mother was all impatience to hear what had befallen her at the fountain. But no sooner did Puccia open her lips, than a shower of toads fell from them, at the sight of which her mother added the fire of rage to the snow of envy, sending forth flame and smoke through nose and mouth.

Now it happened some time afterwards that Ciommo, the brother of Marziella, was at the court of the King of Chiunzo; and the conversation turning on the beauty of various women, he stepped forward, unasked, and said that all the handsome women might hide their heads when his sister made her appearance, who beside the beauty of her form, which made harmony on the song of a noble soul, possessed also a wonderful virtue in her hair, mouth, and feet, which was given to her by a fairy. When the King heard these praises he told Ciommo to bring his sister to the court; adding that, if he found her such as he had represented, he would take her to wife.

Now Ciommo thought this a chance not to be lost; so he forthwith sent a messenger post-haste to his mother, telling her what had happened, and begging her to come instantly with her daughter, in order not to let slip the good luck. But Luceta, who was very unwell, commending the lamb to the wolf, begged her sister to have the kindness to accompany Marziella to the court of Chiunzo for such and such a thing. Whereupon Troccola, who saw that matters were playing into her hand, promised her sister to take Marziella safe and sound to her brother, and then embarked with her niece and Puccia in a boat. But when they were some way out at sea, whilst the sailors were asleep, she threw Marziella into the water; and just as the poor girl was on the point of being drowned there came a most beautiful syren, who took her in her arms and carried her off.

When Troccola arrived at Chiunzo, Ciommo, who had not seen his sister for so long a time, mistook Puccia, and received her as if she were Marziella, and led her instantly to the King. But no sooner did she open her lips than toads dropped on the ground; and when the King looked at her more closely he saw, that as she breathed hard from the fatigue of the journey, she made a lather at her mouth, which looked just like a washtub; then looking down on the ground, he saw a meadow of stinking plants, the sight of which made him quite ill. Upon this he drove Puccia and her mother away, and sent Ciommo in disgrace to keep the geese of the court.

Then Ciommo, in despair and not knowing what had happened to him, drove the geese into the fields, and letting them go their way along the seashore, he used to retire into a little straw shed, where he bewailed his lot until evening, when it was time to return home. But whilst the geese were running about on the shore, Marziella would come out of the water, and feed them with sweetmeats, and give them rose-water to drink; so that the geese grew as big as sheep, and were so fat that they could not see out of their eyes. And in the evening when they came into a little garden under the King's window, they began to sing—

"Pire, pire pire!
The sun and the moon are bright and clear,
But she who feeds us is still more fair."

Now the King, hearing this goose-music every evening, ordered Ciommo to be called, and asked him where, and how, and upon what he fed his geese. And Ciommo replied, "I give them nothing to eat but the fresh grass of the field." But the King, who was not satisfied with this answer, sent a trusty servant after Ciommo to watch and observe where he drove the geese. Then the man followed in his footsteps, and saw him go into the little straw shed, leaving the geese to themselves; and going their way they had no sooner come to the shore than Marziella rose up out of the sea; and I do not believe that even the mother of that blind boy who, as the poet says, "desires no other alms than tears," ever rose from the waves so fair. When the servant of the King saw this, he ran back to his master, beside himself with amazement, and told him the pretty spectacle he had seen upon the seashore.

The curiosity of the King was increased by what the man told him, and he had a great desire to go himself and see the beautiful sight. So the next morning, when the Cock, the ringleader of the birds, excited them all to arm mankind against the Night, and Ciommo went with the geese to the accustomed spot, the King followed him closely; and when the geese came to the seashore, without Ciommo, who remained as usual in the little shed, the King saw Marziella rise out of the water. And after giving the geese a trayful of sweetmeats to eat and a cupful of rose-water to drink, she seated herself on a rock and began to comb her locks, from which fell handfuls of pearls and garnets; at the same time a cloud of flowers dropped from her mouth, and under her feet was a Syrian carpet of lilies and violets.

When the King saw this sight, he ordered Ciommo to be called, and, pointing to Marziella, asked him whether he knew that beautiful maiden. Then Ciommo, recognising his sister, ran to embrace her, and in the presence of the King heard from her all the treacherous conduct of Troccola, and how the envy of that wicked creature had brought that fair fire of love to dwell in the waters of the sea.

The joy of the King is not to be told at the acquisition of so fair a jewel; and turning to the brother he said that he had good reason to praise Marziella so much, and indeed that he found her three times more beautiful than he had described her; he deemed her, therefore, more than worthy to be his wife if she would be content to receive the sceptre of his kingdom.

"Alas, would to Heaven it could be so!" answered Marziella, "and that I could serve you as the slave of your crown! But see you not this golden chain upon my foot, by which the sorceress holds me prisoner? When I take too much fresh air, and tarry too long on the shore, she draws me into the waves, and thus keeps me held in rich slavery by a golden chain."

"What way is there," said the King, "to free you from the claws of this syren?"

"The way," replied Marziella, "would be to cut this chain with a smooth file, and to loose me from it."

"Wait till to-morrow morning," answered the King; "I will then come with all that is needful, and take you home with me, where you shall be the pupil of my eye, the core of my heart, and the life of my soul." And then exchanging a shake of the hands as the earnest-money of their love, she went back into the water and he into the fire—and into such a fire indeed that he had not an hour's rest the whole day long. And when the black old hag of the Night came forth to have a country-dance with the Stars, he never closed an eye, but lay ruminating in his memory over the beauties of Marziella, discoursing in thought of the marvels of her hair, the miracles of her mouth, and the wonders of her feet; and applying the gold of her graces to the touchstone of judgment, he found that it was four-and-twenty carats fine. But he upbraided the Night for not leaving off her embroidery of the Stars, and chided the Sun for not arriving with the chariot of light to enrich his house with the treasure he longed for—a mine of gold which produced pearls, a pearl-shell from which sprang flowers.

But whilst he was thus at sea, thinking of her who was all the while in the sea, behold the pioneers of the Sun appeared, who smooth the road along which he has to pass with the army of his rays. Then the King dressed himself, and went with Ciommo to the seashore, where he found Marziella; and the King with his own hand cut the chain from the foot of the beloved object with the file which they had brought, but all the while he forged a still stronger one for his heart; and setting her on the saddle behind him, she who was already fixed on the saddle of his heart, he set out for the royal palace, where by his command all the handsome ladies of the land were assembled, who received Marziella as their mistress with all due honour. Then the King married her, and there were great festivities; and among all the casks which were burnt for the illuminations, the King ordered that Troccola should be shut up in a tub, and made to suffer for the treachery she had shown to Marziella. Then sending for Luceta, he gave her and Ciommo enough to live upon like princes; whilst Puccia, driven out of the kingdom, wandered about as a beggar; and, as the reward of her not having sown a little bit of cake, she had now to suffer a constant want of bread; for it is the will of Heaven that—

"He who shows no pity finds none."

XXIV

THE SEVEN DOVES

He who gives pleasure meets with it: kindness is the bond of friendship and the hook of love: he who sows not reaps not; of which truth Ciulla has given you the foretaste of example, and I will give you the dessert, if you will bear in mind what Cato says, "Speak little at table." Therefore have the kindness to lend me your ears awhile; and may Heaven cause them to stretch continually, to listen to pleasant and amusing things.

There was once in the county of Arzano a good woman who every year gave birth to a son, until at length there were seven of them, who looked like the pipes of the god Pan, with seven reeds, one larger than another. And when they had changed their first teeth, they said to Jannetella their mother, "Hark ye, mother, if, after so many sons, you do not this time have a daughter, we are resolved to leave home, and go wandering through the world like the sons of the blackbirds."

When their mother heard this sad announcement, she prayed Heaven to remove such an intention from her sons, and prevent her losing seven such jewels as they were. And when the hour of the birth was at hand, the sons said to Jannetella, "We will retire to the top of yonder hill or rock opposite; if you give birth to a son, put an inkstand and a pen up at the window; but if you have a little girl, put up a spoon and a distaff. For if we see the signal of a daughter, we shall return home and spend the rest of our lives under your wings; but if we see the signal of a son, then forget us, for you may know that we have taken ourselves off."

Soon after the sons had departed it pleased Heaven that Jannetella should bring forth a pretty little daughter; then she told the nurse to make the signal to the brothers, but the woman was so stupid and confused that she put up the inkstand and the pen. As soon as the seven brothers saw this signal, they set off, and walked on and on, until at the end of three years they came to a wood, where the trees were performing the sword-dance to the sound of a river which made music upon the stones. In this wood was the house of an ogre whose eyes having been blinded whilst asleep by a woman, he was such an enemy to the sex that he devoured all whom he could catch.

When the youths arrived at the ogre's house, tired out with walking and exhausted with hunger, they begged him for pity's sake to give them a morsel of bread. And the ogre replied that if they would serve him he would give them food, and they would have nothing else to do but to watch over him like a dog, each in turn for a day. The youths, upon hearing this, thought they had found father and mother; so they consented, and remained in the service of the ogre, who, having gotten their names by heart, called once for Giangrazio, at another time for Cecchitiello, now for Pascale, now Nuccio, now Pone, now Pezzillo, and now Carcavecchia, for so the brothers were named; and giving them a room in the lower part of the house, he allowed them enough to live upon.

Meanwhile their sister had grown up; and hearing that her seven brothers, owing to the stupidity of the nurse, had set out to walk through the world, and that no tidings of them had ever been received, she took it into her head to go in search of them. And she begged and prayed her mother so long, that at last, overcome by her entreaties, she gave her leave to go, and dressed her like a pilgrim. Then the maiden walked and walked, asking at every place she came to whether any one had seen seven brothers. And thus she journeyed on, until at length she got news of them at an inn, where having enquired the way to the wood, one morning, at the hour when the Sun with the penknife of his rays scratches out the inkspots made by Night upon the sheet of Heaven, she arrived at the ogre's house, where she was recognised by her brothers with great joy, who cursed the inkstand and the pen for writing falsely such misfortune for them. Then giving her a thousand caresses, they told her to remain quiet in their chamber, that the ogre might not see her; bidding her at the same time give a portion of whatever she had to eat to a cat which was in the room, or otherwise she would do her some harm. Cianna (for so the sister was named) wrote down this advice in the pocket-book of her heart, and shared everything with the cat, like a good companion, always cutting justly, and saying, "This for me—this for thee,—this for the daughter of the king," giving the cat a share to the last morsel.

Now it happened one day that the brothers, going to hunt for the ogre, left Cianna a little basket of chick-peas to cook; and as she was picking them, by ill-luck she found among them a hazel-nut, which was the stone of disturbance to her quiet; for having swallowed it without giving half to the cat, the latter out of spite jumped on the table and blew out the candle. Cianna seeing this, and not knowing what to do, left the room, contrary to the command of her brothers, and going into the ogre's chamber begged him for a little light. Then the ogre, hearing a woman's voice, said, "Welcome, madam! wait awhile,—you have found what you are seeking." And so saying he took a Genoa stone, and daubing it with oil he fell to whetting his tusks. But Cianna, who saw the cart on a wrong track, seizing a lighted stick ran to her chamber; and bolting the door inside, she placed against it bars, stools, bedsteads, tables, stones, and everything there was in the room.

As soon as the ogre had put an edge on his teeth he ran to the chamber of the brothers, and finding the door fastened, he fell to kicking it to break it open. At this noise and disturbance the seven brothers at once came home, and hearing themselves accused by the ogre of treachery for making their chamber a refuge for one of his women enemies, Giangrazio, who was the eldest and had more sense than the others, and saw matters going badly, said to the ogre, "We know nothing of this affair, and it may be that this wicked woman has perchance come into the room whilst we were at the chase; but as she has fortified herself inside, come with me and I will take you to a place where we can seize her without her being able to defend herself."

Then they took the ogre by the hand, and led him to a deep, deep pit, where, giving him a push, they sent him headlong to the bottom; and taking a shovel, which they found on the ground, they covered him with earth. Then they bade their sister unfasten the door, and they rated her soundly for the fault she had committed, and the danger in which she had placed herself; telling her to be more careful in future, and to beware of plucking grass upon the spot where the ogre was buried, or they would be turned into seven doves.

"Heaven keep me from bringing such a misfortune upon you!" replied Cianna. So taking possession of all the ogre's goods and chattels, and making themselves masters of the whole house, they lived there merrily enough, waiting until winter should pass away, and the Sun, on taking possession of the house of the Bull, give a present to the Earth of a green gown embroidered with flowers, when they might set out on their journey home.

Now it happened one day, when the brothers were gone to the mountains to get firewood to defend themselves against the cold, which increased from day to day, that a poor pilgrim came to the ogre's wood, and made faces at an ape that was perched up in a pine-tree; whereupon the ape threw down one of the fir-apples from the tree upon the man's pate, which made such a terrible bump that the poor fellow set up a loud cry. Cianna hearing the noise went out, and taking pity on his disaster, she quickly plucked a sprig of rosemary from a tuft which grew upon the ogre's grave; then she made him a plaster of it with boiled bread and salt, and after giving the man some breakfast she sent him away.

Whilst Cianna was laying the cloth, and expecting her brothers, lo! she saw seven doves come flying, who said to her, "Ah! better that your hand had been cut off, you cause of all our misfortune, ere it plucked that accursed rosemary and brought such a calamity upon us! Have you eaten the brains of a cat, O sister, that you have driven our advice from your mind? Behold us, turned to birds, a prey to the talons of kites, hawks, and falcons! Behold us made companions of water-hens, snipes, goldfinches, woodpeckers, jays, owls, magpies, jackdaws, rooks, starlings, woodcocks, cocks, hens and chickens, turkey-cocks, blackbirds, thrushes, chaffinches, tomtits, jenny-wrens, lapwings, linnets, greenfinches, crossbills, flycatchers, larks, plovers, kingfishers, wagtails, redbreasts, redfinches, sparrows, ducks, fieldfares, woodpigeons and bullfinches! A rare thing you have done! And now we may return to our country to find nets laid and twigs limed for us! To heal the head of a pilgrim, you have broken the heads of seven brothers; nor is there any help for our misfortune, unless you find the Mother of Time, who will tell you the way to get us out of trouble."

Cianna, looking like a plucked quail at the fault she had committed, begged pardon of her brothers, and offered to go round the world until she should find the dwelling of the old woman. Then praying them not to stir from the house until she returned, lest any ill should betide them, she set out, and journeyed on and on without ever tiring; and though she went on foot, her desire to aid her brothers served her as a sumpter-mule, with which she made three miles an hour. At last she came to the seashore, where with the blows of the waves the sea was banging the rocks which would not repeat the Latin it gave them to do. Here she saw a huge whale, who said to her, "My pretty maiden, what go you seeking?" And she replied, "I am seeking the dwelling of the Mother of Time." "Hear then what you must do," replied the whale; "go straight along this shore, and on coming to the first river, follow it up to its source, and you will meet with some one who will show you the way: but do me one kindness,—when you find the good old woman, beg of her the favour to tell me some means by which I may swim about safely, without so often knocking upon the rocks and being thrown on the sands."

"Trust to me," said Cianna, then thanking the whale for pointing out the way, she set off walking along the shore; and after a long journey she came to the river, which like a clerk of the treasury was disbursing silver money into the bank of the sea. Then taking the way up to its source, she arrived at a beautiful open country, where the meadow vied with the heaven, displaying her green mantle starred over with flowers; and there she met a mouse who said to her, "Whither are you going thus alone, my pretty girl?" And Cianna replied, "I am seeking the Mother of Time."

"You have a long way to go," said the mouse; "but do not lose heart, everything has an end. Walk on, therefore, toward yon mountains, which, like the free lords of these fields, assume the title of Highness, and you will soon have more news of what you are seeking. But do me one favour,—when you arrive at the house you wish to find, get the good old woman to tell you what you can do to rid us of the tyranny of the cats; then command me, and I am your slave."

Cianna, after promising to do the mouse this kindness, set off towards the mountains, which, although they appeared to be close at hand, seemed never to be reached. But having come to them at length, she sat down tired out upon a stone; and there she saw an army of ants, carrying a large store of grain, one of whom turning to Cianna said, "Who art thou, and whither art thou going?" And Cianna, who was courteous to every one, said to her, "I am an unhappy girl, who, for a matter that concerns me, am seeking the dwelling of the Mother of Time."

"Go on farther," said the ant, "and where these mountains open into a large plain you will obtain more news. But do me a great favour,—get the secret from the old woman, what we ants can do to live a little longer; for it seems to me a folly in worldly affairs to be heaping up such a large store of food for so short a life, which, like an auctioneer's candle, goes out just at the best bidding of years."

"Be at ease," said Cianna, "I will return the kindness you have shown me."

Then she passed the mountains and arrived at a wide plain; and proceeding a little way over it, she came to a large oak-tree,—a memorial of antiquity, whose fruit (a mouthful which Time gives to this bitter age of its lost sweetness) tasted like sweetmeats to the maiden, who was satisfied with little. Then the oak, making lips of its bark and a tongue of its pith, said to Cianna, "Whither are you going so sad, my little daughter? Come and rest under my shade." Cianna thanked him much, but excused herself, saying that she was going in haste to find the Mother of Time. And when the oak heard this he replied, "You are not far from her dwelling; for before you have gone another day's journey, you will see upon a mountain a house, in which you will find her whom you seek. But if you have as much kindness as beauty, I prithee learn for me what I can do to regain my lost honour; for instead of being food for great men, I am now only made the food of hogs."

"Leave that to me," replied Cianna, "I will take care to serve you." So saying, she departed, and walking on and on without ever resting, she came at length to the foot of an impertinent mountain, which was poking its head into the face of the clouds. There she found an old man, who, wearied and wayworn, had lain down upon some hay; and as soon as he saw Cianna, he knew her at once, and that it was she who had cured his bump.

When the old man heard what she was seeking, he told her that he was carrying to Time the rent for the piece of earth which he had cultivated, and that Time was a tyrant who usurped everything in the world, claiming tribute from all, and especially from people of his age; and he added that, having received kindness from Cianna, he would now return it a hundredfold by giving her some good information about her arrival at the mountain; and that he was sorry he could not accompany her thither, since his old age, which was condemned rather to go down than up, obliged him to remain at the foot of those mountains, to cast up accounts with the clerks of Time—which are the labours, the sufferings, and the infirmities of life—and to pay the debt of Nature. So the old man said to her, "Now, my pretty, innocent child, listen to me. You must know that on the top of this mountain you will find a ruined house, which was built long ago, time out of mind. The walls are cracked, the foundations crumbling away, the doors worm-eaten, the furniture all worn out—and, in short, everything is gone to wrack and ruin. On one side are seen shattered columns, on another broken statues; and nothing is left in a good state except a coat-of-arms over the door, quartered on which you will see a serpent biting its tail, a stag, a raven, and a phoenix. When you enter, you will see on the ground, files, saws, scythes, sickles, pruning-hooks, and hundreds and hundreds of vessels full of ashes, with the names written on them, like gallipots in an apothecary's shop; and there may be read Corinth, Saguntum, Carthage, Troy, and a thousand other cities, the ashes of which Time preserved as trophies of his conquests.

"When you come near the house, hide yourself until Time goes out; and as soon as he has gone forth, enter, and you will find an old, old woman, with a beard that touches the ground and a hump reaching to the sky. Her hair, like the tail of a dapple-grey horse, covers her heels; her face looks like a plaited collar, with the folds stiffened by the starch of years. The old woman is seated upon a clock, which is fastened to a wall; and her eyebrows are so large that they overshadow her eyes, so that she will not be able to see you. As soon as you enter, quickly take the weights off the clock, then call to the old woman, and beg her to answer your questions; whereupon she will instantly call her son to come and eat you up. But the clock upon which the old woman sits having lost its weights, her son cannot move, and she will therefore be obliged to tell you what you wish. But do not trust any oath she may make, unless she swears by the wings of her son, and you will be content."

So saying, the poor old man fell down and crumbled away, like a dead body brought from a catacomb to the light of day. Then Cianna took the ashes, and mixing them with a pint of tears, she made a grave and buried them, praying Heaven to grant them quiet and repose. And ascending the mountain till she was quite out of breath, she waited until Time came out, who was an old man with a long, long beard, and who wore a very old cloak covered with slips of paper, on which were worked the names of various people. He had large wings, and ran so fast that he was out of sight in an instant.

When Cianna entered the house of his mother, she started with affright at the sight of that black old chip; and instantly seizing the weights of the clock, she told what she wanted to the old woman, who, setting up a loud cry, called to her son. But Cianna said to her, "You may butt your head against the wall as long as you like, for you will not see your son whilst I hold these clock-weights."

Thereupon the old woman, seeing herself foiled, began to coax Cianna, saying, "Let go of them, my dear, and do not stop my son's course; for no man living has ever done that. Let go of them, and may Heaven preserve you! for I promise you, by the acid of my son, with which he corrodes everything, that I will do you no harm."

"That's time lost," answered Cianna, "you must say something better if you would have me quit my hold."

"I swear to you by those teeth, which gnaw all mortal things, that I will tell you all you desire."

"That is all nothing," answered Cianna, "for I know you are deceiving me."

"Well, then," said the old woman, "I swear to you by those wings which fly over all that I will give you more pleasure than you imagine."

Thereupon Cianna, letting go the weights, kissed the old woman's hand, which had a mouldy feel and a nasty smell. And the old woman, seeing the courtesy of the damsel, said to her, "Hide yourself behind this door, and when Time comes home I will make him tell me all you wish to know. And as soon as he goes out again—for he never stays quiet in one place—you can depart. But do not let yourself be heard or seen, for he is such a glutton that he does not spare even his own children; and when all fails, he devours himself and then springs up anew."

Cianna did as the old woman told her; and, lo! soon after Time came flying quick, quick, high and light, and having gnawed whatever came to hand, down to the very mouldiness upon the walls, he was about to depart, when his mother told him all she had heard from Cianna, beseeching him by the milk she had given him to answer exactly all her questions. After a thousand entreaties, her son replied, "To the tree may be answered, that it can never be prized by men so long as it keeps treasures buried under its roots; to the mice, that they will never be safe from the cat unless they tie a bell to her leg to tell them when she is coming; to the ants, that they will live a hundred years if they can dispense with flying—for when the ant is going to die she puts on wings; to the whale, that it should be of good cheer, and make friends with the sea-mouse, who will serve him as a guide, so that he will never go wrong; and to the doves, that when they alight on the column of wealth, they will return to their former state."

So saying, Time set out to run his accustomed post; and Cianna, taking leave of the old woman, descended to the foot of the mountain, just at the very time that the seven doves, who had followed their sister's footsteps, arrived there. Wearied with flying so far, they stopped to rest upon the horn of a dead ox; and no sooner had they alighted than they were changed into handsome youths as they were at first. But while they were marvelling at this, they heard the reply which Time had given, and saw at once that the horn, as the symbol of plenty, was the column of wealth of which Time had spoken. Then embracing their sister with great joy, they all set out on the same road by which Cianna had come. And when they came to the oak-tree, and told it what Cianna had heard from Time, the tree begged them to take away the treasure from its roots, since it was the cause why its acorns had lost their reputation. Thereupon the seven brothers, taking a spade which they found in a garden, dug and dug, until they came to a great heap of gold money, which they divided into eight parts and shared among themselves and their sister, so that they might carry it away conveniently. But being wearied with the journey and the load, they laid themselves down to sleep under a hedge. Presently a band of robbers coming by, and seeing the poor fellows asleep, with their heads upon the clothfuls of money, bound them hand and foot to some trees and took away their money, leaving them to bewail not only their wealth—which had slipped through their fingers as soon as found—but their life; for being without hope of succour, they were in peril of either soon dying of hunger or allaying the hunger of some wild beast.

As they were lamenting their unhappy lot, up came the mouse, who, as soon as she heard the reply which Time had given, in return for the good service, nibbled the cords with which they were bound and set them free. And having gone a little way farther, they met on the road the ant, who, when she heard the advice of Time, asked Cianna what was the matter that she was so pale-faced and cast down. And when Cianna told her their misfortune, and the trick which the robbers had played them, the ant replied, "Be quiet, I can now requite the kindness you have done me. You must know, that whilst I was carrying a load of grain underground, I saw a place where these dogs of assassins hide their plunder. They have made some holes under an old building, in which they shut up all the things they have stolen. They are just now gone out for some new robbery, and I will go with you and show you the place, so that you may recover your money."

So saying, she took the way towards some tumbled-down houses, and showed the seven brothers the mouth of the pit; whereupon Giangrazio, who was bolder than the rest, entering it, found there all the money of which they had been robbed. Then taking it with them, they set out, and walked towards the seashore, where they found the whale, and told him the good advice which Time—who is the father of counsel—had given them. And whilst they stood talking of their journey and all that had befallen them, they saw the robbers suddenly appear, armed to the teeth, who had followed in their footsteps. At this sight they exclaimed, "Alas, alas! we are now wholly lost, for here come the robbers armed, and they will not leave the skin on our bodies."

"Fear not," replied the whale, "for I can save you out of the fire, and will thus requite the love you have shown me; so get upon my back, and I will quickly carry you to a place of safety."

Cianna and her brothers, seeing the foe at their heels and the water up to their throats, climbed upon the whale, who, keeping far off from the rocks, carried them to within sight of Naples. But being afraid to land them on account of the shoals and shallows, he said, "Where would you like me to land you? On the shore of Amalfi?" And Giangrazio answered, "See whether that cannot be avoided, my dear fish. I do not wish to land at any place hereabouts; for at Massa they say barely good-day, at Sorrento thieves are plenty, at Vico they say you may go your way, at Castel-a-mare no one says how are ye."

Then the whale, to please them, turned about and went toward the Salt-rock, where he left them; and they got put on shore by the first fishing-boat that passed. Thereupon they returned to their own country, safe and sound and rich, to the great joy and consolation of their mother and father. And, thanks to the goodness of Cianna, they enjoyed a happy life, verifying the old saying—

"Do good whenever you can, and forget it."

XXV

THE RAVEN

It is truly a great proverb—"Rather a crooked sight than a crooked judgment"; but it is so difficult to adopt it that the judgment of few men hits the nail on the head. On the contrary, in the sea of human affairs, the greater part are fishers in smooth waters, who catch crabs; and he who thinks to take the most exact measure of the object at which he aims often shoots widest of the mark. The consequence of this is that all are running pell-mell, all toiling in the dark, all thinking crookedly, all acting child's-play, all judging at random, and with a haphazard blow of a foolish resolution bringing upon themselves a bitter repentance; as was the case with the King of Shady-Grove; and you shall hear how it fared with him if you summon me within the circle of modesty with the bell of courtesy, and give me a little attention.

It is said that there was once a king of Shady-Grove named Milluccio, who was so devoted to the chase, that he neglected the needful affairs of his state and household to follow the track of a hare or the flight of a thrush. And he pursued this road so far that chance one day led him to a thicket, which had formed a solid square of earth and trees to prevent the horses of the Sun from breaking through. There, upon a most beautiful marble stone, he found a raven, which had just been killed.

The King, seeing the bright red blood sprinkled upon the white, white marble, heaved a deep sigh and exclaimed, "O heavens! and cannot I have a wife as white and red as this stone, and with hair and eyebrows as black as the feathers of this raven?" And he stood for a while so buried in this thought that he became a counterpart to the stone, and looked like a marble image making love to the other marble. And this unhappy fancy fixing itself in his head, as he searched for it everywhere with the lanthorn of desire, it grew in four seconds from a picktooth to a pole, from a crab-apple to an Indian pumpkin, from barber's embers to a glass furnace, and from a dwarf to a giant; insomuch that he thought of nothing else than the image of that object encrusted in his heart as stone to stone. Wherever he turned his eyes that form was always presented to him which he carried in his breast; and forgetting all besides, he had nothing but that marble in his head; in short, he became in a manner so worn away upon the stone that he was at last as thin as the edge of a penknife; and this marble was a millstone which crushed his life, a slab of porphyry upon which the colours of his days were ground and mixed, a tinder-box which set fire to the brimstone match of his soul, a loadstone which attracted him, and lastly, a rolling-stone which could never rest.

At length his brother Jennariello, seeing him so pale and half-dead, said to him, "My brother, what has happened to you, that you carry grief lodged in your eyes, and despair sitting under the pale banner of your face? What has befallen you? Speak—open your heart to your brother: the smell of charcoal shut up in a chamber poisons people—powder pent up in a mountain blows it into the air; open your lips, therefore, and tell me what is the matter with you; at all events be assured that I would lay down a thousand lives if I could to help you."

Then Milluccio, mingling words and sighs, thanked him for his love, saying that he had no doubt of his affection, but that there was no remedy for his ill, since it sprang from a stone, where he had sown desires without hope of fruit—a stone from which he did not expect a mushroom of content—a stone of Sisyphus, which he bore to the mountain of designs, and when it reached the top rolled over and over to the bottom. At length, however, after a thousand entreaties, Milluccio told his brother all about his love; whereupon Jennariello comforted him as much as he could, and bade him be of good cheer, and not give way to an unhappy passion; for that he was resolved, in order to satisfy him, to go all the world over until he found a woman the counterpart of the stone.

Then instantly fitting out a large ship, filled with merchandise, and dressing himself like a merchant, he sailed for Venice, the wonder of Italy, the receptacle of virtuous men, the great book of the marvels of art and nature; and having procured there a safe-conduct to pass to the Levant, he set sail for Cairo. When he arrived there and entered the city, he saw a man who was carrying a most beautiful falcon, and Jennariello at once purchased it to take to his brother, who was a sportsman. Soon afterwards he met another man with a splendid horse, which he also bought; whereupon he went to an inn to refresh himself after the fatigues he had suffered at sea.

The following morning, when the army of the Star, at the command of the general of the Light, strikes the tents in the camp of the sky and abandons the post, Jennariello set out to wander through the city, having his eyes about him like a lynx, looking at this woman and that, to see whether by chance he could find the likeness to a stone upon a face of flesh. And as he was wandering about at random, turning continually to this side and that, like a thief in fear of the constables, he met a beggar carrying an hospital of plasters and a mountain of rags upon his back, who said to him, "My gallant sir, what makes you so frightened?"

"Have I, forsooth, to tell you my affairs?" answered Jennariello. "Faith I should do well to tell my reason to the constable."

"Softly, my fair youth!" replied the beggar, "for the flesh of man is not sold by weight. If Darius had not told his troubles to a groom he would not have become king of Persia. It will be no great matter, therefore, for you to tell your affairs to a poor beggar, for there is not a twig so slender but it may serve for a toothpick."

When Jennariello heard the poor man talking sensibly and with reason, he told him the cause that had brought him to that country; whereupon the beggar replied, "See now, my son, how necessary it is to make account of every one; for though I am only a heap of rubbish, yet I shall be able to enrich the garden of your hopes. Now listen—under the pretext of begging alms, I will knock at the door of the young and beautiful daughter of a magician; then open your eyes wide, look at her, contemplate her, regard her, measure her from head to foot, for you will find the image of her whom your brother desires." So saying, he knocked at the door of a house close by, and Liviella opening it threw him a piece of bread.

As soon as Jennariello saw her, she seemed to him built after the model which Milluccio had given him; then he gave a good alms to the beggar and sent him away, and going to the inn he dressed himself like a pedlar, carrying in two caskets all the wealth of the world. And thus he walked up and down before Liviella's house crying his wares, until at length she called him, and took a view of the beautiful net-caps, hoods, ribands, gauze, edgings, lace, handkerchiefs, collars, needles, cups of rouge, and head-gear fit for a queen, which he carried. And when she had examined all the things again and again, she told him to show her something else; and Jennariello answered, "My lady, in these caskets I have only cheap and paltry wares; but if you will deign to come to my ship, I will show you things of the other world, for I have there a host of beautiful goods worthy of any great lord."

Liviella, who was full of curiosity, not to belie the nature of her sex, replied, "If my father indeed were not out he would have given me some money."

"Nay, you can come all the better if he is out," replied Jennariello, "for perhaps he might not allow you the pleasure; and I'll promise to show you such splendid things as will make you rave—such necklaces and earrings, such bracelets and sashes, such workmanship in paper—in short I will perfectly astound you."

When Liviella heard all this display of finery she called a gossip of hers to accompany her, and went to the ship. But no sooner had she embarked than Jennariello, whilst keeping her enchanted with the sight of all the beautiful things he had brought, craftily ordered the anchor to be weighed and the sails to be set, so that before Liviella raised her eyes from the wares and saw that she had left the land, they had already gone many miles. When at length she perceived the trick, she began to act Olympia the reverse way; for whereas Olympia bewailed being left upon a rock, Liviella lamented leaving the rocks. But when Jennariello told her who he was, whither he was carrying her, and the good fortune that awaited her, and pictured to her, moreover, Milluccio's beauty, his valour, his virtues, and lastly the love with which he would receive her, he succeeded in pacifying her, and she even prayed the wind to bear her quickly to see the colouring of the design which Jennariello had drawn.

As they were sailing merrily along they heard the waves grumbling beneath the ship; and although they spoke in an undertone, the captain of the ship, who understood in an instant what it meant, cried out, "All hands aboard! for here comes a storm, and Heaven save us!" No sooner had he spoken these words than there came the testimony of a whistling of the wind; and behold the sky was overcast with clouds, and the sea was covered with white-crested waves. And whilst the waves on either side of the ship, curious to know what the others were about, leaped uninvited to the nuptials upon the deck, one man baled them with a bowl into a tub, another drove them off with a pump; and whilst every sailor was hard at work—as it concerned his own safety—one minding the rudder, another hauling the foresail, another the mainsheet, Jennariello ran up to the topmast, to see with a telescope if he could discover any land where they might cast anchor. And lo! whilst he was measuring a hundred miles of distance with two feet of telescope, he saw a dove and its mate come flying up and alight upon the sail-yard. Then the male bird said, "Rucche, rucche!" And his mate answered, "What's the matter, husband, that you are lamenting so?" "This poor Prince," replied the other, "has bought a falcon, which as soon as it shall be in his brother's hands will pick out his eyes; but if he does not take it to him, or if he warns him of the danger, he will turn to marble." And thereupon he began again to cry, "Rucche, rucche!" And his mate said to him, "What, still lamenting! Is there anything new?" "Ay, indeed," answered the male dove, "he has also bought a horse, and the first time his brother rides him the horse will break his neck; but if he does not take it to him, or if he warns him of the danger, he will turn to marble." "Rucche, rucche!" he cried again. "Alas, with all these RUCCHE, RUCCHE," said the female dove, "what's the matter now?" And her mate said, "This man is taking a beautiful wife to his brother; but the first night, as soon as they go to sleep, they will both be devoured by a frightful dragon; yet if he does not take her to him, or if he warns him of the danger, he will turn to marble."

As he spoke, the tempest ceased, and the rage of the sea and the fury of the wind subsided. But a far greater tempest arose in Jennariello's breast, from what he had heard, and more than twenty times he was on the point of throwing all the things into the sea, in order not to carry to his brother the cause of his ruin. But on the other hand he thought of himself, and reflected that charity begins at home; and fearing that, if he did not carry these things to his brother, or if he warned him of the danger, he should turn to marble, he resolved to look rather to the fact than to the possibility, since the shirt was closer to him than the jacket.

When he arrived at Shady-Grove, he found his brother on the shore, awaiting with great joy the return of the ship, which he had seen at a distance. And when he saw that it bore her whom he carried in his heart, and confronting one face with the other perceived that there was not the difference of a hair, his joy was so great that he was almost weighed down under the excessive burden of delight. Then embracing his brother fervently, he said to him, "What falcon is that you are carrying on your fist?" And Jennariello answered, "I have bought it on purpose to give to you." "I see clearly that you love me," replied Milluccio, "since you go about seeking to give me pleasure. Truly, if you had brought me a costly treasure, it could not have given me greater delight than this falcon." And just as he was going to take it in his hand, Jennariello quickly drew a large knife which he carried at his side and cut off its head. At this deed the King stood aghast, and thought his brother mad to have done such a stupid act; but not to interrupt the joy at his arrival, he remained silent. Presently, however, he saw the horse, and on asking his brother whose it was, heard that it was his own. Then he felt a great desire to ride him, and just as he was ordering the stirrup to beheld, Jennariello quickly cut off the horse's legs with his knife. Thereat the King waxed wrath, for his brother seemed to have done it on purpose to vex him, and his choler began to rise. However, he did not think it a right time to show resentment, lest he should poison the pleasure of the bride at first sight, whom he could never gaze upon enough.

When they arrived at the royal palace, he invited all the lords and ladies of the city to a grand feast, at which the hall seemed just like a riding-school full of horses, curveting and prancing, with a number of foals in the form of women. But when the ball was ended, and a great banquet had been despatched, they all retired to rest.

Jennariello, who thought of nothing else than to save his brother's life, hid himself behind the bed of the bridal pair; and as he stood watching to see the dragon come, behold at midnight a fierce dragon entered the chamber, who sent forth flames from his eyes and smoke from his mouth, and who, from the terror he carried in his look, would have been a good agent to sell all the antidotes to fear in the apothecaries' shops. As soon as Jennariello saw the monster, he began to lay about him right and left with a Damascus blade which he had hidden under his cloak; and he struck one blow so furiously that it cut in halves a post of the King's bed, at which noise the King awoke, and the dragon disappeared.

When Milluccio saw the sword in his brother's hand, and the bedpost cut in two, he set up a loud cry, "Help here! hola! help! This traitor of a brother is come to kill me!" Whereupon, hearing the noise, a number of servants who slept in the antechamber came running up, and the King ordered Jennariello to be bound, and sent him the same hour to prison.

The next morning, as soon as the Sun opened his bank to deliver the deposit of light to the Creditor of the Day, the King summoned the council; and when he told them what had passed, confirming the wicked intention shown in killing the falcon and the horse on purpose to vex him, they judged that Jennariello deserved to die. The prayers of Liviella were all unavailing to soften the heart of the King, who said, "You do not love me, wife, for you have more regard for your brother-in-law than for my life. You have seen with your own eyes this dog of an assassin come with a sword that would cut a hair in the air to kill me; and if the bedpost (the column of my life) had not protected me, you would at this moment have been a widow." So saying, he gave orders that justice should take its course.

When Jennariello heard this sentence, and saw himself so ill-rewarded for doing good, he knew not what to think or to do. If he said nothing, bad; if he spoke, worse; and whatever he should do was a fall from the tree into the wolf's mouth. If he remained silent, he should lose his head under an axe; if he spoke, he should end his days in a stone. At length, after various resolutions, he made up his mind to disclose the matter to his brother; and since he must die at all events, he thought it better to tell his brother the truth, and to end his days with the title of an innocent man, than to keep the truth to himself and be sent out of the world as a traitor. So sending word to the King that he had something to say of importance to his state, he was led into his presence, where he first made a long preamble of the love he had always borne him; then he went on to tell of the deception he had practiced on Liviella in order to give him pleasure; and then what he had heard from the doves about the falcon, and how, to avoid being turned to marble, he had brought it him, and without revealing the secret had killed it in order not to see him without eyes.

As he spoke, he felt his legs stiffen and turn to marble. And when he went on to relate the affair of the horse in the same manner, he became visibly stone up to the waist, stiffening miserably—a thing which at another time he would have paid in ready money, but which now his heart wept at. At last, when he came to the affair of the dragon, he stood like a statue in the middle of the hall, stone from head to foot. When the King saw this, reproaching himself for the error he had committed, and the rash sentence he had passed upon so good and loving a brother, he mourned him more than a year, and every time he thought of him he shed a river of tears.

Meanwhile Liviella gave birth to two sons, who were two of the most beautiful creatures in the world. And after a few months, when the Queen was gone into the country for pleasure, and the father and his two little boys chanced to be standing in the middle of the hall, gazing with tearful eyes on the statue—the memorial of his folly, which had taken from him the flower of men—behold a stately and venerable old man entered, whose long hair fell upon his shoulders and whose beard covered his breast. And making a reverence to the King, the old man said to him, "What would your Majesty give to have this noble brother return to his former state?" And the King answered, "I would give my kingdom." "Nay," replied the old man, "this is not a thing that requires payment in wealth; but being an affair of life, it must be paid for with as much again of life."

Then the King, partly out of the love he bore Jennariello, and partly from hearing himself reproached with the injury he had done him, answered, "Believe me, my good sir, I would give my own life for his life; and provided that he came out of the stone, I should be content to be enclosed in a stone."

Hearing this the old man said, "Without putting your life to the risk—since it takes so long to rear a man—the blood of these, your two little boys, smeared upon the marble, would suffice to make him instantly come to life." Then the King replied, "Children I may have again, but I have a brother, and another I can never more hop to see." So saying, he made a pitiable sacrifice of two little innocent kids before an idol of stone, and besmearing the statue with their blood, it instantly became alive; whereupon the King embraced his brother, and their joy is not to be told. Then they had these poor little creatures put into a coffin, in order to give them burial with all due honour. But just at that instant the Queen returned home, and the King, bidding his brother hide himself, said to his wife, "What would you give, my heart, to have my brother restored to life?" "I would give this whole kingdom," replied Liviella. And the King answered, "Would you give the blood of your children?" "Nay, not that, indeed," replied the Queen; "for I could not be so cruel as to tear out with my own hands the apple of my eyes." "Alas!" said the King, "in order to see a brother alive, I have killed my own children! for this was the price of Jennariello's life!"

So saying, he showed the Queen the little boys in the coffin; and when she saw this sad spectacle, she cried aloud like one mad, saying, "O my children! you props of my life, joys of my heart, fountains of my blood! Who has painted red the windows of the sun? Who has without a doctor's licence bled the chief vein of my life? Alas, my children, my children! my hope now taken from me, my light now darkened, my joy now poisoned, my support now lost! You are stabbed by the sword, I am pierced by grief; you are drowned in blood, I in tears. Alas that, to give life to an uncle, you have slain your mother! For I am no longer able to weave the thread of my days without you, the fair counterpoises of the loom of my unhappy life. The organ of my voice must be silent, now that its bellows are taken away. O children, children! why do ye not give answer to your mother, who once gave you the blood in your veins, and now weeps it for you from her eyes? But since fate shows me the fountain of my happiness dried up, I will no longer live the sport of fortune in the world, but will go at once to find you again!"

So saying, she ran to a window to throw herself out; but just at that instant her father entered by the same window in a cloud, and called to her, "Stop, Liviella! I have now accomplished what I intended, and killed three birds with one stone. I have revenged myself on Jennariello, who came to my house to rob me of my daughter, by making him stand all these months like a marble statue in a block of stone. I have punished you for your ill-conduct in going away in a ship without my permission, by showing you your two children, your two jewels, killed by their own father. And I have punished the King for the caprice he took into his head, by making him first the judge of his brother, and afterwards the executioner of his children. But as I have wished only to shear and not to flay you, I desire now that all the poison may turn into sweetmeats for you. Therefore, go, take again your children and my grandchildren, who are more beautiful than ever. And you, Milluccio, embrace me. I receive you as my son-in-law and as my son. And I pardon Jennariello his offence, having done all that he did out of love to so excellent a brother."

And as he spoke, the little children came, and the grandfather was never satisfied with embracing and kissing them; and in the midst of the rejoicings Jennariello entered, as a third sharer in them, who, after suffering so many storms of fate, was now swimming in macaroni broth. But notwithstanding all the after pleasures that he enjoyed in life, his past dangers never went from his mind; and he was always thinking on the error his brother had committed, and how careful a man ought to be not to fall into the ditch, since—

"All human judgment is false and perverse."

XXVI

THE MONTHS

It is a saying worthy to be written in letters as big as those on a monument, that silence never harmed any one: and let it not be imagined that those slanderers who never speak well of others, but are always cutting and stinging, and pinching and biting, ever gain anything by their malice; for when the bags come to be shaken out, it has always been seen, and is so still, that whilst a good word gains love and profit, slander brings enmity and ruin; and when you shall have heard how this happens, you will say I speak with reason.

Once upon a time there were two brothers—Cianne, who was as rich as a lord, and Lise, who had barely enough to live upon: but poor as one was in fortune, so pitiful was the other in mind, for he would not have given his brother a farthing were it to save his life; so that poor Lise in despair left his country, and set out to wander over the world. And he wandered on and on, till one wet and cold evening he came to an inn, where he found twelve youths seated around a fire, who, when they saw poor Lise benumbed with cold, partly from the severe season and partly from his ragged clothes, invited him to sit down by the fire.

Lise accepted the invitation, for he needed it greatly, and began to warm himself. And as he was warming himself, one of the young men whose face was such a picture of moroseness as to make you die of fright, said to him, "What think you, countryman, of this weather?"

"What do I think of it?" replied Lise; "I think that all the months of the year perform their duty; but we, who know not what we would have, wish to give laws to Heaven; and wanting to have things our own way, we do not fish deeply enough to the bottom, to find out whether what comes into our fancy be good or evil, useful or hurtful. In winter, when it rains, we want the sun in Leo, and in the month of August the clouds to discharge themselves; not reflecting, that were this the case, the seasons would be turned topsy-turvy, the seed sown would be lost, the crops would be destroyed, the bodies of men would faint away, and Nature would go head over heels. Therefore let us leave Heaven to its own course; for it has made the tree to mitigate with its wood the severity of winter, and with its leaves the heat of summer."

"You speak like Samson!" replied the youth; "but you cannot deny that this month of March, in which we now are, is very impertinent to send all this frost and rain, snow and hail, wind and storm, these fogs and tempests and other troubles, that make one's life a burden."

"You tell only the ill of this poor month," replied Lisa, "but do not speak of the benefits it yields us; for, by bringing forward the Spring, it commences the production of things, and is alone the cause that the Sun proves the happiness of the present time, by leading him into the house of the Ram."

The youth was greatly pleased at what Lise said, for he was in truth no other than the month of March itself, who had arrived at that inn with his eleven brothers; and to reward Lise's goodness, who had not even found anything ill to say of a month so sad that the shepherds do not like to mention it, he gave him a beautiful little casket, saying, "Take this, and if you want anything, only ask for it, and when you open this box you will see it before you." Lise thanked the youth, with many expressions of respect, and laying the little box under his head by way of a pillow, he went to sleep.

As soon, however, as the Sun, with the pencil of his rays, had retouched the dark shadows of Night, Lise took leave of the youths and set out on his way. But he had hardly proceeded fifty steps from the inn, when, opening the casket, he said, "Ah, my friend, I wish I had a litter lined with cloth, and with a little fire inside, that I might travel warm and comfortable through the snow!" No sooner had he uttered the words than there appeared a litter, with bearers, who, lifting him up, placed him in it; whereupon he told them to carry him home.

When the hour was come to set the jaws to work Lise opened the little box and said, "I wish for something to eat." And instantly there appeared a profusion of the choicest food, and there was such a banquet that ten crowned kings might have feasted on it.

One evening, having come to a wood which did not give admittance to the Sun because he came from suspected places, Lise opened the little casket, and said, "I should like to rest to-night on this beautiful spot, where the river is making harmony upon the stones as accompaniment to the song of the cool breezes." And instantly there appeared, under an oilcloth tent, a couch of fine scarlet, with down mattresses, covered with a Spanish counterpane and sheets as light as a feather. Then he asked for something to eat, and in a trice there was set out a sideboard covered with silver and gold fit for a prince, and under another tent a table was spread with viands, the savoury smell of which extended a hundred miles.

When he had eaten enough, he laid himself down to sleep; and as soon as the Cock, who is the spy of the Sun, announced to his master that the Shades of Night were worn and wearied, and it was now time for him, like a skilful general, to fall upon their rear and make a slaughter of them, Lise opened his little box and said, "I wish to have a handsome dress, for to-day I shall see my brother, and I should like to make his mouth water." No sooner said than done: immediately a princely dress of the richest black velvet appeared, with edgings of red camlet and a lining of yellow cloth embroidered all over, which looked like a field of flowers. So dressing himself, Lise got into the litter and soon reached his brother's house.

When Cianne saw his brother arrive, with all this splendour and luxury, he wished to know what good fortune had befallen him. Then Lise told him of the youths whom he had met in the inn, and of the present they had made him; but he kept to himself his conversation with the youths.

Cianne was now all impatience to get away from his brother, and told him to go and rest himself, as he was no doubt tired; then he started post-haste, and soon arrived at the inn, where, finding the same youths, he fell into chat with them. And when the youth asked him the same question, what he thought of that month of March, Cianne, making a big mouth, said, "Confound the miserable month! the enemy of shepherds, which stirs up all the ill-humours and brings sickness to our bodies. A month of which, whenever we would announce ruin to a man, we say, Go, March has shaved you!' A month of which, when you want to call a man presumptuous, you say, What cares March?' A month in short so hateful, that it would be the best fortune for the world, the greatest blessing to the earth, the greatest gain to men, were it excluded from the band of brothers."

March, who heard himself thus slandered, suppressed his anger till the morning, intending then to reward Cianne for his calumny; and when Cianne wished to depart, he gave him a fine whip, saying to him, "Whenever you wish for anything, only say, Whip, give me a hundred!' and you shall see pearls strung upon a rush."

Cianne, thanking the youth, went his way in great haste, not wishing to make trial of the whip until he reached home. But hardly had he set foot in the house, when he went into a secret chamber, intending to hide the money which he expected to receive from the whip. Then he said, "Whip, give me a hundred!" and thereupon the whip gave him more than he looked for, making a score on his legs and face like a musical composer, so that Lise, hearing his cries, came running to the spot; and when he saw that the whip, like a runaway horse, could not stop itself, he opened the little box and brought it to a standstill. Then he asked Cianne what had happened to him, and upon hearing his story, he told him he had no one to blame but himself; for like a blockhead he alone had caused his own misfortune, acting like the camel, that wanted to have horns and lost its ears; but he bade him mind another time and keep a bridle on his tongue, which was the key that had opened to him the storehouse of misfortune; for if he had spoken well of the youths, he would perhaps have had the same good fortune, especially as to speak well of any one is a merchandise that costs nothing, and usually brings profit that is not expected. In conclusion Lise comforted him, bidding him not seek more wealth than Heaven had give him, for his little casket would suffice to fill the houses of thirty misers, and Cianne should be master of all he possessed, since to the generous man Heaven is treasurer; and he added that, although another brother might have borne Cianne ill-will for the cruelty with which he had treated him in his poverty, yet he reflected that his avarice had been a favourable wind which had brought him to this port, and therefore wished to show himself grateful for the benefit.

When Cianne heard these things, he begged his brother's pardon for his past unkindness, and entering into partnership they enjoyed together their good fortune, and from that time forward Cianne spoke well of everything, however bad it might be; for—

"The dog that was scalded with hot water, for ever dreads that which is cold."

XXVII

PINTOSMALTO

It has always been more difficult for a man to keep than to get; for in the one case fortune aids, which often assists injustice, but in the other case sense is required. Therefore we frequently find a person deficient in cleverness rise to wealth, and then, from want of sense, roll over heels to the bottom; as you will see clearly from the story I am going to tell you, if you are quick of understanding.

A merchant once had an only daughter, whom he wished greatly to see married; but as often as he struck this note, he found her a hundred miles off from the desired pitch, for the foolish girl would never consent to marry, and the father was in consequence the most unhappy and miserable man in the world. Now it happened one day that he was going to a fair; so he asked his daughter, who was named Betta, what she would like him to bring her on his return. And she said, "Papa, if you love me, bring me half a hundredweight of Palermo sugar, and as much again of sweet almonds, with four to six bottles of scented water, and a little musk and amber, also forty pearls, two sapphires, a few garnets and rubies, with some gold thread, and above all a trough and a little silver trowel." Her father wondered at this extravagant demand, nevertheless he would not refuse his daughter; so he went to the fair, and on his return brought her all that she had requested.

As soon as Betta received these things, she shut herself up in a chamber, and began to make a great quantity of paste of almonds and sugar, mixed with rosewater and perfumes, and set to work to form a most beautiful youth, making his hair of gold thread, his eyes of sapphires, his teeth of pearls, his lips of rubies; and she gave him such grace that speech alone was wanting to him. When she had done all this, having heard say that at the prayers of a certain King of Cyprus a statue had once come to life, she prayed to the goddess of Love so long that at last the statue began to open its eyes; and increasing her prayers, it began to breathe; and after breathing, words came out; and at last, disengaging all its limbs, it began to walk.

With a joy far greater than if she had gained a kingdom, Betta embraced and kissed the youth, and taking him by the hand, she led him before her father and said, "My lord and father, you have always told me that you wished to see me married, and in order to please you I have now chosen a husband after my own heart." When her father saw the handsome youth come out of his daughter's room, whom he had not seen enter it, he stood amazed, and at the sight of such beauty, which folks would have paid a halfpenny a head to gaze at, he consented that the marriage should take place. So a great feast was made, at which, among the other ladies present, there appeared a great unknown Queen, who, seeing the beauty of Pintosmalto (for that was the name Betta gave him), fell desperately in love with him. Now Pintosmalto, who had only opened his eyes on the wickedness of the world three hours before, and was as innocent as a babe, accompanied the strangers who had come to celebrate his nuptials to the stairs, as his bride had told him; and when he did the same with this Queen, she took him by the hand and led him quietly to her coach, drawn by six horses, which stood in the courtyard; then taking him into it, she ordered the coachman to drive off and away to her country.

After Betta had waited a while in vain expecting Pintosmalto to return, she sent down into the courtyard to see whether he were speaking with any one there; then she sent up to the roof to see if he had gone to take fresh air; but finding him nowhere, she directly imagined that, on account of his great beauty, he had been stolen from her. So she ordered the usual proclamations to be made; but at last, as no tidings of him were brought, she formed the resolution to go all the world over in search of him, and dressing herself as a poor girl, she set out on her way. After some months she came to the house of a good old woman, who received her with great kindness; and when she had heard Betta's misfortune, she took compassion on her, and taught her three sayings. The first was, "Tricche varlacche, the house rains!" the second, "Anola tranola, the fountain plays!"; the third, "Scatola matola, the sun shines!"—telling her to repeat these words whenever she was in trouble, and they would be of good service to her.

Betta wondered greatly at this present of chaff, nevertheless she said to herself, "He who blows into your mouth does not wish to see you dead, and the plant that strikes root does not wither; everything has its use; who knows what good fortune may be contained in these words?" So saying, she thanked the old woman, and set out upon her way. And after a long journey she came to a beautiful city called Round Mount, where she went straight to the royal palace, and begged for the love of Heaven a little shelter in the stable. So the ladies of the court ordered a small room to be given her on the stairs; and while poor Betta was sitting there she saw Pintosmalto pass by, whereat her joy was so great that she was on the point of slipping down from the tree of life. But seeing the trouble she was in, Betta wished to make proof of the first saying which the old woman had told her; and no sooner had she repeated the words, "Tricche varlacche, the house rains!" than instantly there appeared before her a beautiful little coach of gold set all over with jewels, which ran about the chamber of itself and was a wonder to behold.

When the ladies of the court saw this sight they went and told the Queen, who without loss of time ran to Betta's chamber; and when she saw the beautiful little coach, she asked whether she would sell it, and offered to give whatever she might demand. But Betta replied that, although she was poor she would not sell it for all the gold in the world, but if the Queen wished for the little coach, she must allow her to pass one night at the door of Pintosmalto's chamber.

The Queen was amazed at the folly of the poor girl, who although she was all in rags would nevertheless give up such riches for a mere whim; however, she resolved to take the good mouthful offered her, and, by giving Pintosmalto a sleeping-draught, to satisfy the poor girl but pay her in bad coin.

As soon as the Night was come, when the stars in the sky and the glowworms on the earth were to pass in review, the Queen gave a sleeping-draught to Pintosmalto, who did everything he was told, and sent him to bed. And no sooner had he thrown himself on the mattress than he fell as sound asleep as a dormouse. Poor Betta, who thought that night to relate all her past troubles, seeing now that she had no audience, fell to lamenting beyond measure, blaming herself for all that she had done for his sake; and the unhappy girl never closed her mouth, nor did the sleeping Pintosmalto ever open his eyes until the Sun appeared with the aqua regia of his rays to separate the shades from the light, when the Queen came down, and taking Pintosmalto by the hand, said to Betta, "Now be content."

"May you have such content all the days of your life!" replied Betta in an undertone; "for I have passed so bad a night that I shall not soon forget it."

The poor girl, however, could not resist her longing, and resolved to make trial of the second saying; so she repeated the words, "Anola tranola, the fountain plays!" and instantly there appeared a golden cage, with a beautiful bird made of precious stones and gold, which sang like a nightingale. When the ladies saw this they went and told it to the Queen, who wished to see the bird; then she asked the same question as about the little coach, and Betta made the same reply as before. Whereupon the Queen, who perceived, as she thought, what a silly creature Betta was, promised to grant her request, and took the cage with the bird. And as soon as night came she gave Pintosmalto a sleeping-draught as before, and sent him to bed. When Betta saw that he slept like a dead person, she began again to wail and lament, saying things that would have moved a flintstone to compassion; and thus she passed another night, full of trouble, weeping and wailing and tearing her hair. But as soon as it was day the Queen came to fetch her captive, and left poor Betta in grief and sorrow, and biting her hands with vexation at the trick that had been played her.

In the morning when Pintosmalto went to a garden outside the city gate to pluck some figs, he met a cobbler, who lived in a room close to where Betta lay and had not lost a word of all she had said. Then he told Pintosmalto of the weeping, lamentation, and crying of the unhappy beggar-girl; and when Pintosmalto, who already began to get a little more sense, heard this, he guessed how matters stood, and resolved that, if the same thing happened again, he would not drink what the Queen gave him.

Betta now wished to make the third trial, so she said the words, "Scatola matola, the sun shines!" and instantly there appeared a quantity of stuffs of silk and gold, and embroidered scarfs, with a golden cup; in short, the Queen herself could not have brought together so many beautiful ornaments. When the ladies saw these things they told their mistress, who endeavoured to obtain them as she had done the others; but Betta replied as before, that if the Queen wished to have them she must let her spend the night at the door of the chamber. Then the Queen said to herself, "What can I lose by satisfying this silly girl, in order to get from her these beautiful things?" So taking all the treasures which Betta offered her, as soon as Night appeared, the instrument for the debt contracted with Sleep and Repose being liquidated, she gave the sleeping-draught to Pintosmalto; but this time he did not swallow it, and making an excuse to leave the room, he spat it out again, and then went to bed.

Betta now began the same tune again, saying how she had kneaded him with her own hands of sugar and almonds, how she had made his hair of gold, and his eyes and mouth of pearls and precious stones, and how he was indebted to her for his life, which the gods had granted to her prayers, and lastly how he had been stolen from her, and she had gone seeking him with such toil and trouble. Then she went on to tell him how she had watched two nights at the door of his room, and for leave to do so had given up two treasures, and yet had not been able to hear a single word from him, so that this was the last night of her hopes and the conclusion of her life.

When Pintosmalto, who had remained awake, heard these words, and called to mind as a dream all that had passed, he rose and embraced her; and as Night had just come forth with her black mask to direct the dance of the Stars, he went very quietly into the chamber of the Queen, who was in a deep sleep, and took from her all the things that she had taken from Betta, and all the jewels and money which were in a desk, to repay himself for his past troubles. Then returning to his wife, they set off that very hour, and travelled on and on until they arrived at her father's house, where they found him alive and well; and from the joy of seeing his daughter again he became like a boy of fifteen years. But when the Queen found neither Pintosmalto, nor beggar-girl, nor jewels, she tore her hair and rent her clothes, and called to mind the saying—

"He who cheats must not complain if he be cheated."

XXVIII

THE GOLDEN ROOT

A person who is over-curious, and wants to know more than he ought, always carries the match in his hand to set fire to the powder-room of his own fortunes; and he who pries into others' affairs is frequently a loser in his own; for generally he who digs holes to search for treasures, comes to a ditch into which he himself falls—as happened to the daughter of a gardener in the following manner.

There was once a gardener who was so very very poor that, however hard he worked, he could not manage to get bread for his family. So he gave three little pigs to his three daughters, that they might rear them, and thus get something for a little dowry. Then Pascuzza and Cice, who were the eldest, drove their little pigs to feed in a beautiful meadow; but they would not let Parmetella, who was the youngest daughter, go with them, and sent her away, telling her to go and feed her pig somewhere else. So Parmetella drove her little animal into a wood, where the Shades were holding out against the assaults of the Sun; and coming to a pasture—in the middle of which flowed a fountain, that, like the hostess of an inn where cold water is sold, was inviting the passers-by with its silver tongue—she found a certain tree with golden leaves. Then plucking one of them, she took it to her father, who with great joy sold it for more than twenty ducats, which served to stop up a hole in his affairs. And when he asked Parmetella where she had found it, she said, "Take it, sir, and ask no questions, unless you would spoil your good fortune." The next day she returned and did the same; and she went on plucking the leaves from the tree until it was entirely stript, as if it had been plundered by the winds of Autumn. Then she perceived that the tree had a large golden root, which she could not pull up with her hands; so she went home, and fetching an axe set to work to lay bare the root around the foot of the tree; and raising the trunk as well as she could, she found under it a beautiful porphyry staircase.

Parmetella, who was curious beyond measure, went down the stairs, and walking through a large and deep cavern, she came to a beautiful plain, on which was a splendid palace, where only gold and silver were trodden underfoot, and pearls and precious stones everywhere met the eye. And as Parmetella stood wondering at all these splendid things, not seeing any person moving among so many beautiful fixtures, she went into a chamber, in which were a number of pictures; and on them were seen painted various beautiful things—especially the ignorance of man esteemed wise, the injustice of him who held the scales, the injuries avenged by Heaven—things truly to amaze one. And in the same chamber also was a splendid table, set out with things to eat and to drink.

Seeing no one, Parmetella, who was very hungry, sat down at a table to eat like a fine count; but whilst she was in the midst of the feast, behold a handsome Slave entered, who said, "Stay! do not go away, for I will have you for my wife, and will make you the happiest woman in the world." In spite of her fear, Parmetella took heart at this good offer, and consenting to what the Slave proposed, a coach of diamonds was instantly given her, drawn by four golden steeds, with wings of emeralds and rubies, who carried her flying through the air to take an airing; and a number of apes, clad in cloth of gold, were given to attend on her person, who forthwith arrayed her from head to foot, and adorned her so that she looked just like a Queen.

When night was come, and the Sun—desiring to sleep on the banks of the river of India untroubled by gnats—had put out the light, the Slave said to Parmetella, "My dear, now go to rest in this bed; but remember first to put out the candle, and mind what I say, or ill will betide you." Then Parmetella did as he told her; but no sooner had she closed her eyes than the blackamoor, changing to a handsome youth, lay down to sleep. But the next morning, ere the Dawn went forth to seek fresh eggs in the fields of the sky the youth arose and took his other form again, leaving Parmetella full of wonder and curiosity.

And again the following night, when Parmetella went to rest, she put out the candle as she had done the night before, and the youth came as usual and lay down to sleep. But no sooner had he shut his eyes than Parmetella arose, took a steel which she had provided, and lighting the tinder applied a match; then taking the candle, she raised the coverlet, and beheld the ebony turned to ivory, and the coal to chalk. And whilst she stood gazing with open mouth, and contemplating the most beautiful pencilling that Nature had ever given upon the canvas of Wonder, the youth awoke, and began to reproach Parmetella, saying, "Ah, woe is me! for your prying curiosity I have to suffer another seven years this accursed punishment. But begone! Run, scamper off! Take yourself out of my sight! You know not what good fortune you lose." So saying, he vanished like quicksilver.

The poor girl left the palace, cold and stiff with affright, and with her head bowed to the ground. And when she had come out of the cavern she met a fairy, who said to her, "My child, how my heart grieves at your misfortune! Unhappy girl, you are going to the slaughter-house, where you will pass over the bridge no wider than a hair. Therefore, to provide against your peril, take these seven spindles with these seven figs, and a little jar of honey, and these seven pairs of iron shoes, and walk on and on without stopping, until they are worn out; then you will see seven women standing upon a balcony of a house, and spinning from above down to the ground, with the thread wound upon the bone of a dead person. Remain quite still and hidden, and when the thread comes down, take out the bone and put in its place a spindle besmeared with honey, with a fig in the place of the little button. Then as soon as the women draw up the spindles and taste the honey, they will say—

'He who has made my spindle sweet,
Shall in return with good fortune meet!'

And after repeating these words, they will say, one after another, 'O you who brought us these sweet things appear!' Then you must answer, Nay, for you will eat me.' And they will say, We swear by our spoon that we will not eat you!' But do not stir; and they will continue, We swear by our spit that we will not eat you!' But stand firm, as if rooted to the spot; and they will say, We swear by our broom that we will not eat you!' Still do not believe them; and when they say, We swear by our pail that we will not eat you!' shut your mouth, and say not a word, or it will cost you your life. At last they will say, We swear by Thunder-and-Lightning that we will not eat you!' Then take courage and mount up, for they will do you no harm."

When Parmetella heard this, she set off and walked over hill and dale, until at the end of seven years the iron shoes were worn out; and coming to a large house, with a projecting balcony, she saw the seven women spinning. So she did as the fairy had advised her; and after a thousand wiles and allurements, they swore by Thunder-and-Lightning, whereupon she showed herself and mounted up. Then they all seven said to her, "Traitress, you are the cause that our brother has lived twice seven long years in the cavern, far away from us, in the form of a blackamoor! But never mind; although you have been clever enough to stop our throat with the oath, you shall on the first opportunity pay off both the old and the new reckoning. But now hear what you must do. Hide yourself behind this trough, and when our mother comes, who would swallow you down at once, rise up and seize her behind her back; hold her fast, and do not let her go until she swears by Thunder-and-Lightning not to harm you."

Parmetella did as she was bid, and after the ogress had sworn by the fire-shovel, by the spinning-wheel, by the reel, by the sideboard, and by the peg, at last she swore by Thunder-and-Lightning; whereupon Parmetella let go her hold, and showed herself to the ogress, who said, "You have caught me this time; but take care, Traitress! for, at the first shower, I'll send you to the Lava."

One day the ogress, who was on the look-out for an opportunity to devour Parmetella, took twelve sacks of various seeds—peas, chick-peas, lentils, vetches, kidney-beans, beans, and lupins—and mixed them all together; then she said to her, "Traitress, take these seeds and sort them all, so that each kind may be separated from the rest; and if they are not all sorted by this evening, I'll swallow you like a penny tart."

Poor Parmetella sat down beside the sacks, weeping, and said, "O mother, mother, how will this golden root prove a root of woes to me! Now is my misery completed; by seeing a black face turned white, all has become black before my eyes. Alas! I am ruined and undone—there is no help for it. I already seem as if I were in the throat of that horrid ogress; there is no one to help me, there is no one to advise me, there is no one to comfort me!"

As she was lamenting thus, lo! Thunder-and-Lightning appeared like a flash, for the banishment laid upon him by the spell had just ended. Although he was angry with Parmetella, yet his blood could not turn to water, and seeing her grieving thus he said to her, "Traitress, what makes you weep so?" Then she told him of his mother's ill-treatment of her, and her wish to make an end of her, and eat her up. But Thunder-and-Lightning replied, "Calm yourself and take heart, for it shall not be as she said." And instantly scattering all the seeds on the ground he made a deluge of ants spring up, who forthwith set to work to heap up all the seeds separately, each kind by itself, and Parmetella filled the sacks with them.

When the ogress came home and found the task done, she was almost in despair, and cried, "That dog Thunder-and-Lightning has played me this trick; but you shall not escape thus! So take these pieces of bed-tick, which are enough for twelve mattresses, and mind that by this evening they are filled with feathers, or else I will make mincemeat of you."

The poor girl took the bed-ticks, and sitting down upon the ground began to weep and lament bitterly, making two fountains of her eyes. But presently Thunder-and-Lightning appeared, and said to her, "Do not weep, Traitress,—leave it to me, and I will bring you to port; so let down your hair, spread the bed-ticks upon the ground, and fall to weeping and wailing, and crying out that the king of the birds is dead, then you'll see what will happen."

Parmetella did as she was told, and behold a cloud of birds suddenly appeared that darkened the air; and flapping their wings they let fall their feathers by basketfuls, so that in less than an hour the mattresses were all filled. When the ogress came home and saw the task done, she swelled up with rage till she almost burst, saying, "Thunder-and-Lightning is determined to plague me, but may I be dragged at an ape's tail if I let her escape!" Then she said to Parmetella, "Run quickly to my sister's house, and tell her to send me the musical instruments; for I have resolved that Thunder-and-Lightning shall marry, and we will make a feast fit for a king." At the same time she sent to bid her sister, when the poor girl came to ask for the instruments, instantly to kill and cook her, and she would come and partake of the feast.

Parmetella, hearing herself ordered to perform an easier task, was in great joy, thinking that the weather had begun to grow milder. Alas, how crooked is human judgment! On the way she met Thunder-and-Lightning, who, seeing her walking at a quick pace, said to her, "Whither are you going, wretched girl? See you not that you are on the way to the slaughter; that you are forging your own fetters, and sharpening the knife and mixing the poison for yourself; that you are sent to the ogress for her to swallow you? But listen to me and fear not. Take this little loaf, this bundle of hay, and this stone; and when you come to the house of my aunt, you will find a bulldog, which will fly barking at you to bite you; but give him this little loaf, and it will stop his throat. And when you have passed the dog, you will meet a horse running loose, which will run up to kick and trample on you; but give him the hay, and you will clog his feet. At last you will come to a door, banging to and fro continually; put this stone before it, and you will stop its fury. Then mount upstairs and you find the ogress, with a little child in her arms, and the oven ready heated to bake you. Whereupon she will say to you, Hold this little creature, and wait here till I go and fetch the instruments.' But mind—she will only go to whet her tusks, in order to tear you in pieces. Then throw the little child into the oven without pity, take the instruments which stand behind the door, and hie off before the ogress returns, or else you are lost. The instruments are in a box, but beware of opening it, or you will repent."

Parmetella did all that Thunder-and-Lightning told her; but on her way back with the instruments she opened the box, and lo and behold! they all flew out and about—here a flute, there a flageolet, here a pipe, there a bagpipe, making a thousand different sounds in the air, whilst Parmetella stood looking on and tearing her hair in despair.

Meanwhile the ogress came downstairs, and not finding Parmetella, she went to the window, and called out to the door, "Crush that traitress!" But the door answered:

"I will not use the poor girl ill,
For she has made me at last stand still."

Then the ogress cried out to the horse, "Trample on the thief!" But the horse replied:

"Let the poor girl go her way,
For she has given me the hay."

And lastly, the ogress called to the dog, saying, "Bite the rogue!" But the dog answered:

"I'll not hurt a hair of her head,
For she it was who gave me the bread."

Now as Parmetella ran crying after the instruments, she met Thunder-and-Lightning, who scolded her well, saying, "Traitress, will you not learn at your cost that by your fatal curiosity you are brought to this plight?" Then he called back the instruments with a whistle, and shut them up again in the box, telling Parmetella to take them to his mother. But when the ogress saw her, she cried aloud, "O cruel fate! even my sister is against me, and refuses to give me this pleasure."

Meanwhile the new bride arrived—a hideous pest, a compound of ugliness, a harpy, an evil shade, a horror, a monster, a large tub, who with a hundred flowers and boughs about her looked like a newly opened inn. Then the ogress made a great banquet for her; and being full of gall and malice, she had the table placed close to a well, where she seated her seven daughters, each with a torch in one hand; but she gave two torches to Parmetella, and made her sit at the edge of the well, on purpose that, when she fell asleep, she might tumble to the bottom.

Now whilst the dishes were passing to and fro, and their blood began to get warm, Thunder-and-Lightning, who turned quite sick at the sight of the new bride, said to Parmetella, "Traitress, do you love me?" "Ay, to the top of the roof," she replied. And he answered, "If you love me, give me a kiss." "Nay," said Parmetella, "YOU indeed, who have such a pretty creature at your side! Heaven preserve her to you a hundred years in health and with plenty of sons!" Then the new bride answered, "It is very clear that you are a simpleton, and would remain so were you to live a hundred years, acting the prude as you do, and refusing to kiss so handsome a youth, whilst I let a herdsman kiss me for a couple of chestnuts."

At these words the bridegroom swelled with rage like a toad, so that his food remained sticking in his throat; however, he put a good face on the matter and swallowed the pill, intending to make the reckoning and settle the balance afterwards. But when the tables were removed, and the ogress and his sisters had gone away, Thunder-and-Lightning said to the new bride, "Wife, did you see this proud creature refuse me a kiss?" "She was a simpleton," replied the bride, "to refuse a kiss to such a handsome young man, whilst I let a herdsman kiss me for a couple of chestnuts."

Thunder-and-Lightning could contain himself no longer; the mustard got up into his nose, and with the flash of scorn and the thunder of action, he seized a knife and stabbed the bride, and digging a hole in the cellar he buried her. Then embracing Parmetella he said to her, "You are my jewel, the flower of women, the mirror of honour! Then turn those eyes upon me, give me that hand, put out those lips, draw near to me, my heart! for I will be yours as long as the world lasts."

The next morning, when the Sun aroused his fiery steeds from their watery stable, and drove them to pasture on the fields sown by the Dawn, the ogress came with fresh eggs for the newly married couple, that the young wife might be able to say, "Happy is she who marries and gets a mother-in-law!" But finding Parmetella in the arms of her son, and hearing what had passed, she ran to her sister, to concert some means of removing this thorn from her eyes without her son's being able to prevent it. But when she found that her sister, out of grief at the loss of her daughter, had crept into the oven herself and was burnt, her despair was so great, that from an ogress she became a ram, and butted her head against the wall under she broke her pate. Then Thunder-and-Lightning made peace between Parmetella and her sisters-in-law, and they all lived happy and content, finding the saying come true, that—

"Patience conquers all."

XXIX

SUN, MOON, AND TALIA

It is a well-known fact that the cruel man is generally his own hangman; and he who throws stones at Heaven frequently comes off with a broken head. But the reverse of the medal shows us that innocence is a shield of fig-tree wood, upon which the sword of malice is broken, or blunts its point; so that, when a poor man fancies himself already dead and buried, he revives again in bone and flesh, as you shall hear in the story which I am going to draw from the cask of memory with the tap of my tongue.

There was once a great Lord, who, having a daughter born to him named Talia, commanded the seers and wise men of his kingdom to come and tell him her fortune; and after various counsellings they came to the conclusion, that a great peril awaited her from a piece of stalk in some flax. Thereupon he issued a command, prohibiting any flax or hemp, or such-like thing, to be brought into his house, hoping thus to avoid the danger.

When Talia was grown up, and was standing one day at the window, she saw an old woman pass by who was spinning. She had never seen a distaff or a spindle, and being vastly pleased with the twisting and twirling of the thread, her curiosity was so great that she made the old woman come upstairs. Then, taking the distaff in her hand, Talia began to draw out the thread, when, by mischance, a piece of stalk in the flax getting under her finger-nail, she fell dead upon the ground; at which sight the old woman hobbled downstairs as quickly as she could.

When the unhappy father heard of the disaster that had befallen Talia, after weeping bitterly, he placed her in that palace in the country, upon a velvet seat under a canopy of brocade; and fastening the doors, he quitted for ever the place which had been the cause of such misfortune to him, in order to drive all remembrance of it from his mind.

Now, a certain King happened to go one day to the chase, and a falcon escaping from him flew in at the window of that palace. When the King found that the bird did not return at his call, he ordered his attendants to knock at the door, thinking that the palace was inhabited; and after knocking for some time, the King ordered them to fetch a vine-dresser's ladder, wishing himself to scale the house and see what was inside. Then he mounted the ladder, and going through the whole palace, he stood aghast at not finding there any living person. At last he came to the room where Talia was lying, as if enchanted; and when the King saw her, he called to her, thinking that she was asleep, but in vain, for she still slept on, however loud he called. So, after admiring her beauty awhile, the King returned home to his kingdom, where for a long time he forgot all that had happened.

Meanwhile, two little twins, one a boy and the other a girl, who looked like two little jewels, wandered, from I know not where, into the palace and found Talia in a trance. At first they were afraid because they tried in vain to awaken her; but, becoming bolder, the girl gently took Talia's finger into her mouth, to bite it and wake her up by this means; and so it happened that the splinter of flax came out. Thereupon she seemed to awake as from a deep sleep; and when she saw those little jewels at her side, she took them to her heart, and loved them more than her life; but she wondered greatly at seeing herself quite alone in the palace with two children, and food and refreshment brought her by unseen hands.

After a time the King, calling Talia to mind, took occasion one day when he went to the chase to go and see her; and when he found her awakened, and with two beautiful little creatures by her side, he was struck dumb with rapture. Then the King told Talia who he was, and they formed a great league and friendship, and he remained there for several days, promising, as he took leave, to return and fetch her.

When the King went back to his own kingdom he was for ever repeating the names of Talia and the little ones, insomuch that, when he was eating he had Talia in his mouth, and Sun and Moon (for so he named the children); nay, even when he went to rest he did not leave off calling on them, first one and then the other.

Now the King's stepmother had grown suspicious at his long absence at the chase, and when she heard him calling thus on Talia, Sun, and Moon, she waxed wroth, and said to the King's secretary, "Hark ye, friend, you stand in great danger, between the axe and the block; tell me who it is that my stepson is enamoured of, and I will make you rich; but if you conceal the truth from me, I'll make you rue it."

The man, moved on the one side by fear, and on the other pricked by interest, which is a bandage to the eyes of honour, the blind of justice, and an old horse-shoe to trip up good faith, told the Queen the whole truth. Whereupon she sent the secretary in the King's name to Talia, saying that he wished to see the children. Then Talia sent them with great joy, but the Queen commanded the cook to kill them, and serve them up in various ways for her wretched stepson to eat.

Now the cook, who had a tender heart, seeing the two pretty little golden pippins, took compassion on them, and gave them to his wife, bidding her keep them concealed; then he killed and dressed two little kids in a hundred different ways. When the King came, the Queen quickly ordered the dishes served up; and the King fell to eating with great delight, exclaiming, "How good this is! Oh, how excellent, by the soul of my grandfather!" And the old Queen all the while kept saying, "Eat away, for you know what you eat." At first the King paid no attention to what she said; but at last, hearing the music continue, he replied, "Ay, I know well enough what I eat, for YOU brought nothing to the house." And at last, getting up in a rage, he went off to a villa at a little distance to cool his anger.

Meanwhile the Queen, not satisfied with what she had done, called the secretary again, and sent him to fetch Talia, pretending that the King wished to see her. At this summons Talia went that very instant, longing to see the light of her eyes, and not knowing that only the smoke awaited her. But when she came before the Queen, the latter said to her, with the face of a Nero, and full of poison as a viper, "Welcome, Madam Sly-cheat! Are you indeed the pretty mischief-maker? Are you the weed that has caught my son's eye and given me all this trouble."

When Talia heard this she began to excuse herself; but the Queen would not listen to a word; and having a large fire lighted in the courtyard, she commanded that Talia should be thrown into the flames. Poor Talia, seeing matters come to a bad pass, fell on her knees before the Queen, and besought her at least to grant her time to take the clothes from off her back. Whereupon the Queen, not so much out of pity for the unhappy girl, as to get possession of her dress, which was embroidered all over with gold and pearls, said to her, "Undress yourself—I allow you." Then Talia began to undress, and as she took off each garment she uttered an exclamation of grief; and when she had stripped off her cloak, her gown, and her jacket, and was proceeding to take off her petticoat, they seized her and were dragging her away. At that moment the King came up, and seeing the spectacle he demanded to know the whole truth; and when he asked also for the children, and heard that his stepmother had ordered them to be killed, the unhappy King gave himself up to despair.

He then ordered her to be thrown into the same fire which had been lighted for Talia, and the secretary with her, who was the handle of this cruel game and the weaver of this wicked web. Then he was going to do the same with the cook, thinking that he had killed the children; but the cook threw himself at the King's feet and said, "Truly, sir King, I would desire no other sinecure in return for the service I have done you than to be thrown into a furnace full of live coals; I would ask no other gratuity than the thrust of a spike; I would wish for no other amusement than to be roasted in the fire; I would desire no other privilege than to have the ashes of the cook mingled with those of a Queen. But I look for no such great reward for having saved the children, and brought them back to you in spite of that wicked creature who wished to kill them."

When the King heard these words he was quite beside himself; he appeared to dream, and could not believe what his ears had heard. Then he said to the cook, "If it is true that you have saved the children, be assured I will take you from turning the spit, and reward you so that you shall call yourself the happiest man in the world."

As the King was speaking these words, the wife of the cook, seeing the dilemma her husband was in, brought Sun and Moon before the King, who, playing at the game of three with Talia and the other children, went round and round kissing first one and then another. Then giving the cook a large reward, he made him his chamberlain; and he took

Talia to wife, who enjoyed a long life with her husband and the children, acknowledging that—

"He who has luck may go to bed,
And bliss will rain upon his head."

XXX

NENNILLO AND NENNELLA

Woe to him who thinks to find a governess for his children by giving them a stepmother! He only brings into his house the cause of their ruin. There never yet was a stepmother who looked kindly on the children of another; or if by chance such a one were ever found, she would be regarded as a miracle, and be called a white crow. But beside all those of whom you may have heard, I will now tell you of another, to be added to the list of heartless stepmothers, whom you will consider well deserving the punishment she purchased for herself with ready money.

There was once a good man named Jannuccio, who had two children, Nennillo and Nennella, whom he loved as much as his own life. But Death having, with the smooth file of Time, severed the prison-bars of his wife's soul, he took to himself a cruel woman, who had no sooner set foot in his house than she began to ride the high horse, saying, "Am I come here indeed to look after other folk's children? A pretty job I have undertaken, to have all this trouble and be for ever teased by a couple of squalling brats! Would that I had broken my neck ere I ever came to this place, to have bad food, worse drink, and get no sleep at night! Here's a life to lead! Forsooth I came as a wife, and not as a servant; but I must find some means of getting rid of these creatures, or it will cost me my life: better to blush once than to grow pale a hundred times; so I've done with them, for I am resolved to send them away, or to leave the house myself for ever."

The poor husband, who had some affection for this woman, said to her, "Softly, wife! Don't be angry, for sugar is dear; and to-morrow morning, before the cock crows, I will remove this annoyance in order to please you." So the next morning, ere the Dawn had hung out the red counterpane at the window of the East to air it, Jannuccio took the children, one by each hand, and with a good basketful of things to eat upon his arm, he led them to a wood, where an army of poplars and beech-trees were holding the shades besieged. Then Jannuccio said, "My little children, stay here in this wood, and eat and drink merrily; but if you want anything, follow this line of ashes which I have been strewing as we came along; this will be a clue to lead you out of the labyrinth and bring you straight home." Then giving them both a kiss, he returned weeping to his house.

But at the hour when all creatures, summoned by the constables of Night, pay to Nature the tax of needful repose, the two children began to feel afraid at remaining in that lonesome place, where the waters of a river, which was thrashing the impertinent stones for obstructing its course, would have frightened even a hero. So they went slowly along the path of ashes, and it was already midnight ere they reached their home. When Pascozza, their stepmother, saw the children, she acted not like a woman, but a perfect fury; crying aloud, wringing her hands, stamping with her feet, snorting like a frightened horse, and exclaiming, "What fine piece of work is this? Is there no way of ridding the house of these creatures? Is it possible, husband, that you are determined to keep them here to plague my very life out? Go, take them out of my sight! I'll not wait for the crowing of cocks and the cackling of hens; or else be assured that to-morrow morning I'll go off to my parents' house, for you do not deserve me. I have not brought you so many fine things, only to be made the slave of children who are not my own."

Poor Jannuccio, who saw that matters were growing rather too warm, immediately took the little ones and returned to the wood; where giving the children another basketful of food, he said to them, "You see, my dears, how this wife of mine—who is come to my house to be your ruin and a nail in my heart—hates you; therefore remain in this wood, where the trees, more compassionate, will give you shelter from the sun; where the river, more charitable, will give you drink without poison; and the earth, more kind, will give you a pillow of grass without danger. And when you want food, follow this little path of bran which I have made for you in a straight line, and you can come and seek what you require." So saying, he turned away his face, not to let himself be seen to weep and dishearten the poor little creatures.

When Nennillo and Nennella had eaten all that was in the basket, they wanted to return home; but alas! a jackass—the son of ill-luck—had eaten up all the bran that was strewn upon the ground; so they lost their way, and wandered about forlorn in the wood for several days, feeding on acorns and chestnuts which they found fallen on the ground. But as Heaven always extends its arm over the innocent, there came by chance a Prince to hunt in that wood. Then Nennillo, hearing the baying of the hounds, was so frightened that he crept into a hollow tree; and Nennella set off running at full speed, and ran until she came out of the wood, and found herself on the seashore. Now it happened that some pirates, who had landed there to get fuel, saw Nennella and carried her off; and their captain took her home with him where he and his wife, having just lost a little girl, took her as their daughter.

Meantime Nennillo, who had hidden himself in the tree, was surrounded by the dogs, which made such a furious barking that the Prince sent to find out the cause; and when he discovered the pretty little boy, who was so young that he could not tell who were his father and mother, he ordered one of the huntsmen to set him upon his saddle and take him to the royal palace. Then he had him brought up with great care, and instructed in various arts, and among others, he had him taught that of a carver; so that, before three or four years had passed, Nennillo became so expert in his art that he could carve a joint to a hair.

Now about this time it was discovered that the captain of the ship who had taken Nennella to his house was a sea-robber, and the people wished to take him prisoner; but getting timely notice from the clerks in the law-courts, who were his friends, and whom he kept in his pay, he fled with all his family. It was decreed, however, perhaps by the judgment of Heaven, that he who had committed his crimes upon the sea, upon the sea should suffer the punishment of them; for having embarked in a small boat, no sooner was he upon the open sea than there came such a storm of wind and tumult of the waves, that the boat was upset and all were drowned—all except Nennella, who having had no share in the corsair's robberies, like his wife and children, escaped the danger; for just then a large enchanted fish, which was swimming about the boat, opened its huge throat and swallowed her down.

The little girl now thought to herself that her days were surely at an end, when suddenly she found a thing to amaze her inside the fish,—beautiful fields and fine gardens, and a splendid mansion, with all that heart could desire, in which she lived like a Princess. Then she was carried quickly by the fish to a rock, where it chanced that the Prince had come to escape the burning heat of a summer, and to enjoy the cool sea-breezes. And whilst a great banquet was preparing, Nennillo had stepped out upon a balcony of the palace on the rock to sharpen some knives, priding himself greatly on acquiring honour from his office. When Nennella saw him through the fish's throat, she cried aloud,

"Brother, brother, your task is done,
The tables are laid out every one;
But here in the fish I must sit and sigh,
O brother, without you I soon shall die."

Nennillo at first paid no attention to the voice, but the Prince, who was standing on another balcony and had also heard it, turned in the direction whence the sound came, and saw the fish. And when he again heard the same words, he was beside himself with amazement, and ordered a number of servants to try whether by any means they could ensnare the fish and draw it to land. At last, hearing the words "Brother, brother!" continually repeated, he asked all his servants, one by one, whether any of them had lost a sister. And Nennillo replied, that he recollected, as a dream, having had a sister when the Prince found him in the wood, but that he had never since heard any tidings of her. Then the Prince told him to go nearer to the fish, and see what was the matter, for perhaps this adventure might concern him. As soon as Nennillo approached the fish, it raised up its head upon the rock, and opening its throat six palms wide, Nennella stepped out, so beautiful that she looked just like a nymph in some interlude, come forth from that animal at the incantation of a magician. And when the Prince asked her how it had all happened, she told him a part of her sad story, and the hatred of their stepmother; but not being able to recollect the name of their father nor of their home, the Prince caused a proclamation to be issued, commanding that whoever had lost two children, named Nennillo and Nennella, in a wood, should come to the royal palace, and he would there receive joyful news of them.

Jannuccio, who had all this time passed a sad and disconsolate life, believing that his children had been devoured by wolves, now hastened with the greatest joy to seek the Prince, and told him that he had lost the children. And when he had related the story, how he had been compelled to take them to the wood, the Prince gave him a good scolding, calling him a blockhead for allowing a woman to put her heel upon his neck till he was brought to send away two such jewels as his children. But after he had broken Jannuccio's head with these words, he applied to it the plaster of consolation, showing him the children, whom the father embraced and kissed for half an hour without being satisfied. Then the Prince made him pull off his jacket, and had him dressed like a lord; and sending for Jannuccio's wife, he showed her those two golden pippins, asked her what that person would deserve who should do them any harm, and even endanger their lives. And she replied, "For my part, I would put her into a closed cask, and send her rolling down a mountain."

"So it shall be done!" said the Prince. "The goat has butted at herself. Quick now! you have passed the sentence, and you must suffer it, for having borne these beautiful stepchildren such malice." So he gave orders that the sentence should be instantly executed. Then choosing a very rich lord among his vassals, he gave him Nennella to wife, and the daughter of another great lord to Nennillo; allowing them enough to live upon, with their father, so that they wanted for nothing in the world. But the stepmother, shut into the cask and shut out from life, kept on crying through the bunghole as long as she had breath—

"To him who mischief seeks, shall mischief fall;
There comes an hour that recompenses all."

XXXI

THE THREE CITRONS

Well was it in truth said by the wise man, "Do not say all you know, nor do all you are able"; for both one and the other bring unknown danger and unforeseen ruin; as you shall hear of a certain slave (be it spoken with all reverence for my lady the Princess), who, after doing all the injury in her power to a poor girl, came off so badly in the court, that she was the judge of her own crime, and sentenced herself to the punishment she deserved.

The King of Long-Tower had once a son, who was the apple of his eye, and on whom he had built all his hopes; and he longed impatiently for the time when he should find some good match for him. But the Prince was so averse to marriage and so obstinate that, whenever a wife was talked of, he shook his head and wished himself a hundred miles off; so that the poor King, finding his son stubborn and perverse, and foreseeing that his race would come to an end, was more vexed and melancholy, cast down and out of spirits, than a merchant whose correspondent has become bankrupt, or a peasant whose ass has died. Neither could the tears of his father move the Prince, nor the entreaties of the courtiers soften him, nor the counsel of wise men make him change his mind; in vain they set before his eyes the wishes of his father, the wants of the people, and his own interest, representing to him that he was the full-stop in the line of the royal race; for with the obstinacy of Carella and the stubbornness of an old mule with a skin four fingers thick, he had planted his foot resolutely, stopped his ears, and closed his heart against all assaults. But as frequently more comes to pass in an hour than in a hundred years, and no one can say, Stop here or go there, it happened that one day, when all were at table, and the Prince was cutting a piece of new-made cheese, whilst listening to the chit-chat that was going on, he accidentally cut his finger; and two drops of blood, falling upon the cheese, made such a beautiful mixture of colours that—either it was a punishment inflicted by Love, or the will of Heaven to console the poor father—the whim seized the Prince to find a woman exactly as white and red as that cheese tinged with blood. Then he said to his father, "Sir, unless I have a wife as white and red as this cheese, it is all over with me; so now resolve, if you wish to see me alive and well, to give me all I require to go through the world in search of a beauty exactly like this cheese, or else I shall end my life and die by inches."

When the King heard this mad resolution, he thought the house was falling about his ears; his colour came and went, but as soon as he recovered himself and could speak, he said, "My son, the life of my soul, the core of my heart, the prop of my old age, what mad-brained fancy has made you take leave of your senses? Have you lost your wits? You want either all or nothing: first you wish not to marry, on purpose to deprive me of an heir, and now you are impatient to drive me out of the world. Whither, O whither would you go wandering about, wasting your life? And why leave your house, your hearth, your home? You know not what toils and peril he brings on himself who goes rambling and roving. Let this whim pass, my son; be sensible, and do not wish to see my life worn out, this house fall to the ground, my household go to ruin."

But these and other words went in at one ear and out at the other, and were all cast upon the sea; and the poor King, seeing that his son was as immovable as a rook upon a belfry, gave him a handful of dollars and two or three servants; and bidding him farewell, he felt as if his soul was torn out of his body. Then weeping bitterly, he went to a balcony, and followed his son with his eyes until he was lost to sight.

The Prince departed, leaving his unhappy father to his grief, and hastened on his way through fields and woods, over mountain and valley, hill and plain, visiting various countries, and mixing with various peoples, and always with his eyes wide awake to see whether he could find the object of his desire. At the end of several months he arrived at the coast of France, where, leaving his servants at a hospital with sore feet, he embarked alone in a Genoese boat, and set out towards the Straits of Gibraltar. There he took a larger vessel and sailed for the Indies, seeking everywhere, from kingdom to kingdom, from province to province, from country to country, from street to street, from house to house, in every hole and corner, whether he could find the original likeness of that beautiful image which he had pictured to his heart. And he wandered about and about until at length he came to the Island of the Ogresses, where he cast anchor and landed. There he found an old, old woman, withered and shrivelled up, and with a hideous face, to whom he related the reason that had brought him to the country. The old woman was beside herself with amazement when she heard the strange whim and the fancy of the Prince, and the toils and perils he had gone through to satisfy himself; then she said to him, "Hasten away, my son! for if my three daughters meet you I would not give a farthing for your life; half-alive and half-roasted, a frying-pan would be your bier and a belly your grave. But away with you as fast as a hare, and you will not go far before you find what you are seeking!"

When the Prince heard this, frightened, terrified, and aghast, he set off running at full speed, and ran till he came to another country, where he again met an old woman, more ugly even than the first, to whom he told all his story. Then the old woman said to him in like manner, "Away with you! unless you wish to serve as a breakfast to the little ogresses my daughters; but go straight on, and you will soon find what you want."

The Prince, hearing this, set off running as fast as a dog with a kettle at its tail; and he went on and on, until he met another old woman, who was sitting upon a wheel, with a basket full of little pies and sweetmeats on her arm, and feeding a number of jackasses, which thereupon began leaping about on the bank of a river and kicking at some poor swans. When the Prince came up to the old woman, after making a hundred salaams, he related to her the story of his wanderings; whereupon the old woman, comforting him with kind words, gave him such a good breakfast that he licked his fingers after it. And when he had done eating she gave him three citrons, which seemed to be just fresh gathered from the tree; and she gave him also a beautiful knife, saying, "You are now free to return to Italy, for your labour is ended, and you have what you were seeking. Go your way, therefore, and when you are near your own kingdom stop at the first fountain you come to and cut a citron. Then a fairy will come forth from it, and will say to you, 'Give me to drink.' Mind and be ready with the water or she will vanish like quicksilver. But if you are not quick enough with the second fairy, have your eyes open and be watchful that the third does not escape you, giving her quickly to drink, and you shall have a wife after your own heart."

The Prince, overjoyed, kissed the old woman's hairy hand a hundred times, which seemed just like a hedgehog's back. Then taking his leave he left that country, and coming to the seashore sailed for the Pillars of Hercules, and arrived at our Sea, and after a thousand storms and perils, he entered port a day's distance from his own kingdom. There he came to a most beautiful grove, where the Shades formed a palace for the Meadows, to prevent their being seen by the sun; and dismounting at a fountain, which, with a crystal tongue, was inviting the people to refresh their lips, he seated himself on a Syrian carpet formed by the plants and flowers. Then he drew his knife from the sheath and began to cut the first citron, when lo! there appeared like a flash of lightning a most beautiful maiden, white as milk and red as a strawberry, who said, "Give me to drink!" The Prince was so amazed, bewildered, and captivated with the beauty of the fairy that he did not give her the water quick enough, so she appeared and vanished at one and the same moment. Whether this was a rap on the Prince's head, let any one judge who, after longing for a thing, gets it into his hands and instantly loses it again.

Then the Prince cut the second citron, and the same thing happened again; and this was a second blow he got on his pate; so making two little fountains of his eyes, he wept, face to face, tear for tear, drop for drop, with the fountain, and sighing he exclaimed, "Good heavens, how is it that I am so unfortunate? Twice I have let her escape, as if my hands were tied; and here I sit like a rock, when I ought to run like a greyhound. Faith indeed I have made a fine hand of it! But courage, man! there is still another, and three is the lucky number; either this knife shall give me the fay, or it shall take my life away." So saying he cut the third citron, and forth came the third fairy, who said like the others, "Give me to drink." Then the Prince instantly handed her the water; and behold there stood before him a delicate maiden, white as a junket with red streaks,—a thing never before seen in the world, with a beauty beyond compare, a fairness beyond the beyonds, a grace more than the most. On that hair Jove had showered down gold, of which Love made his shafts to pierce all hearts; that face the god of Love had tinged with red, that some innocent soul should be hung on the gallows of desire; at those eyes the sun had lighted two fireworks, to set fire to the rockets of sighs in the breast of the beholder; to the roses on those lips Venus had given their colour, to wound a thousand enamoured hearts with their thorns. In a word, she was so beautiful from head to foot, that a more exquisite creature was never seen. The Prince knew not what had happened to him, and stood lost in amazement, gazing on such a beautiful offspring of a citron; and he said to himself, "Are you asleep or awake, Ciommetiello? Are your eyes bewitched, or are you blind? What fair white creature is this come forth from a yellow rind? What sweet fruit, from the sour juice of a citron? What lovely maiden sprung from a citron-pip?"

At length, seeing that it was all true and no dream, he embraced the fairy, giving her a hundred and a hundred kisses; and after a thousand tender words had passed between them—words which, as a setting, had an accompaniment of sugared kisses—the Prince said, "My soul, I cannot take you to my father's kingdom without handsome raiment worthy of so beautiful a person, and an attendance befitting a Queen; therefore climb up into this oak-tree, where Nature seems purposely to have made for us a hiding-place in the form of a little room, and here await my return; for I will come back on wings, before a tear can be dry, with dresses and servants, and carry you off to my kingdom." So saying, after the usual ceremonies, he departed.

Now a black slave, who was sent by her mistress with a pitcher to fetch water, came to the well, and seeing by chance the reflection of the fairy in the water, she thought it was herself, and exclaimed in amazement, "Poor Lucia, what do I see? Me so pretty and fair, and mistress send me here. No, me will no longer bear." So saying she broke the pitcher and returned home; and when her mistress asked her, "Why have you done this mischief?" she replied, "Me go to the well alone, pitcher break upon a stone." Her mistress swallowed this idle story, and the next day she gave her a pretty little cask, telling her to go and fill it with water. So the slave returned to the fountain, and seeing again the beautiful image reflected in the water, she said with a deep sigh, "Me no ugly slave, me no broad-foot goose, but pretty and fine as mistress mine, and me not go to the fountain!" So saying, smash again! she broke the cask into seventy pieces, and returned grumbling home, and said to her mistress, "Ass come past, tub fell down at the well, and all was broken in pieces." The poor mistress, on hearing this, could contain herself no longer, and seizing a broomstick she beat the slave so soundly that she felt it for many days; then giving her a leather bag, she said, "Run, break your neck, you wretched slave, you grasshopper-legs, you black beetle! Run and fetch me this bag full of water, or else I'll hang you like a dog, and give you a good thrashing."

Away ran the slave heels over head, for she had seen the flash and dreaded the thunder; and while she was filling the leather bag, she turned to look again at the beautiful image, and said, "Me fool to fetch water! better live by one's wits; such a pretty girl indeed to serve a bad mistress!" So saying, she took a large pin which she wore in her hair, and began to pick holes in the leather bag, which looked like an open place in a garden with the rose of a watering-pot making a hundred little fountains. When the fairy saw this she laughed outright; and the slave hearing her, turned and espied her hiding-place up in the tree; whereat she said to herself, "O ho! you make me be beaten? but never mind!" Then she said to her, "What you doing up there, pretty lass?" And the fairy, who was the very mother of courtesy, told her all she knew, and all that had passed with the Prince, whom she was expecting from hour to hour and from moment to moment, with fine dresses and servants, to take her with him to his father's kingdom where they would live happy together.

When the slave, who was full of spite, heard this, she thought to herself that she would get this prize into her own hands; so she answered the fairy, "You expect your husband,—me come up and comb your locks, and make you more smart." And the fairy said, "Ay, welcome as the first of May!" So the slave climbed up the tree, and the fairy held out her white hand to her, which looked in the black paws of the slave like a crystal mirror in a frame of ebony. But no sooner did the slave begin to comb the fairy's locks, than she suddenly stuck a hairpin into her head. Then the fairy, feeling herself pricked, cried out, "Dove, dove!" and instantly she became a dove and flew away; whereupon the slave stripped herself, and making a bundle of all the rags that she had worn, she threw them a mile away; and there she sat, up in the tree, looking like a statue of jet in a house of emerald.

In a short time the Prince returned with a great cavalcade, and finding a cask of caviar where he had left a pan of milk, he stood for awhile beside himself with amazement. At length he said, "Who has made this great blot of ink on the fine paper upon which I thought to write the brightest days of my life? Who has hung with mourning this newly white-washed house, where I thought to spend a happy life? How comes it that I find this touchstone, where I left a mine of silver, that was to make me rich and happy?" But the crafty slave, observing the Prince's amazement, said, "Do not wonder, my Prince; for me turned by a wicked spell from a white lily to a black coal."

The poor Prince, seeing that there was no help for the mischief, drooped his head and swallowed this pill; and bidding the slave come down from the tree, he ordered her to be clothed from head to foot in new dresses. Then sad and sorrowful, cast-down and woe-begone, he took his way back with the slave to his own country, where the King and Queen, who had gone out six miles to meet them, received them with the same pleasure as a prisoner feels at the announcement of a sentence of hanging, seeing the fine choice their foolish son had made, who after travelling about so long to find a white dove had brought home at last a black crow. However, as they could do no less, they gave up the crown to their children, and placed the golden tripod upon that face of coal.

Now whilst they were preparing splendid feasts and banquets, and the cooks were busy plucking geese, killing little pigs, flaying kids, basting the roast meat, skimming pots, mincing meat for dumplings, larding capons, and preparing a thousand other delicacies, a beautiful dove came flying to the kitchen window, and said,

"O cook of the kitchen, tell me, I pray,
What the King and the slave are doing to-day."

The cook at first paid little heed to the dove; but when she returned a second and a third time, and repeated the same words, he ran to the dining-hall to tell the marvellous thing. But no sooner did the lady hear this music than she gave orders for the dove to be instantly caught and made into a hash. So the cook went, and he managed to catch the dove, and did all that the slave had commanded. And having scalded the bird in order to pluck it, he threw the water with the feathers out from a balcony on to a garden-bed, on which, before three days had passed, there sprang up a beautiful citron-tree, which quickly grew to its full size.

Now it happened that the King, going by chance to a window that looked upon the garden, saw the tree, which he had never observed before; and calling the cook, he asked him when and by whom it had been planted. No sooner had he heard all the particulars from Master Pot-ladle, than he began to suspect how matters stood. So he gave orders, under pain of death, that the tree should not be touched, but that it should be tended with the greatest care.

At the end of a few days three most beautiful citrons appeared, similar to those which the ogress had given Ciommetiello. And when they were grown larger, he plucked them; and shutting himself up in a chamber, with a large basin of water and the knife, which he always carried at his side, he began to cut the citrons. Then it all fell out with the first and second fairy just as it had done before; but when at last he cut the third citron, and gave the fairy who came forth from it to drink, behold, there stood before him the self-same maiden whom he had left up in the tree, and who told him all the mischief that the slave had done.

Who now can tell the least part of the delight the King felt at this good turn of fortune? Who can describe the shouting and leaping for joy that there was? For the King was swimming in a sea of delight, and was wafted to Heaven on a tide of rapture. Then he embraced the fairy, and ordered her to be handsomely dressed from head to foot; and taking her by the hand he led her into the middle of the hall, where all the courtiers and great folks of the city were met to celebrate the feast. Then the King called on them one by one, and said, "Tell me, what punishment would that person deserve who should do any harm to this beautiful lady!" And one replied that such a person would deserve a hempen collar; another, a breakfast of stones; a third, a good beating; a fourth, a draught of poison; a fifth, a millstone for a brooch—in short, one said this thing and another that. At last he called on the black Queen, and putting the same question, she replied, "Such a person would deserve to be burned, and that her ashes should be thrown from the roof of the castle."

When the King heard this, he said to her, "You have struck your own foot with the axe, you have made your own fetters, you have sharpened the knife and mixed the poison; for no one has done this lady so much harm as yourself, you good-for-nothing creature! Know you that this is the beautiful maiden whom you wounded with the hairpin? Know you that this is the pretty dove which you ordered to be killed and cooked in a stewpan? What say you now? It is all your own doing; and one who does ill may expect ill in return." So saying, he ordered the slave to be seized and cast alive on to a large burning pile of wood; and her ashes were thrown from the top of the castle to all the winds of Heaven, verifying the truth of the saying that—

"He who sows thorns should not go barefoot."

XXXII

CONCLUSION

All sat listening to Ciommetella's last story. Some praised the skill with which she had told it, while others murmured at her indiscretion, saying that, in the presence of the Princess, she ought not to have exposed to blame the ill-deeds of another slave, and run the risk of stopping the game. But Lucia herself sat upon thorns, and kept turning and twisting herself about all the time the story was being told; insomuch that the restlessness of her body betrayed the storm that was in her heart, at seeing in the tale of another slave the exact image of her own deceit. Gladly would she have dismissed the whole company, but that, owing to the desire which the doll had given her to hear stories, she could not restrain her passion for them. And, partly also not to give Taddeo cause for suspicion, she swallowed this bitter pill, intending to take a good revenge in proper time and place. But Taddeo, who had grown quite fond of the amusement, made a sign to Zoza to relate her story; and, after making her curtsey, she began—

"Truth, my Lord Prince, has always been the mother of hatred, and I would not wish, therefore, by obeying your commands, to offend any one of those about me. But as I am not accustomed to weave fictions or to invent stories, I am constrained, both by nature and habit, to speak the truth; and, although the proverb says, Tell truth and fear nothing, yet knowing well that truth is not welcome in the presence of princes, I tremble lest I say anything that may offend you."

"Say all you wish," replied Taddeo, "for nothing but what is sweet can come from those pretty lips."

These words were stabs to the heart of the Slave, as all would have seen plainly if black faces were, as white ones, the book of the soul. And she would have given a finger of her hand to have been rid of these stories, for all before her eyes had grown blacker even than her face. She feared that the last story was only the fore-runner of mischief to follow; and from a cloudy morning she foretold a bad day. But Zoza, meanwhile, began to enchant all around her with the sweetness of her words, relating her sorrows from first to last, and beginning with her natural melancholy, the unhappy augury of all she had to suffer. Then she went on to tell of the old woman's curse, her painful wanderings, her arrival at the fountain, her bitter weeping, and the treacherous sleep which had been the cause of her ruin.

The Slave, hearing Zoza tell the story in all its breadth and length, and seeing the boat go out of its course, exclaimed, "Be quiet and hold your tongue! or I will not answer for the consequences." But Taddeo, who had discovered how matters stood, could no longer contain himself; so, stripping off the mask and throwing the saddle on the ground, he exclaimed, "Let her tell her story to the end, and have done with this nonsense. I have been made a fool of for long enough, and, if what I suspect is true, it were better that you had never been born." Then he commanded Zoza to continue her story in spite of his wife; and Zoza, who only waited for the sign, went on to tell how the Slave had found the pitcher and had treacherously robbed her of her good fortune. And, thereupon, she fell to weeping in such a manner, that every person present was affected at the sight.

Taddeo, who, from Zoza's tears and the Slave's silence, discerned the truth of the matter, gave Lucia a rare scolding, and made her confess her treachery with her own lips. Then he gave instant orders that she should be buried alive up to her neck, that she might die a more painful death. And, embracing Zoza, he caused her to be treated with all honour as his Princess and wife, sending to invite the King of Wood-Valley to come to the feast.

With these fresh nuptials terminated the greatness of the Slave and the amusement of these stories. And much good may they do you, and promote your health! And may you lay them down as unwillingly as I do, taking my leave with regret at my heels and a good spoonful of honey in my mouth.

Made in the USA
Las Vegas, NV
26 June 2025